HAPPILY EVER ISLAND

HAPPILY EVER ISLAND

CRYSTAL CESTARI

Disney • HYPERION

First Edition, June 2022
10 9 8 7 6 5 4 3 2 1
FAC-004510-22089
Printed in the United States of America

This book is set in Cochin/Monotype
Designed by Marci Senders

Library of Congress Cataloging-in-Publication Data

Names: Cestari, Crystal, author.
Title: Happily Ever Island / by Crystal Cestari.
Description: First edition. • Los Angeles ; New York : Disney-Hyperion, 2022. • Audience: Ages 14–18. • Audience: Grades 10–12. • Summary: "When Disney superfan and hopeless romantic Madison gets the chance to test-run Disney's newest fully-immersive vacation destination that allows guests to become their favorite Disney character for a week, the eighteen-year-old college freshman jumps at the opportunity and begs her best friend Lanie to come along" —Provided by publisher.
Identifiers: LCCN 2021027084 • ISBN 9781368075473 (hardcover) • ISBN 9781368075718 (ebook)
Subjects: CYAC: Role playing—Fiction. • Disney characters—Fiction. • Fans (Persons)—Fiction. • Best friends—Fiction. • Friendship—Fiction. • Lesbians—Fiction. • Spring break—Fiction. • LCGFT: Novels.
Classification: LCC PZ7.1.C465 Hap 2022 • DDC [Fic]—dc23
LC record available at https://lccn.loc.gov/2021027084

Reinforced binding

Visit www.DisneyBooks.com

TO TIFFANY,
MY FAVORITE PERSON TO GO
TO DISNEY WITH

TO ALL WHO COME
TO THIS HAPPY PLACE,
WELCOME.
—WALT DISNEY

Thank you for your interest in Happily Ever Island,
the most pixie-dusted vacation a Disney fan could ever imagine!

Located in the Florida Keys, this brand-new interactive
Disney Resort allows guests to fully immerse themselves in their
favorite Disney movies through a chosen fairy-tale character persona.
Guests will engage in live-action role-play scenarios of iconic
moments in Disney filmography, experiencing all the sights,
sounds, and sensations that will bring movie scenes to life.

This contest is open to adults 18+ only. Winners will receive
two free guest passes to Happily Ever Island's inaugural run,
including airfare and accommodations
for a one-week stay at the end of March.

In order to create the most magical experience for contest winners,
please fill out the following information to
complete your contest entry.

Name: _____

Phone number: _____

Email address: _____

Please list your top three Disney characters you'd like to play in priority order, and we'll do our best to accommodate (human characters only, although mermaids permitted):

_____

_____

_____

Add the character choices for your plus one: _____

_____

_____

Measurements (we'll create a custom wardrobe based on your character): _____

Shoe size: _____

Allergies/dietary restrictions (food is included in your stay):

_____

Any other important accommodations: _____

Please attach a short essay describing your personal connection to your chosen character.

Good luck!

MADISON

"I'M LATE"

I t's times like this that I really wish cartoon birds and mice were available for personal grooming and tailoring services. It would be so helpful for people like me who, against all honest efforts, manage to sleep through ten alarms set to maximum volume and need nothing short of magic to get to work on time.

"Ugghhhhh," I moan, hitting snooze again while bleary eyes struggle to make out the time on my phone. 5:53 a.m. Crap. I thought changing my alarm tone to old-timey car horns would shock me out of bed, but I guess a year of falling asleep to my roommate Wren's death metal playlists has trained me to snooze through anything. I kick my comforter and SLEEPING BEAUTY AT WORK pillow off the bed, which flops onto Wren's side of the dorm. Thankfully, she's still asleep at this unholy hour, or I'd get a laser-beamed side-eye over my personal belongings crossing into her territory. To say that we are not the fast friends I always dreamed my first-year living quarters would create is the understatement of the century, but I mean, Wren *is* a Scorpio, so the stars were never on my side there.

I check my email before clumsily pulling on some jeans and stumbling around in the dark to find a hair tie and my silver sparkly flats. Still no news, argh. When are they going to announce the contest winners already?!

This is the third time I'll be late this week, pushing the limits of professional work behavior with my best friend, Lanie Golding, who I know is already at the coffee shop grinding the morning's beans. Unlike me, Lanie would probably burst into flames before arriving late to work, and she's had to cover for me more times than what's fair. She's my Java Jam! coworker, and luckily I know she won't be too mad, unless I leave her alone to the caffeine-craving overachievers who demand their triple espressos before their early morning study groups. Dealing with the public before proper coffee consumption is a challenge few people should have to endure, but least of all Lanie, who doesn't like talking to people even during the best circumstances.

I need to get to work before the Americano demons descend.

Running out of University Hall makeup-free and sloppily

dressed, I feel a freezing midwestern March wind blow back my hair, the winter cold hanging on for dear life despite spring being just around the corner. I spot a sliver of sunlight peeking over the top of the Schmitt Academic Center, otherwise known as SAC, one of the largest buildings on DePaul's campus. The surrounding Chicago neighborhoods continue their slumber as I race across the quad to Java Jam! conveniently located on SAC's first floor. Since I'm almost always running there, I know it will take me exactly two minutes and thirty-seven seconds to arrive, and when I burst through the door to the mostly empty building, Lanie doesn't even look up from under her coffee-colored baseball cap.

"Barry's not here," she says, referring to our boss and shop owner, who's itching to fire me. "There was some kind of deep-fryer emergency over at one of his other carts."

"Oh, thank god," I exhale, clutching a pain in my side. I should be used to these pre-dawn sprints by now, but my body really resists violent bursts of exercise.

"Also, I clocked you in at 5:58," Lanie continues. She pulls out a tray of muffins from the fridge, the same selection of mixed-flavor pastries we've been taking in and out of the display case for three days. I would be grossed out, but since no one ever buys them, I guess it doesn't matter.

"You are my actual fairy godmother," I tell her. "In fact, you're my Merryweather. No, Flora. No—"

"I don't know what any of that means." Lanie stops me. "But thanks?"

"Oh, yes you do. The good fairies! From *Sleeping Beauty*!"

She refills the half-and-half pitcher, nodding along as I continue. "The three of them protect Aurora when she's at her most vulnerable. They practically save the entire day! In fact, that whole movie should just be called *Three Kick-Ass Fairies.*"

She gives me a quick, placating smile. "Okay."

Lanie is a Very Serious Person. Or at least she pretends to be. Most of her days are spent in labs swimming with academia sharks, all waiting to strike for the top spot in the biology sciences program. This forces her to stay focused on school at all times, even on the weekends, reading textbooks with super-boring titles like *Investigations into Human Cells and Genomes.* Blech. Her GPA is a number I didn't think was mathematically possible, and she works so hard she sometimes forgets to take off her game face. But we've had enough late nights laughing over trash TV and ramen for me to know she's really fun when she lets loose.

I tie on my brown apron, smoothing my long blonde waves under my Java Jam! cap before getting to work. The two of us fall into our daily opening checklist, brewing coffee, prepping teas, filling ice bins, and, my favorite, whipping cream. This coffee cart's claim to fame is real whipped cream on every drink, and it's so good, I don't even mind having to make fresh batches constantly. Mostly because a lot of it ends up in my mouth.

Everything's brewed and ready by the time our 7:00 a.m. regulars roll through, eager to caffeinate before the day of learning begins. It's a steady stream of dark roasts, chai lattes, and iced mochas, Lanie and I dancing back and forth between milk frothers and coffee pots until the line mercifully dies down. There's always a lull after that initial push, giving my best friend and me time to chat and play around with the different menu ingredients.

"Hey, so, um, I heard back from that lab assistant summer internship thing," Lanie says quietly after cleaning the coffee grinder.

"What? Are you only just telling me now?" I exclaim. "You're in, right? Tell me you're in."

A red flush blossoms across her pale cheeks. "I'm in."

"LANIE!" I throw my arms around her, squeezing until she gasps for air. As a full head taller, I rest my cheek on the top of her Java Jam! cap, pressing her face into me. "This is amazing! We have to celebrate!"

She wiggles free, ears turning pink against her dark brown pixie cut. "Thanks. I wasn't sure if it would happen."

"Oh, please. They'd have been stupid not to pick you."

"Well, it's pretty competitive, so you never know."

"Whatever. I knew."

She can't help but smile, yet quickly deflects attention by immediately asking, "Did you pick a major yet? You have that meeting with your adviser soon, right?"

I turn away, busying myself with another batch of whipped cream. "Still deciding."

"I can help, you know," she offers. When I don't respond, she adds, "Maybe craft a pro-con list? I'm sure there are lots of cool majors here, but if you wait too long, you may not graduate on time. And there are summer internships to apply for . . . Next week *is* spring break —"

"I get it!" I say a little too forcefully, causing her to cringe. I swallow hard and reset my tone. "I get it. It's just . . . how am I supposed to choose things when every class or internship I look at makes me want to fall asleep? Like, I'm pretty sure I won't do great in a role if I can't even read through the description without yawning. I don't know what I want out of school or in an internship . . . or a job . . . or . . ." I give my bowl of cream a few vigorous stirs with my whisk, swirling the sugar into a fluffy cloud. "I just . . . haven't found the right thing. . . . The thing that makes me say, *Yes! This is it!* You know?"

Lanie frowns, twisting her fingers around in a nervous knot. Because she doesn't know. How could she? Lanie declared her major from the womb and has been hurtling toward a career in health care ever since, falling in line with her mom's expectation of landing a job with an "MD" at the end. Unlike me, she doesn't have to think about what's next, her academic path set in cement. Unlike me, she knows exactly where she's going and what to do. I keep hoping that something — anything — will set me on a trajectory, but so far My Calling is playing hard to get, leaving me to wander through random 101 classes until something clicks. I thought being in college would give me time to find myself, but lately it feels like everyone completed their journeys a long time ago.

But how? What am I missing?

"Well, maybe after class I can help you look," Lanie

suggests sweetly. "We could meet at the career center, browse the job boards? That could spark something. Because . . . and I hate to be the one to tell you this . . . but I don't think there will ever be a magic answer. As enchanting as you are, you're not some sleeping princess waiting for a miracle to wake you up."

"See, I *knew* you knew that movie!" I laugh, happy to be changing subjects. If there's anything I hate dwelling on, it's The Future, a fact my adviser is probably tired of hearing about. "But fine. We can quickly check the job boards, but only if we do something fun immediately afterward to celebrate your internship." I throw my hands up in a silent party, biting my bottom lip to the imaginary beat. "Oh! That reminds me: one dark chocolate pumpkin marshmallow chai coming right up!"

"Really?" Lanie does a little bounce on her toes, anticipating our favorite coffee concoction. When we first started working together, we thought it would be fun to cram as many flavors into a cup as possible to push the boundaries of caffeine consumption. While we mixed up some truly horrifying combinations (matcha mint hazelnut, may you never return from your watery grave), dark chocolate pumpkin marshmallow chai was an instant classic. Even though Barry keeps warning us that excessive flavor pumping is a "drain on his profits" and "cause for termination," we still whip up this winner every time one of us aces a test, finishes a paper, or simply makes it through a challenging day in one piece.

I quickly fill a large cup with the world's most delicious drink, adding a pinch of cinnamon to the massive scoop of whipped cream topping. "To Lanie, my best friend and biology genius, soon to rule over all the frog dissections and secret experiments of the world as a lab manager."

"Lab *intern*," she corrects.

"Lab *badass*," I retort, handing her the cup. She's blushing all over again, closing her eyes as she savors the first sip.

"God, this is so good." After another gulp, she adds, "Maybe you could be a chef?"

"What? No, too messy. I don't like touching raw meat. Besides, I only know how to make drinks."

"Mixologist? I feel like that's a thing."

"Um, no. That's just a fancy way of saying *bartender*."

"It's always something with this one," says a voice behind us. I turn to see Tessa, my on-again, off-again, current-status-unclear girlfriend standing on the other side of the counter with a shy grin. With her tight black curls pulled into a bouncy pony and crop top revealing just enough toned brown skin to get my attention, she looks amazing, and it's hard not to get swept away. When Tessa says things like, "Hey, you up?" I hear, "I miss you, I need you! Let's go on a romantic adventure together!" when really what she means is "I'm doing laundry; got any detergent?" Pairing socks is not whimsical. Feeling discouraged because one person wants burritos and the other wants to run through the rain hand in hand until we tumble into a mess of perfect kisses and shimmering fireworks is not a fantasy that works. Still, I keep hoping one day she'll want to ride off in the sunset together.

Lanie lets out a barely audible sigh, removing herself from

the conversation by ducking behind the refrigerator. But I perk up, eager to see what brought this elusive creature to my coffee cart.

"But that's what you love about me, right?" I ask. "Always full of surprises?"

"Hmm." She wrinkles her nose. "I'd say I *appreciate* your spontaneity."

Well, it's not love, but I'll take it. "Can I get you anything? Barry says we're not supposed to give stuff away, but you can have my free daily drink if you want."

Her body tenses, which is a strange reaction toward complimentary coffee. "Um, sure." She scans the chalkboard menu, biting the end of her thumb. "How about one of those unicorn lattes?"

"You got it!" I spin around, grabbing a large-size paper cup. "So, how are you? I missed you at my Disney karaoke night last week."

I peek over my shoulder to catch her dark eyes go wide. "Oh, you were serious about that? I thought you were joking when you said, 'Costumes and accessories will be provided.'"

"Why would I joke about theming?"

Her face bends into one of those uncomfortable smiles you give to a child who just discovered Santa Claus isn't real. "You're right. My mistake. I'm sorry I missed it." I finish adding a massive rainbow-sprinkle pile on top of her drink as she asks, "Do you have a break coming up?"

"I could sneak away for a second," I say mischievously, hoping for a quick mid-morning make-out session. There's a dark hallway just around the corner that would be perfect. "Lanie, cover for me?"

My best friend nods as I untie my apron. I scoot around the cart and reach for Tessa's hand, but she pulls away at the last second, wrapping both palms around her sugary drink.

"There's an empty classroom not far from here," I suggest.

"I was thinking we could talk right here?" She gestures toward an open table in the middle of the room. Talk? That doesn't sound good *or* fun.

We sit across from each other, Tessa doing everything she can to avoid eye contact. The ceiling, floor, and edge of her to-go cup are apparently preferable to looking at my face. Something's up. I mean, we haven't talked in days, which is never a good sign, but her body language is all wrong, sitting stiffly in her chair like she's about to start a business presentation, not a casual conversation with her occasional kissing partner. "So, I've been thinking—"

"Me too," I interrupt, knowing nothing good can come at the end of that sentence. "We're past due for a romantic date night. How about Italian? Ooh, or fondue! A little cheese, a little chocolate . . ." I do a mini seated body roll, flowing like melted cheddar.

She laughs politely. "I love both those things, but that's not where I was going."

"I'm fine with somewhere else—"

"No," she says more sternly before sliding back into her usual calm tone. "I mean, it's about spring break."

"Oh, tell me about it." I shake my head. "I still can't believe we haven't heard back from Disney yet." Ever since Tessa and I entered a contest to win a free trip to Disney's newest themed resort, Happily Ever Island, a few months ago, I haven't been able to stop thinking about it. The Disney Parks blog described it as the "preeminent immersive experience," allowing guests to step into the shoes of their favorite Disney character. The costumes, the settings, the music: Every detail has been brought to life, with the entire island split into themed sections representing all the Disney princess's stories. The concept art alone was enough to make me cry: fly a magic carpet as Jasmine, lead a battle as Mulan, make it snow as Elsa! FOR REAL. I've never done live-action role-play before but found myself in tears over the possibility of playing a character that means so much to me. It took a little coaxing (okay, a lot of coaxing) to get Tessa to enter with me, and I've been obsessively checking my email ever since.

Tessa squirms, taking a long sip of her latte. "I think . . . I'll actually be going out of town—not to the Florida Keys."

I blink, struggling to process her words. "What? Where?"

"Well, you know how my brother lives in LA? He landed a record label job and wants me to come visit." She brightens. "Can you imagine? Getting to visit a real recording studio?"

Reading her mind, I add, "You could sing for them!"

"I know! Wouldn't that be amazing?" Tessa breaks into the first real smile of the day, momentarily shedding the uncomfortable vibes she's been shouldering. My heart pinches at her excitement, loving to see her fired up but sad at what that means for me.

"Totally!" I cheer as my stomach sinks. I met Tessa at the beginning of the year when I heard someone in our dorm belting out "Let It Go" like Idina Menzel herself was in the building. Like a siren she called to me, pulling my fangirl heartstrings with her soaring soprano. I knocked on door after door until I found her singing into her hairbrush, breathless after nailing the elusive final note. My soul leapt: a beautiful girl busting out one of my all-time favorite ballads? Yes, please. We started hanging out, but ever since, I've been chasing that high from our first meeting: me, on the hunt for love; her, like a faraway maiden waiting to be found. I thought we'd bond over a shared passion for Disney and magic, but it turns out the *Frozen* soundtrack is her warm-up playlist, perfectly in her range with no emotional attachments.

From the very start, our relationship cast me as the Immature Dreamer while Tessa played the Grounded Goddess, tolerating my fairy-tale vibes while never really engaging. She's less "when you wish upon a star" and more "becoming the star itself." The Happily Ever Island contest was a chance to show her my world; I'm forever convinced that anyone not under Disney's spell just hasn't had the proper tour guide. And okay, yes, I know we haven't technically won the trip yet. But now it looks like I wouldn't even get the chance to share it with her if, by some mouse-eared miracle, we did.

"I can tell you're upset . . ." Tessa offers, reaching for me. As she squeezes my hand she adds, "And I want you to know, I've had a lot of fun hanging out with you. You're so cute and so . . . unique. But I think we both know we're on different pages here. And I can't miss out on this opportunity."

I nod, even though I don't understand this obsession with hurtling toward the future right this moment. This is our first year of college! Spring break is supposed to be about adventure, not networking. We're only eighteen . . . why can't we just have some fun? Why is everyone around me in a race to the finish line?

"I hope you do win, by the way," she continues with a genuine grin. "I know you'll make the perfect Cinderella." A big part of the contest entry was choosing which character to cosplay, which was not an easy feat. I identify with so many Disney characters, but who is my ultimate princess persona? Sweet, romantic Snow? Daydreaming, underwater-scheming Ariel? I made one of Lanie's pro-con lists, covered my dorm room with princess dream boards (much to Wren's disgust), but in the end, it had to be gentle, ever-hopeful Cinderella, the first heroine whose story grabbed my imagination and never let me go.

Plus, I mean, glass slippers? Hello? Like I'm going to let the chance to wear the most glamorous accessory of all time pass me by.

"Well, I know you'll crush it in California." My voice catches, unable to hide my disappointment. Even if winning this trip was a long shot, I thought Tessa's commitment was less to the destination and more to me, opening herself up to something *I* love and to our possible future together. Who did she think I planned that karaoke night for? I'm certainly not a singer.

Tessa breathes in relief. "Thanks. We're cool, then?" I force a smile as she stands. "Okay, see you around, Madison." I can't believe this is happening. Part of me wants to do something—explode into a flashy romantic gesture to show her how much I care—but instead we wave polite good-byes and I'm left alone in the hustle of students running to class.

I sigh, resting my chin in my hands. This is not how I thought today would go. Dumped. Stuck. Nothing to look forward to. Everyone in my life has something—Tessa and her musical aspirations, Lanie and her academic dominance—and I can't even make spring break plans, let alone declare a major. Typical Gemini spinning in place, trying so hard to make things work yet left with nothing but wishes and dreams. Why is it so different for me? The idea of growing up makes me want to barf: taxes, real estate prices? Complaining about the stock market and how the weather is affecting my lawn care routine? Gross. Does no one else see that adulthood is a plague from which there is no escape?

It's a good thing I didn't have time for mascara this morning or else I'd have black streaks running down my face. I let my long hair hang over my cheeks until I calm down. It's not fair to leave Lanie alone for so long, but I imagine no one wants to get a pick-me-up from a crying barista.

My phone buzzes in my back jeans pocket, and I naively hope it's Tessa saying she's changed her mind. But no, it's just an email.

Wait. Not just *an* email.

An email from Disney.

I drop my phone, nearly shattering the screen as I scramble to open the message. On my hands and knees from underneath the table I read:

CONGRATULATIONS!

You have been chosen for the inaugural journey
to Happily Ever Island!

Please see below for your travel arrangements.

Oh my god. OH MY GOD! I hit my head on the table, knocking it over onto a nearby study group, who looks at me like I escaped from the Lincoln Park Zoo. The entire hall stops and stares as I climb up off the floor, questioning why this splotchy-face girl is making a scene. But I don't care—let them judge. I'm about to be a freaking PRINCESS!

Happily Ever Island, here I come!

LANIE

"BE PREPARED"

Watching Madison and Tessa break up is a solid reminder of why I don't date. That, and the fact that I haven't made eye contact with a guy my age since I got to DePaul, but it's mostly the first part. Dating seems exhausting, and I don't have the time or energy to focus on another human being right now, unless that human is a cadaver in my biology classes.

From the safety of Java Jam! I watch Tessa walk away, leaving my best friend to bury her face in her hands in frustration. I fill a cup full of whipped cream as a post-breakup offering and tiptoe over to her table as she suddenly falls to the floor, looking at her phone like it's displaying the meaning of life before flipping over the whole seating arrangement, rising victoriously as everyone in SAC stares.

Um. That was unexpected.

"Madison?" I ask, approaching nervously. "Are you . . . What is happening?"

"LANIE!" She scoops me up in a rib-crushing hug. "I WON! I'm going to Happily Ever Island!"

I pull back in need of air. For someone who hates working out she's surprisingly strong. "That Disney dress-up vacation thing?"

She laughs, too excited to roll her eyes. "Oh my god, it's not just dress-up!"

I know this; of course I know this. Anyone within a one-mile radius of Madison has become aware of Happily Ever Island and all it entails, but as her best friend, I've listened to her talk about this trip to an almost-but-not-quite-nauseating degree.

"I'm so happy for you!" I cheer, but I can't help glancing back at the empty coffee counter, knowing Barry will pop a vein if he sees no one there. As the owner of eight different quick-service food shops and carts around campus, Barry's built a strange little empire for himself and enjoys randomly dropping by at least once a day to try and catch someone messing up. He loves any excuse to exert the very limited power he has in this world, and Madison, who admittedly is terrible at punctuality and overall rule adherence, is his latest target. He already yelled at her two days ago for wearing a sparkly castle pin on her apron, a violation of the company guidebook that I don't think actually exists, and I don't want him railing on her again when she's clearly in an emotional state. "But can we get back to the counter?" I ask with urgency. Our shift is almost over; Barry should be here any second.

"Ugh, who even cares about coffee right now?" she moans. "I just had my heart smashed to pieces and then glued back together with pixie dust in, like, sixty seconds! I need to go shopping! I need to pack!"

Okay, I can tell I'm losing her. She may not care about getting fired, but I do; this job would be insufferable without her at my side. Nothing motivates Madison more than talking about Disney, so if I want her feet on the ground and back at the counter, I have to rile her up fast.

"Why do you need clothes? Won't you just be walking around in a poufy princess dress?" I tease, instantly drawing her ire.

"Lanie, what even? I showed you the website! It's a completely immersive fantasy experience where guests actually *become* their favorite characters."

"Uh-huh," I say, slowly stepping backward toward the cart. "But isn't believing in all this stuff a little . . . juvenile?"

She stomps one of her sparkly flats. "Argh! What is with everyone today? Why can't adults believe in magic, huh? Do we all have to wring the joy out of our hearts in order to grow up?" I take another step back; she steps forward. "Is there some sort of age limit on dreams?" Step, step. "Because I'm not having it, Lanie." Almost there. "I don't care how old I get,

I like dreaming about happy endings, okay? I like fairy dust and glass slippers, and damn it, I don't care who knows it!"

She says the last part so emphatically, her cap falls forward on her face. Her chest heaves with the stubborn passion burning inside while a few waiting Java Jam! customers give her a slow clap.

"I'm with you, friend," I say, rubbing her shoulder. "Never stop dreaming, okay?"

She eyes me suspiciously, circling a finger around my face. "You did that on purpose, didn't you?"

"Yes."

"So that I wouldn't incur the wrath of Barry."

"Yes."

"Ugh, Lanie!" She throws her arms around me for the third time this shift. In my whole life I've never been as frequently embraced as during my one-year friendship with Madison. It used to weird me out, but now it feels strange if she doesn't hug me at least once a day. "Thank god! For a second, I thought you were abandoning me, too."

"Never."

"Uh, can I get a cappuccino, or are you two girls just gonna keep talking about your feelings and stuff?" asks the random guy at the front of the line.

We turn to him slowly. I am not above spitting in someone's coffee. Well, in theory. I'd never actually do it, but I'd think about it. A lot. Madison, on the other hand, would have no problem leaving some saliva as a parting gift, but only after giving exceptional customer service that tricks the jerk into sipping the contaminated drink.

"Sooooo sorry about that!" she says with a sunny smile. "One cappuccino coming up!" It isn't until after the line's died back down that she admits, "I hate it when customers interrupt. Can't they see I'm going through something right now?"

"Agreed, so rude of them to want coffee while we're talking."

"Right?"

"Seriously, though, are you okay?" I say to her as she brews another dark roast. "You walked away for five minutes and were suddenly flipping tables."

"I know, so random. Honestly I'm feeling all the things right now. I did not expect Tessa to dump me. Like, things haven't been great, but they haven't been bad, you know? She stole my heart, just like Maui did to Te Fiti!"

"Huh?"

"And then to find out moments later that the trip we planned together is officially on? My horoscope did NOT mention this." She closes her eyes, breathing deeply through her nose.

I can't help but laugh to myself. The way Madison looks at the world will never cease to amaze me. She's got this heart-on-her-sleeve, everything-will-be-okay breeziness that blows my anxiety-riddled mind.

I wish I could be more like that.

"Oh, Madison, you give hope to the rest of us," I admit.

She cocks her head, blonde waves falling over her shoulder. "What does that mean?"

"It's . . ." My skin starts to burn, an unwelcome heat radiating from my chest, up my neck, and around my ears. A fire so frequent, I'm surprised my pale skin hasn't permanently charred by now. It really doesn't take much to trigger it: a passing look from a stranger, a fallen book in a quiet room, an existential dread unearthed from simple conversation that makes me question every single decision I've ever made my entire life. Basically, the whole world is a trigger I can't avoid. But me alluding to the secret fear that's been building a nest of anguish in my head for the past several weeks? No, that's a path I'm not ready to trek right now. "Don't worry about it."

Madison twists her mouth in a question but lets it slide, choosing instead to tidy up the sugar packets while I stand in front of the fridge to let my chest return to its regular ghostly white. While I'm at it, I refill the various milk containers, and just before I can ask Madison more about her win, she says, "So, what should I do about Tessa? Tell her we won? Decorate her dorm in sparkly streamers and convince her to run away with me? I mean, this changes everything, right?"

I cringe, knowing I certainly wouldn't want to come home to a room covered in glitter. "I don't think she'd like that."

Her blue eyes flash with mischief. "I have an idea."

I freeze, a few beans spilling over the side of the grinder. "Which is?"

She flips her hair, grinning from ear to ear. "Can't say yet. But it'll be epic."

I grab both her hands and try yanking her down from whatever cloud she just floated away on. "Promise me you won't do anything too over the top, okay? Remember that you and Tessa are different people who respond to different things." She nods, but I can tell she's not really listening, already planning some romantic gesture that is unlikely to end in her desired result. The last time she tried to win Tessa's heart, she filled her room with stargazer lilies, only to find out later that Tessa's allergic. I hate seeing my friend throw her heart out with no one to catch it.

"Don't worry, I got this." Madison winks just as Barry saunters up to the cart.

"Well hello, girls. You managing not to burn the place down today?" He chuckles, wiping his nose on his sleeve. Barry, a middle-aged balding white guy who demands extreme cleanliness of his businesses but not of himself, always reminds me of a cranky old bull raring for a fight. It's not uncommon for him and Madison to go head-to-head, and judging by the exasperation on her face, the next round is about to start.

"As you can see, Barry, everything is perfect," she says, gesturing dramatically to the coffee-ground-free workstation. "But, as we've said to *you* multiple times, calling us 'girls' in that condescending tone is really inappropriate."

My cheeks burn at her comment, though I wholeheartedly agree. I don't know how she says these things so easily without breaking into hives.

Barry rolls his eyes, walking behind the counter. "Danny called in sick, so I'm covering the next shift. You two *WOMEN* are off the clock."

Madison mutters something under her breath as we untie

our brown aprons, grabbing our backpacks from the little storage space beneath the espresso machine. I heave my bag over my shoulder, my biology textbooks weighing an actual ton. My upper body strength has seen a dramatic improvement this year from carrying books alone.

We head outside of SAC into the quad, a biting blast of Chicago wind whipping both our faces. I zip my jacket up to my nose and pull a beanie over my pixie cut.

"Happily Ever Island is in the Florida Keys," my friend says with a sigh. "It will be so nice to get a break from this cold, bleak Chicago grossness and feel actual sunshine on my skin."

I nod, earlobes turning to ice.

"Text me later. Have fun learning about stem cells or muscle tissue or whatever." She waves a pink-mittened hand as she skips off in the opposite direction. "Love you!"

My mouth peeks out of my coat long enough to reply, "Love you too!" before I trudge off to class for another thrilling lecture on the miracle that is the human body. I get there early, choose a seat in the way back, and watch the room fill up with America's future doctors, all ready to soak up knowledge for their big, perfectly planned futures. No one really talks to one other, which is fine, because if anyone chatted with me right now, I'd probably accidentally blabber about princesses. The lingering buzz from Madison's dark chocolate marshmallow pumpkin chai fades as I pull out my notebook and favorite gel pen, stretching my fingers before the rush of note taking begins. I've found that taking notes longhand helps me retain information better, but it does result in hand cramps.

Eventually, the lights dim, my professor firing up a PowerPoint on the spinal cord, and I zone out, filling up the page with words like *cerebrospinal fluid* and *medulla oblongata*, adding bullet points, headers, and underlines as I go. My note-taking system evolved over time, but I perfected it my senior year of high school during my heated valedictorian race. Back then, being the top student in my class and securing a stellar SAT score felt like the fight of my life, but now that I'm in college, living out this "dream" I worked so hard for, the monotony of academia has settled in. Study for the grade, get the grade; study for the grade, get the grade: The game never changes, and I figured out how to win years ago. I thought taking more advanced classes would shake things up a bit, present a new challenge and reignite my desire to learn, but as second semester winds down, I find myself more and more detached. I should be excited, finally diving into subjects I'll actually use in my career, but the more I look at the road ahead, the more it feels like a life already lived, every choice already made.

And here I am bored before it's even begun.

An hour later, my notebook is full, my peers packing up for the next sojourn into science. I should say something to one of them, make plans for a study group or ask a follow-up question on the lecture, but making the first move turns my mouth into glue, so I quietly wait until the room clears. I'd hoped to make a friend in my program before the end of the year, but that outlook is grim.

My phone rings, Mom's face lighting up the screen. I swear she has an alarm schedule set to call me every time a class lets out. "Hi, Mom."

"How was the lecture?" she asks, tone crisp.

"Fine."

"Tell me the most interesting thing you learned."

I sigh. Resistance is futile. "Hold on," I groan, awkwardly pressing my phone to my cheek while grabbing my notebook back out of my backpack.

"Lanie?" Mom warbles. "Is something wrong?"

"No, just . . . referring to my notes."

She huffs with disapproval. "You shouldn't need your notes; the information should be fresh. When you're a doctor, you'll need to recall thousands of facts at the drop of a hat—"

"I know," I stress, but she doesn't stop.

"And if you're falling behind—"

"Mom!"

She pauses, I imagine to take a deep, cleansing breath. "Are you okay, hon? I'm worried about you."

"I'm fine. Just . . . tired."

"You know, I read an excellent study about a new supplement the other day, it's supposed to help with sleep patterns. . . ."

This goes on for the entire walk back to my dorm room, until she finally exhausts herself on the subject of my well-being and academic excellence. It's much better to let her get it all out over the phone, otherwise she'll send a stream of aggressively worded texts with more emojis than a respectable adult should ever use, and I don't really feel like listening to my phone buzz all night long.

"Call me after your test later, okay?" she demands, and I can almost feel her pacing back and forth from her office. "I'll be thinking of you."

"I'm fine, Mom. Don't worry." Ha. *Don't worry.* That's like telling someone in our family, *Don't breathe.* But she accepts my reassurance and hangs up, my room suddenly quiet without academic warning signs being shoved down my throat.

Honestly, it could be worse. I could have a parent who doesn't care at all, uninterested in my future and leaving me to fend entirely for myself. Madison's parents are some kind of wanderlusting globetrotters who left her to be raised by her grandmother. They certainly aren't checking on her grades or if she ate a vegetable this week; my mom wants what's best for me, even if her love burns so bright it feels like I'm being engulfed by the sun.

I curl up on the small corner of my bed not covered in books, looking at my Post-it Note–encrusted beige wall. At the beginning of the semester, I broke down each syllabus into what I call study bites: individual topics I can commit to memory each day. Every new vocabulary word or subject matter gets its own Post-it, and once I have it mastered, I move it from my "must learn" side of the wall to the "mastered" section. It should be a progress snapshot broken into rainbow squares, but lately, the mastered section is really slowing down.

I scan the available topics, eyes glazing over at terms like *afferent fibers* and *sensory cortex*, until I spot a square with swirling handwriting that reads, "I believe in you!"

Madison. She must have snuck that up there the other night when she was hiding from Wren. She'd promised to help me study, but we ended up binging some very old episodes of *America's Next Top Model* because Madison was incensed that I did not grow up learning how to "smize" and find my light. She is truly the weirdest and yet most wonderful friend I've ever had.

I stare at the Post-its, knowing I should be studying for the chemistry test I have in an hour. I have to study, but I don't want to. There's nothing inside me begging to understand the molecular breakdown of organic matter. And that is what worries me.

As Madison would say, I think this is a bad sign.

MADISON

"SHOW YOURSELF"

The trick to surprising someone who doesn't like surprises is to give them something they never knew they wanted. Like Lanie: She lives in a constant state of fear, so it makes no sense to jump out and startle her. Instead, my planned wonderments have to be sneakier, like leaving a bowl of mac 'n' cheese at her door when she's deep in study mode. Tessa *says* she doesn't play make-believe, but she's never really tried; the fact that we've actually won this once-in-a-lifetime trip has to make her reconsider. Time to make her a believer.

I head back to my dorm and pull out my arts-and-crafts box from under my bed. It's packed with all the basics: glitter, cardstock, stickers. Necessities. Wren's not here, so I can craft in peace; she never lets me decorate our room with seasonally appropriate paper crafts, which is pretty rude because why does she think I brought these supplies to college in the first place? Next year I hope to live with Lanie because she won't object to sparkly orange pumpkins or candy-coated hearts all over the place.

Anytime a Disney trip was officially on the books, Grandma Jean would surprise me with some kind of festive announcement. One time she filled my bedroom with Mickey-shaped balloons; another, she picked me up from school with a banner reading WE'RE GOING TO DISNEYLAND! taped to the side of her car. These moments were almost as special as the trips themselves; I still have the countdown calendar she made to keep track of the days leading up to our first visit.

For Tessa, I decide on something more low-key: a fake admission ticket announcing our win. I cut out an oversize rectangle from light green cardstock, mimicking the design of the old-school Disneyland ticket books. Tessa may not know what an E ticket is, but I know this vacation is worth the top-tier pass. With a Sharpie, I do my best to letter in the right font, adding little flourishes here and there.

GOOD FOR ONE MAGICAL VACATION WITH YOUR MAGICAL GIRL

I set down my pen. I still can't believe we won. Part of the application was a short essay on your favorite character and why. I poured my heart on the page, going way past the word-count requirement to detail my love for Cinderella, glass slippers, and basically all things Disney. There may have been a side story about the time I tried (and instantly failed) to sneak into the Cinderella Castle Suite at Walt Disney World, but the judges must have found that more charming than wrongful. God, I can't wait to see what this place looks like and to be one of the first guests to be there! I feel like my whole life has been building to this.

Peeking at my phone, I realize it's almost 3:30 p.m.: Tessa will be getting out of her vocal performance class soon. I blow off the excess glitter and slip the ticket into my coat pocket, dashing out the door. The music building is all the way across campus, but it's not like I haven't run there before. I book it down Fullerton Avenue, passing under the L tracks and out to the farthest end of DePaul. Eyes watering with windburn, I make it there with two minutes to spare, fired up and ready to change Tessa's world. Phew! I sit on the entry steps, bouncing in my seat.

Music majors start trickling out into the cold, and I look for Tessa's curls tucked under her red knit cap. Eventually, I spot her chatting with her fellow soprano Jenna. I leap up behind them without them noticing me, but before I can launch into my big surprise, I catch the tail end of their conversation.

"So, you finally dumped Madison?" Jenna asks with a disappointing amount of glee. Whoa. Excuse me? I thought we were friends. I let her borrow my favorite silver cardigan!

"*Dumped* is a little strong, but yeah, it's over," Tessa confirms. I bury my face in my scarf.

"You're too nice. She was hot and all, but so immature. Do you know she once asked if she could read my tea leaves? Who does that?"

Tessa shrugs. "She was sweet. And a good kisser. We could never really go anywhere, though. She just needs to grow up a little."

I stop in my tracks, letting Tessa and Jenna walk away in their cloud of gossip.

Grow up? Is that what she really thinks? My heart catches in my throat as I hear Jenna laughing from a distance. So that's all I am . . . some immature girl who's fun to make out with? When did celebrating the things you love become childish? Was I supposed to switch off my whimsy the day I became a legal adult? Tessa never called me immature to my face; she'd say she appreciated my lighthearted nature. But I guess what she really meant was that she could never fall for someone as juvenile as me.

A parade of students passes around me as tears begin to form, the cardstock ticket suddenly heavy in my pocket. What was I thinking? Why do I always find myself here? Throwing myself at people, jobs, and hobbies that aren't right, aren't me. Tessa was clear about what she wanted, but still I kept dreaming it would transform into something else. I'm so, so tired of being the fool. I wipe my frozen face on my coat, charging over to the nearest trash can to tear my handmade gesture to shreds. But before I destroy the evidence of my naiveté, a CTA bus comes barreling by, hitting a pothole and spraying a stream of melted snow and slush all over my face and coat.

Are. You. KIDDING ME?!?

I don't even move at first, feeling the gray sludge drip down my cheeks. A few students pass by and cringe, thankful they missed the spatter. I pull off a mitten to wipe mud and city grime off my face as more of it slides into my ballet flats; I consider myself a pretty positive person, but COME ON.

"WHYYYYYY?" I scream to no one in particular. Furious and freezing, I shake the ice out of my hair as I stomp down the sidewalk, promptly running straight into my academic adviser, Ms. Creeney, accidently spilling her cappuccino all over the ground. I have never in my entire life experienced such a rapid-fire turn of ridiculous events.

"Oh my god! I'm so sorry!" I cringe as she scowls at me through her scarf. We both look at the puddle of coffee, steam rising from the sidewalk.

"Ms. Turner," she grumbles. "Did you forget something?"

"Um . . . I can get you a fresh cup? Let me run over to Java Jam! real quick—"

"No. I meant, our two o'clock appointment? To discuss your declaring a major?"

Efff. I totally forgot. "I, um . . . something came up."

"And what was it this time?" she asks, crossing her arms. At this point, she's heard all my excuses.

"Would you believe I'm having a catastrophically bad day?" I gesture to the dirty water dripping from my coat.

She tightens her jaw, clearly not interested in my drama. "I'm concerned about your future, Madison. At this rate, you're not going to graduate in four years. Is that what you want? To be left behind?"

Wow, the stars are really not on my side today. First Tessa, now Ms. Creeney: Can't a girl just be without The Future breathing down her neck every five seconds?

I sigh. "No. I promise I'm working on it." She frowns. "Can we reschedule?"

She tells me she's booked until after spring break, but it's not like it matters anyway. I can't sit down with her *again* and tell her *again* that I'm just as lost. No, I don't know what I want to be when I grow up, because apparently I'm not even close to being a grown-up.

After she leaves, I watch the final rush of students hurry by before the next class hour begins. With nowhere to be, I stand in my misery, feet literally freezing to the sidewalk. I should be vibrating with happiness right now, hours deep in a Disney marathon to mentally prepare for the journey ahead. But the world seems very committed to a darker story line for me today, so instead I listen to the L train rattle by, watching all the passengers inside who know where they're going and supposed to be.

My phone chimes, and I almost don't check it, unwilling to tempt the fates with another potential calamity. But I can't leave notifications unread, so I peek at a text from my best friend:

Hey, hope your surprise went as planned.
Either way, I'm here for you.

Even though she has so much on her plate, Lanie always makes time to check in on me. She doesn't make fun of my efforts; she may not be a Disney girl, but she can at least appreciate what it's all about. Because yes, I made a fake admission pass for a girl who was clear about her disinterest. And yes, it looks like a class project made by a small child. But . . . I still like it. If someone made something like this for me, I'd be hers forever. Does that mean I'm not a grown-up? Too silly to be taken seriously? Then I guess so be it, because I'd rather keep my heart on my sleeve than let it shrivel up and harden forever.

I sigh, pulling the ticket out of my pocket, my glitter-pen details only slightly smudged by the puddle water. Maybe this is a sign that I should hit the brakes on romance right now. Take some time to focus on myself. . . . That's a thing people do, right? Every princess has a journey, an obstacle she must overcome. Maybe mine is figuring out how not to fall head-over-heels over and over again. What if I just let this magical Disney vacay sweep me away? Forget worrying about what-ifs and happily-ever-afters with girls that don't seem to get me and instead make a happily-ever-after of my own!

Yes, I can totally do that. And if I'm about to embark on a life-changing experiences without a significant other in tow, I know exactly who I want by my side.

Hoping to catch Lanie before her next class, I make a beeline back for SAC, reignited with fresh, joyful energy. I should've asked Lanie from the start! A spring break filled with something more than studying will be good for her, a nice change of pace before she continues careening down the path to lab coats and stethoscopes.

I pull out my phone to see where she's at, texting her a stream of messages including whether or not she wants to hear her horoscope. She never says yes, but I send it anyway:

> Aquarius: You've been on a nonstop conveyor belt of goal chasing, and while your overachieving ways have served you well, eventually you need to hit pause. Be a little adventurous this month and see how the world looks on the other side.

Then I add a GIF of Merida, triumphantly releasing an arrow into the sky, hair wild in the wind but loving every minute of it. Lanie won't know what this means, but she will.

Oh yes, she will.

LANIE

"LOST IN THE WOODS"

cing tests isn't just about studying. You have to know your stuff, but there are extra elements that can give you an edge. Peppermints to soothe a nervous stomach, spare pencils and pens in case they break, and never—ever—sit next to a window or door. Sight lines to the outside world are strictly forbidden, lest anything pull you away from your intended subject matter.

I flip through my flash cards one last time on the way to chemistry, but it's not really about the vocab words. In middle school, I convinced myself that osmosis was crucial to my success, and now I can't break the habit of physically touching my study materials right before an exam. I wonder if I'll still be doing this when I become a doctor, thumbing through medical texts before seeing patients. I stop in my tracks, trying to picture it.

But I can't.

Madison's dark chocolate marshmallow pumpkin chai catches up with me, so I make a quick bathroom stop, and by the time I get to my classroom, all my usual spots are taken, forcing me to sit by the wall of windows. Shit. Thankfully, Professor Callahan is a decent man who keeps the shades shut, cloaking us in the world of chemistry. I fire off a quick text to Madison, fingers crossed that whatever she's doing for Tessa turns out in her favor. Now it's time for my brainy Lanie life.

Test distributed, timer started, I dive in, slipping into that hypnotic state of answer delivery. I'm not even thinking, just doing, my brain eager to expunge all the excess information crammed within. I've made significant progress when our professor randomly says, "It's a little dark in here, don't we think?" and pulls open the blinds, sunlight streaming into the classroom. I squint against the sudden light change. Once my eyes adjust, I try returning my focus to the test, but something catches my attention outside.

A skateboarder circles around the quad, casually rolling like it's a sunny summer's day. At first I worry for him—should he be doing flip tricks when the sidewalk is covered in ice?— but then I'm pulled into his rhythm, joyfully gliding without a care in the world. Classes? Cold temps? Who cares? Not this guy. He's in his own little world, skating and spinning and loving every minute of it.

It's so nice.

"Pencils down!" Professor Callahan calls, breaking me from my trance. Shit. SHIT! I didn't finish the test! It's worth 20 percent of my grade! The last two questions stare up at me, innocent in their emptiness. Shit!

A hot geyser of nerves shoots through me as zombie feet take me to the front of the class. My professor frowns as I hand over my test.

"You all right, Lanie?"

We've never really spoken, unless it's been about proper microscope setup. "Oh. Um. I'm fine," I lie, voice shaky. Because this is the furthest I could be from fine. Heat builds in my chest, an eruption of anxiety about to boil over. I run to the nearest restroom, hiding in a stall as my stomach churns with my mistake.

I didn't finish the test. . . . There's no way I'll get a good grade . . . which will bring down my GPA . . . making it harder to get into medical school . . . delaying my residency . . . failure, failure, failure!

The fears spill into each other, coming in so fast and furious that they eventually merge into one apocalyptic truth: that in one fell swoop I destroyed my entire future.

I rock myself on the toilet seat, arms wrapped tight around my chest. As the worries churn, I fight to breathe deep and pull up my therapist's grounding exercises. When my internal world feels out of control, she encourages me to focus on what's right in front of me, concentrating on what I can see, smell, touch, and hear. I start cataloging my surroundings: I see toilet paper, I smell . . . well, best not to focus on that. But even as I prioritize what's real over what my panicked brain wants me to believe, I keep circling back to my future.

Sometimes it feels like it's all I think about, and yet, I've barely even thought about if that's what I want. The studying, the prep: The goal of becoming a doctor has always just been there, and as the dutiful daughter, I've kept my head down to do whatever it takes along the way. I don't even know what first prompted me to take my eyes off the prize; a few months ago, I was sitting in biology, taking notes like usual, when all of a sudden I thought, *Do I even like learning about the human body?* It was so weird, so out of the blue. I shook it off that day, but now the doubts pop up on a daily basis. Why do I feel like this is? Is it normal? Do other people question their goals?

My phone rings, but I don't even check. I know it's my mom and I don't have the heart to reveal my screwup; nor do I have the courage to lie. As a single mom, she worked her ass off to get me here: years of saving, planning, and not to mention acting as my personal tutor in all the sciences. All while running her own family medicine practice, a place that's expecting my name on the door. How can I turn my nose up at that? How can I even waver? My mom made so many sacrifices on my behalf. It's not something you can walk away from, no matter how much doubt starts piling up.

My phone vibrates again, this time with a rapid series of texts that have to be from Madison. She's the only person who sends me ten-plus messages in a row, so I reach from the toilet to check.

> Lanie
>
> LANIE
>
> I just had a flash of brilliance.
>
> Are you in class?
>
> I need to talk to yooooooooou.
>
> Also, do you want to hear your horoscope?

After reading about the stars wanting me to take an adventure, I text back:

> I'm in the second floor bathroom in SAC.

She writes back:

> Um gross but okay I'll be there in 2.

I force myself out of the stall, splashing water on my face from the sink. The mirror greets me with puffy brown eyes and freckles smeared on top of fading red blotches. Why do I have to wear my feelings on my skin? As if panicking wasn't enough, I have to broadcast to the world that I'm having a hard time. I can't hide it; Madison will demand to know what's wrong. But I don't want to burden her with this, especially since she just got dumped. My academic crisis is not her problem.

She bursts in, cheeks rosy from the wind, blonde hair fluttering down her coat. She always looks like she just belted out a Broadway musical: eyes glowing, chest heaving with joy. I don't think I've ever felt the way she looks.

"Lanie!" She floats over to me. "Lanie?" Her face falls. "What's wrong?"

"Nothing. It's nothing." I shrug, pretending like I didn't spend the past ten minutes crying in public. "Just . . . school, you know?"

"Totally." She studies me for a second, as though waiting for me to say more. Then she exhales loudly. "I'm so ready for a break."

"Did you pull off the secret plan I warned you against?"

She smiles, big and goofy. "Not yet."

"What does that—"

"I've been thinking," she interrupts. "This Happily Ever Island trip is a once-in-a-lifetime experience. I need to share it with someone special." She walks back and forth, tapping her chin as if a literal thought bubble is floating over her head. "Someone who is always there for me. Someone who could maybe use a little magic in her life?" She twinkles her fingers beside her glowing pink face.

Oh no. No, no, no. "Madison . . ." I groan.

"Lanie! It would be SO FUN!"

"Would it, though?" I cringe. The thought of pulling on an itchy taffeta princess dress instead of my usual oversize tee and leggings sounds anything but fun, not to mention how I'm sure this island will be populated with people, strange people, who I have no interest in meeting.

"Um, yes! It would be awesome!" she exclaims. "There will be soooo much to do there!"

"Like what?" I ask, picturing myself sunburned and forced

45

to mingle at a themed beach mixer or something equally awful.

"There's a whole schedule of classes, like making candied apples with Snow White and horseback riding with Mulan. Oh! And book discussions with Belle! You love reading!" Madison shakes my shoulders as if this physical reassurance cements her point.

The truth is, the princess angle has never appealed to me. At all. I never played dress-up as a kid, never played with dolls or anything sparkly. This may be because my mom felt the color pink was loaded with too many gender stereotypes or that all my toys were actually STEM learning sets about robotics or hydroponics or whatever. And that childhood vacation to Disney World? Yeah, right. My mom took me on a guided tour of crumbling European castles instead. I'm not *against* princesses—people are free to like whatever they want—but I wouldn't know the first thing about being one.

"Didn't you and Tessa have your characters all picked out weeks ago?" I ask, remembering the dozens of princess pictures taped to Madison's dorm during the decision-making process. "Who did she pick?"

Madison bites her bottom lip in excitement. "Merida!" she squeals, grabbing my hands as if this is best news ever. "Originally, she wanted Jasmine, because she wanted to rock that killer pony and belt out 'A Whole New World.' But then at the last minute she didn't want to deal with some 'useless Aladdin'—her words, not mine—and chose Merida from *Brave*, which is so much better for us because, Lanie," she gasps, clasping a hand over her mouth, "she's literally perfect for you! A smart, kick-ass woman who straight-up rejects the princess scene in order to chase down her destiny! Why didn't I think of this before?!"

She starts talking a mile a minute, lost in a daze of Disney details that I can barely follow. The more she talks, the more nervous I feel, completely unable to embody even a drop of the ebullient joy exuding from her every pore. I cling to the sink, taking deep breaths as worrisome thoughts flood in about a social situation where I'd be unprepared and unable to hide due to my major starring role.

What does Merida talk like? Would I have to know her lines? What if I say something wrong that's not in character? Do I get a script? What about the clothes? What happens if they don't fit? What if the fabric is uncomfortable? What if I mess everything up and ruin this trip Madison's been so excited about?

But all I say is "I don't even look like Merida."

Madison swats away my comment. "That doesn't matter! No one has to look like their characters."

"But you look exactly like Cinderella."

"That's a coincidence. She's my favorite, yes, but I could've chosen anyone. I could've been Ursula or the Beast! It's about living out your fantasies." She reaches into her pocket, pulling out a glittery piece of paper. "Here. Will you go on an adventure with me?"

As I look at what appears to be a pretend admission ticket, something comes over me. Do I have a burning desire to be a princess? No. But am I burning to do anything, really? I don't know what I'm doing, where I'm going; maybe it would be good to take a break. Try something different and see if any of my doubts become clear. I will 100 percent regret this, but I say, "Okay."

She lets out a high-pitched squeal. "Oh my god, Lanie! We're going to have the best time! And you will love being Merida!"

I force a smile.

Well, at least I'll get to shoot things.

MADISON

"JOLLY HOLIDAY"

The most important part of any Disney trip is the planning."

Lanie scrunches her nose at me. "That doesn't sound right."

I've invaded my best friend's room, pushing her boring textbooks aside for my Disney planning guides, park maps, and sample cosplay ideas. Whereas moments ago the room was a sad Post-it–covered cave where fun times go to die, now at least there's a little bit of sparkle to liven it up. "Well, it is. Your time at Disney is short and precious, which means you need to plan ahead to maximize your magic. Now, I know we're not going to the parks, but normally we'd need to map out our ride strategy, dining reservations, park hopping: It's a subtle science."

"Okay first, I don't think I've ever heard you say the phrase *plan ahead*," Lanie says, reaching for the bag of gummy worms I brought to fuel this planning session. "And second, you lost me with everything after that."

"I only plan when it's important, and nothing takes higher priority than this trip," I confirm. From the second she accepted my offer, I went into high gear, knowing full well that if I don't take lead on making this an exciting experience from start to finish, Lanie will bail. I love her to death, but she's very good at talking herself out of anything that wouldn't look good on a résumé, and I'm pretty sure most employers aren't interested in the details of your freshman-year spring break, no matter how epic. "To start, we're doing a double feature of *Cinderella* and *Brave*."

"I've seen them before."

"Okay, but like when—ten years ago?" She shrugs. "No, this material needs to be top of mind. Lanie, you're about to BECOME Merida. Living in her castle, wearing her clothes. Shooting her arrows! You need to be fresh."

She sighs. "You sound like my mom."

"Well, *you're* already in character, so we're on our way," I say, throwing a pillow on the floor beside her where I fire up Disney+ on my laptop. She snuggles into me, resting her head on my shoulder, and my heart pinches with glee. "I am so, so happy you agreed to do this," I tell her. "Honestly, I don't know why I didn't ask you in the first place."

"Hmm, because you were holding on to a girl who wasn't right for you?" she says sleepily.

"True," I admit. "But I liked her. The heart wants what it wants."

Lanie yawns, adding no further comment. Which is fair. She watched me chase after Tessa for months all while gently suggesting I spend my time on someone who actually *likes* being pursued. And even though I couldn't stop myself, I guess I knew deep down we'd end up this way. We really had nothing in common. Not that the person I'm romantically entwined with has to share all my interests, but I should be able to talk about them without feeling dumb. It would've been fun to traipse around an island with a drop-dead-gorgeous girl on my arm, but now I'm 100 percent committed to *not* being committed. I'm free to flirt with any princess I want.

Besides, Lanie's never even been to Disney, which is basically a crime, but now she can have a true expert by her side for her inaugural experience, and I'm going to do everything in my power to make it magical as hell.

❖

The next few days are spent shopping and packing. Since my class schedule is way less demanding than Lanie's, I take over coordinating all her outfits and necessities in Merida's color scheme: shades of forest green, blue, brown, and, of course, bright pops of fiery red. Finding island plaids proves to be a bit more challenging than expected, but I manage to snag a few tartan-inspired hair accessories including a very cute head-band I will definitely steal when we get back home. From tank tops to flip-flops, my best friend will always be in character, whether she notices or not.

My own vacation wardrobe is all about baby blue, drawing on Cinderella's ball gown palette. If it's not sparkly, it's not in my suitcase. I'm particularly excited to wear my new shimmering blue bikini with silver sandals; it's been so cold in Chicago this spring that the idea of being warm is a fantasy in itself.

Normally, when I pack for Disney, I bring Mickey-ear head-bands to coordinate with daily Disney bounds, my favorite ever being an *Alice in Wonderland*–inspired look with teacup-shaped ears and skirt that read CURIOUSER AND CURIOUSER along the hem. At Disneyland, I posed and twirled in front of the Mad Tea Party until I got the perfect shot, which is still my social profile pic to this day.

Things will work a little differently at Happily Ever Island. According to the island guidelines, guests will be provided with authentic character costumes for something they're calling "hero moments." Even though I signed us up for a variety of princess-themed activities, we won't get our full schedule until we arrive, and it's KILLING ME not to know all the details of what's to come. As a Certified Disney Expert, I like to be prepared, so I stuff every scrap of princess paraphernalia possible into our suitcases, including a framed picture of my grandma Jean during my first trip to Disneyland. Standing in front of Sleeping Beauty Castle grinning like total idiots having the time of their lives, Grandma Jean and I were twinning that day, both of us wearing Cinderella tiaras—me in an accompanying gown, her in a baby-blue sweat suit. I remember dripping in that cheap fabric under the hot California sun, but I didn't care, little six-year-old me just happy to be having fun in a magical place with my magical grandma by my side.

I miss her.

"Are you leaving yet?" Wren grumbles from her dark corner of our dorm. I don't know how she does it, but the girl exists in perpetual shadow.

"That depends," I say, safely securing the Grandma Jean pic in my carry-on bag. "Do you promise not to perform any satanic rituals while I'm gone?"

Wren glares at me through the small opening of the hoodie pulled over her head. "No."

God. It's time to go. I zip up my Mickey Mouse suitcase and head out the door, already wearing shorts even though it's still only forty degrees outside. Soon I'll get to trade my parka for a princess dress, and I am beyond ready.

Only when I get to Lanie's room, it's clear my Disney companion is not yet on island time like me. Through the door, I catch her one-sided snippets of a phone conversation.

". . . but I took the extra study session . . . My professor said it wouldn't be on the test. . . . I haven't taken a break all year. . . ."

Uh-oh, Mom dram. I knock quietly, and Lanie greets me with weary brown eyes, cheeks wet with tears. I tiptoe in, rolling suitcases in tow, as the muffled frustration of Lanie's mom sucks out all vacation energy from the room. On the corner of her textbook-covered bed sits her open laptop with a B+ graded paper—an impressive grade for almost any student unless you're Lanie. She mouths an "I'm sorry" to me, but I shrug it away, especially since I'm not the one getting pelted through the earpiece with words like *irresponsible* and *disappointment*.

After listening to a very long stream of verbal condemnation, Lanie finally interjects with "Mom, I gotta go," and quickly hangs up the phone, looking up at the ceiling as she blinks away more tears.

"Everything okay?" I ask.

She continues staring upward as she says, "Oh, you know, just that my entire future as a doctor is jeopardized due to a bad test."

"Wow, yeah, I see what you mean. A B-plus? Why not give up now?"

But Lanie is not in a joking mood. "My mom doesn't think I should go on this trip. She says I'm too distracted; that vacations are for *after* you've achieved your goals."

Whoa, now that is too far. "I'm sorry, is she implying that you haven't?"

Lanie looks at me, skin pale with exhaustion. "Not implying."

I want to explode with fury, white-hot flames blasting from the top of my head. But I dig deep to stay calm for Lanie's sake, knowing she needs soothing energy right now. "Lanie, you are—and this is not an exaggeration—the most dedicated student I have ever met. Not to mention the hardest worker.

If it wasn't for you, I would've been fired from Java Jam! ten times already. Plus, you're taking six classes instead of four, in super-hard subjects like microcellular genetic sensory systems or whatever."

She tries not to smile. "That's not a thing."

"But see? You know it's not a thing, which makes you way smart and way deserving of a vacation." She doesn't move, trapped in some sort of mental prison. Lanie's mom has some kind of Mother Gothel mind control over her daughter, but even Rapunzel had to break free at some point. If that makes me the Flynn Rider of the trio, I fully accept that responsibility.

"Besides," I add, crossing the room, "once we're airborne, what's your mom gonna do? Chase us down? Storm the shores of Happily Ever Island? These tickets are very exclusive, so trust me, there's no way she's getting to us."

Lanie perks up, a flash of off-brand determination lighting up her face. "Okay. Let's go."

*

A plane ride later, we're standing at a dock in the Florida Keys. Sunlight sparkles on turquoise waves, palm trees sway gently. High above, a white arched sign reads:

HAPPILY EVER ISLAND:

FERRY EVERY 30 MINUTES

I tilt my chin toward the sky, breathing in the salty sea air, my bare legs and shoulders warming in the sun for the first time in months. A thirty-five-degree temperature jump in a matter of hours? Um, yeah, I'd say we're crushing spring break so far.

On my right, Lanie nests in her cardigan, slathering globs of SPF 100 on her freckled cheeks. While I'm anxious to remove every inch of unnecessary fabric from my body, she's hiding away under a large-brimmed visor that she must have snuck in her carry-on, because I most definitely did not pack such hideous headgear.

I stare at the cartoon flamingo on the brim. "What?" she asks, a streak of white sunscreen remaining on her nose.

"Where did this visor come from?"

She touches her head, short brown hair peeking out the opening. "I bought it at the airport gift shop while you were in the bathroom."

"It's ginormous! And not even close to on theme."

"Okay, well, I don't want to spend the week burnt to a crisp!"

I sigh. "A little vitamin D might do you some good, babe."

Lanie pulls the visor farther down her forehead, sticking out her tongue at me before turning her attention to the ocean. She didn't say much on the flight to Key West, her mind busy untangling dilemmas she didn't want to share. I kind of wish she'd use *me* as a sounding board sometimes, but I'm not really one to give advice about overbearing mothers, so instead I distracted her with Disney Pinterest boards and official Happily Ever Island marketing materials, hoping to fill her head with much more frivolous thoughts. I didn't know her in high school, but if I had to guess, teenage rebellion was not high on her to-do list, making this trip a first dip in the disobedience pool. I just hope this time in paradise will shed some of the weight of that inner turmoil, maybe even help her open up a bit.

A group of girls walks up behind us, all wearing matching white T-shirts with pink glittery Greek letters. They giggle nonstop, as if they had too many cocktails on their flight, but either way, I like their vibes.

"Is this where we catch the ferry?" asks a pretty girl with dark hair and tan skin.

I nod, my excitement level cranked up to high. "Are you all going to Happily Ever Island, too?"

"Yes!" the sorority squeals in unison, all hugging and hopping on their toes. These are my people!

"Who are your characters?" I ask the group.

"Well, Zara here is going to be Ariel," reveals a blonde, pointing to the girl who asked about the ferry. The girls cheer her name over and over, clapping as she takes a small bow. "And the rest of us will be her mermaid sisters! Delta Nu goes under the sea!"

They start singing the chorus of "Under the Sea," and it's all so deeply cute I either want to make out with or befriend all of them immediately.

But I can't forget about my actual best friend, who is standing about as far away from the Disney lovefest as possible. I reach for her, refusing to let my introverted pal fade away.

"Nice to meet you, Ariel and various daughters of Triton," I say, once their singing dies down. Ariel gives me a little wink, and I have to stop short from fanning myself. Even though they started offering their real names, I won't be doing the same, because the second we step foot on Disney property, I plan to let the fantasy immersion wash over me and swallow me whole. "I'm Cinderella," I continue, giving a royal flourish with my free hand, "and this is my fiercely independent friend Merida."

All eyes turn to Lanie—much to her horror—a chorus of *ooh*s and *aww*s punctuating an onslaught of commentary.

"Merida! She's one of my favorites!"

"Ugh, I love the part where she rips her dress to shoot her arrow. Iconic."

"Do you know how to ride a horse? I bet they'll teach you!"

Lanie's cheeks redden. Working at Java Jam! all year has increased her tolerance for attention, but she still has room to grow. During our first morning shift, she got so overwhelmed from the stream of orders, she came super close to vomiting in the ice bin. That was my introduction to what she calls her "stress barfs"; until then, I'd never realized how anxiety can take such a physical toll. The girl is a damn warrior for managing that challenge every day.

More and more guests arrive at the docks, each with a hopeful Disney twinkle in their eye. Lanie and I stick with the mermaids, playing a guessing game of who will be playing which Disney character.

"What do you think . . . Gaston?" I guess, pointing to a thirtysomething-year-old dude with serious biceps.

"Ooh, totally." Ariel grins. "What about her?" She nods toward a sweet, elderly woman. "Mrs. Potts?"

"Oh my god, yes." I laugh. "But remember—you don't have to look like your character. Those two could be totally flip-flopped."

"I'm so here for that!" she cheers. Her bare shoulder brushes up against mine, and I turn to catch her beautiful dark eyes. My heart somersaults, but I remind myself to be casual. I've been so dead set on landing a long-term girlfriend that I've forgotten how to just let myself have fun. If there is to be any island romance while I'm here, it's going to be easy, breezy, with no strings attached. Time for some *me* time, to move on from my heartache and immerse myself in Disney magic.

I pull myself away, leaning into Lanie. "Join our game."

"Umm." She looks around. The docks are pretty packed now, making it harder to scope out our fellow islanders. "I don't know, Madison. I'm not good at this."

"Here, let me help." I scan our surroundings, searching for a potential target. "What about—"

A tinkling sound plays over a hidden PA system, as if Tinkerbell herself is flittering above us. Heads turn looking for the iconic pixie, but instead we're drawn to a golden ferry pulling up to the shore. A couple of people chuckle, myself included.

"I don't get it. Why are you laughing?" Lanie asks.

"The announcement for the ferry is a fairy sound. A *fairy* ferry."

"Ah. Got it," she says without judgment. I can only imagine how dorky she must think this all is, but at least she's not showing it.

The double-decker ferry glitters against the water, railings and life preservers all painted in a shimmering gold. Along the side, a dark blue nautical font reads HAPPILY EVER ISLAND, the I of ISLAND drawn into a lighthouse with the light itself shaped like a castle. As everyone excitedly chatters about our approaching ride, I lock fingers with Lanie and pull her to the front of the gates. I want to be the very first person on board.

"Welcome, guests," says a soothing prerecorded female voice. "Once you step off these docks, you'll be transported to an incredible island of Disney magic, celebrating the dreams and heroic moments of your favorite classic characters. Leave your worries behind as you open your heart and imagination to a whole new world where happily ever after happens every day."

I squeeze Lanie's hand. I think I'm going to cry.

No, I'm definitely going to cry.

Two cast members dressed in navy-blue vests and matching shorts open the gate, and I practically throw them our tickets, run-walking onto the ferry and up the stairs, rolling suitcase bumping at my heels. I hear Lanie gasp in surprise as I take off, but I can't stop until I snag a prime viewing spot up front. Approaching Disney properties is A Thing, a magical moment in time where fairy tales are just within reach. Grandma Jean and I would always compete over who could spot the first landmark, whether it was the peak of the Matterhorn peering over Harbor Boulevard or the spires of Cinderella's Castle glistening over the Seven Seas Lagoon. Seeing those silhouettes meant it was really happening, that everything we'd been dreaming of was about to come true.

I don't know what Happily Ever Island will look like, but I have to be the one who sees it first.

Lanie catches up to my coveted spot on the second story, flopping her arms over the railing dramatically. "Uh, did we really have to run?" she asks.

"Yes. Lesson one in Disney fandom is honoring tradition," I say in my best authoritative tone.

Other guests start to crowd around us, each hoping to squirm closer to the very front. We hear someone grumble, "Ugh, how did they get that spot so fast?" and I give Lanie a knowing look.

"I have much to learn from you, Obi-Wan," she says. "Wait, *Star Wars* is Disney now, right?"

I throw an arm over her shoulders. "You're going to be just fine, my friend."

Another chime plays, followed by a cast member announcement. "Good afternoon! Welcome to the Happily Ever Island ferry! We're about to push off for our thirty-minute ride, so please relax and enjoy your journey!" The opening notes from *The Little Mermaid*'s "Fathoms Below" begin to play, gentle horns leading the way as the ferry lurches forward. A few guests begin to clap, and I turn my attention forward, eyes glued to the horizon as sailors sing their tales of time at sea.

About halfway through our sail, Lanie finally removes her cardigan, taking her first relaxed breath since we left Chicago.

"You know, I'm actually kind of excited to see what this island's all about," she admits, but there's no time to answer because: I see it.

Happily Every Island, a growing dot coming into focus on the horizon.

A sprawling yet secluded landscape stretching out against the Atlantic, a gradient of greens punctuated by glittering building tops, each with its own distinctive outline and story. The closer we get, the more details begin flooding my senses, and I have to hold on to the railing so as not to melt onto the ferry floor.

To the far left I see Motunui, lush with tropical plants and Moana's wooden boat pulled up on the sandy beach. To the far right, a desert landscape, the dusty streets of Agrabah partially concealing the golden domes of the Sultan's palace. From the snowy peaks of Arendelle to multiple fairy-tale castles reaching toward the sky, every inch of the island is blanketed in Disney iconography, pulled from the screen and set atop water. It's unlike anything I've ever seen and yet is exactly how I imagined.

Everyone around me whips out their phones, recording our arrival to a turn-of-the-century style boardwalk in the center of the island. But I can't move, can't even blink, for fear of missing one single second.

Tears stream down my cheeks as the ferry slows down, easing its way into its awaiting dock. Lanie looks over at me in surprise.

"Madison? Are you okay?"

I swallow hard, a memory rising in my heart.

"Grandma Jean, what is Disneyland like?"

I'm sitting on her lap, a souvenir park map unfolded before us. I've yet to memorize all the landmarks and don't know how to process what I'm seeing.

"Well, it's a magical place where you can lose yourself in stories," *she says. "Cruise through jungles, fly through space, plunge down mountains: You can try it all."*

My eyes open wide, taking in all the colors and shapes. I'm drawn to a pink castle in the center. . . . Who lives there? Can I go inside? I want to more than anything.

"And see right here?" She points to the bottom of the map where a little train waits at a station. "Once you pass through the gates, anything is possible. No matter what, you're destined for adventure."

"Really?" I ask, breathless.

She smiles, holding me close. "You'll see when we get there."

Oh, Grandma Jean, if only you could see this!

LANIE

"INTO THE UNKNOWN"

When Madison first told me about Happily Ever Island, I couldn't really envision it. The only "immersive experience" I ever had was going to space camp in eighth grade. I got so nervous waiting to get on the gyroscope ride that I threw up everywhere. I had to skip it altogether, completely missing the actual space-like sensation. She told me we were going to live out our dreams, but since she says that on a regular basis, the description didn't hold much weight. The closest I'd been to a theme park was a grocery-store parking lot carnival, so my imagination stopped at the postcard view: a static image of one castle ready for a day's work.

But this . . . this is unreal. There's not one but several

castles rising through the island trees, with topography rang-
ing from sand to snow and back again. Beaches and mountains mash together as the island strives to represent very different terrains in close proximity, yet somehow it all works.
In the center of it all sits a grand boathouse in pristine white,
accented with nautical reds and blues. An arched sign in bold
gold lettering reads HAPPILY EVER ISLAND, with thirteen different flags hanging from a high balcony. Each flag bears a unique
crest that must represent each kingdom; I don't recognize all
the symbols, but I'm instantly drawn to the blue-and-brown
tartan flag that must be for Merida. I stare at the Scottish
print, feeling zero connection to what it represents and my role
here. *How am I going to do this?*

Judging by the absolute glee of the Disney superfans all
around me, no one else is having worries like mine. Everyone
is frozen in awe, mouths agape, eyes glossy. It's eerily quiet as
the guests take it all in, so I turn to Madison, who's suspended
in the same stunned wonder. Golden waves fluttering behind
her, her pale pink nails clutching the railing; she's so still, I
worry she may be having a stroke.

"Madison? Are you okay?"

Her chest heaves, releasing a response so soft, I almost
miss it. But there's a melody behind her whispers, convincing
me she's on the verge of breaking into song.

She closes her eyes, quietly mouthing the same lyrics
Rapunzel sings when she's about to burst free from her tower.
I only know this because Madison regularly sings "When Will
My Life Begin" when we're close to quitting time. In fact, the

last time she sang this song in public was when Barry intro-
duced a new dark fudge sauce to the Java Jam! flavor menu,
and Madison had no problem belting out how this additional
chocolate option made her life begin. At school, the surrounding
students looked at her like she was high, but here —*here* — she
is a ringleader, not an outlier, because it doesn't take long for
her solo to morph into a chorus of voices.

I tap her on the shoulder, trying to break her *Tangled*
trance. "Madison?" I repeat, but it's too late; she won't be able
to answer until the song is done.

She faces me, grabbing my hands and pulling them to her
heart. Tears in her eyes fuel her song, and the second the ferry
docks, we're running again, but this time, everyone on the
second story is following our lead, a herd of quick feet and
bumping suitcases rushing down the stairs.

Madison continues her melody louder now, as we run with
Ariel and all her mermaid sisters joining in. More and more
voices collide as an uncomfortable amount of people brushes
up against me. Everyone is singing except for me. I'm too
focused on not being stampeded to death as we dash to the
docks, Madison leading the way.

But as quickly as we took off we suddenly stop, my best
friend having lost a shoe somewhere between the boat and
the shore. "Shoot!" she yelps, her right foot bare. "Do you see
my shoe?"

I scan the scene, but the frantic scurry of feet and rolling of
suitcases make it hard.

Suddenly, a young East Asian woman dressed in a navy-blue

vest and matching skirt swoops up behind us, holding Madison's silver ballet slipper. "Excuse me, did you lose this?" she asks.

"Oh!" Madison exclaims, sliding it back on. "Th-thank you!" Madison stares, her mouth agape as the woman turns to make her way to the front of the crowd. Then Madison shakes her head, shooting me a little goofy grin, before skipping to catch up with her people.

The whole crowd gathers together in an inward-facing circle, cheeks bursting with excitement. They all clap and laugh as they finish their song, people hugging one another in celebration. I could not feel more out of the loop, yet I plaster on a smile, not wanting to seem like some horrible curmudgeon allergic to fun. I want to sink into the experience, but my points of entry are so limited. Maybe I should have studied for this, swapped out my biology flash cards for Disney-themed ones. But I guess it's too late for that now.

"That's some serious Disney spirit!" shouts a male voice over the group's chatter. We turn toward a pair of island employees, dressed in matching navy-blue vests. The first is the woman who returned Madison's shoe, and the second is a white guy with massively large red curls bouncing on top of his head. "How is everyone's day so far?"

We answer with some tame clapping and a few *woo*s.

But this does not satisfy Big Red. He leans over, comically pressing his palm into his ear like he can't hear us. "I said: How is everyone's day so far?"

Everyone responds more enthusiastically this time, and he breaks out in a toothy smile. "All right, that's more like it!

Well, welcome to Happily Ever Island, everyone! My name is Jared Jones, and I will be your island ambassador this week." His partner gently elbows him in the ribs. "Oh, I'm sorry—*one* of your island ambassadors. With me of course is my fairy-tale partner-in-crime, Valentine Kimura!" He fans her with jazz hands to which she gives a blink-and-you'd-miss-it side-eye, immediately replacing it with a winning smile.

"It's Val, actually, but yes, welcome, everyone! We are so happy you're here for our inaugural run of what is sure to become one of Disney's more beloved vacation destinations. Think of me"—she lowers her voice considerably—"and Jared as your concierge, cruise director, and all-around Disney guru dedicated to your complete and total happiness."

I can already tell I'll be going to Val, not Jared, with any questions. Even from across the way, his overeager energy is making me nervous. People who are loud and aggressive for no reason are what I call "turtle people" because they make me retreat into my shell.

Val continues. "A little background on me. I started with the Disney College Program my junior year at NYU, but when I heard about Happily Every Island, I knew I had to be part of this magical, once-in-a-lifetime experience. I've pretty much always been hooked on all things Disney, but the summer I went to Tokyo Disneyland with my grandparents—they're from Yokohama—I became full-on obsessed. There's literally nothing I don't know, so please, don't hesitate to ask!"

"Hmm, challenge accepted," Madison whispers to me with a smirk.

Jared steps forward, swinging the spotlight back his way. "And about me—"

"Jared?" Val interrupts. "Should we start getting everyone checked in?"

His lips press in a thin line before breaking into a full smile. "Great idea, Valentine! I know I can't wait to get started!"

"It's *Val*," she repeats under her breath, keeping her face bright and cheerful. After a year of grinning and bearing it with Barry, I know this forced expression well.

"Oh my god, they hate each other!" I whisper excitedly to Madison.

She nods emphatically. "This is going to be amazing."

Val looks down at her clipboard, crossing something off with red pen. "Okay!" she chirps, smile beaming. "Behind me is the Boathouse, your one-stop shop for all your accommodation needs. Check-in, guest services, first aid: If you need help during your stay, the boathouse is your best bet. Now, I'm sure you're all eager to slip into your Disney personas, but first we'll get everyone checked in, and you'll receive your itineraries, island maps, and suggested scripts for your big-hero-moment performances. This way, everyone!"

My insides ignite as Val hurries off, leaving Jared behind to escort the group.

Scripts? Performances? WHAT IS THIS? I may not have understood all the terms of this vacation, but I certainly did not sign up for some sort of *Brave* stage show. I would rather be shot into the sun than have an audience of rabid Disney fans critiquing my Merida moves.

I grab Madison, pulling her to the back of the forming line. "You did not tell me about this!" I hiss.

"Babe, relax," she says, clearly unhappy at my preventing us from checking in. "It's not like you'll be doing a play or something. More like . . . a reenactment."

"How is that different?!" I shriek.

"Look, don't stress. You don't have to do anything you don't want to do."

Her calming efforts are only making me spin out further. "But I'm signed up for *Merida*, not Random Villager Number Two. It kind of seems like my participation will be an important component for any guests signed up for the *Brave* story lines!"

Madison must see the sheer panic in my eyes because she grabs me by the shoulders to say, "Hey, this isn't like the time you almost fainted during your genetic testing presentation. There are no grades here, you're not being judged. These people are here to goof around and play pretend. It's going to be fun."

Fun? Fun?! Nothing about being thrown into a situation where I have no sense of control sounds fun. On the other side of that boathouse lies a place where I'm supposed to dive into fantasies I know nothing about, and nothing makes me feel more helpless than being unprepared. My breathing picks up, a rush of adrenaline causing my hands to shake. I twist my fingers into a knot, but before the surge in stress completely takes over, I remember to run through the grounding exercises I learned in therapy.

Five things I can see: a palm tree, a seagull, the ferry, the board-walk, my suitcase.

Four things I can feel: the ocean breeze, the sun on my skin, my cardigan around my waist, Madison gently squeezing my hand.

I run through the rest of the senses and feel a little better. Madison tips up the brim of my visor and asks, "You okay?"

"Yes. Thanks for waiting."

"Duh. Let's go."

We link arms and walk into the Boathouse lobby, a soaring room with curved white ceilings, wicker rocking chairs, and a giant wooden steering wheel looking like it was stolen from a pirate's ship hanging over reception. Madison skips up to the desk and happily retrieves very thick welcome packets for each of us. I start flipping through the binder of information, but my best friend impatiently insists we catch up with the group who are all checked in and waiting outside.

The Boathouse acts as not only guest services but as a gateway to the island itself, and when we exit, we're thrown back in time to a 1920s East Coast boardwalk. Pastel-colored restaurants and shops line the wooden walkway, each with ornate architecture and tasteful princess theming, with names like Belle's Bookstore and Ariel's Thingamabobs. Bright, tropical flowers are tucked into every window box and lamppost: a rainbow of hot-pink hibiscus, purple lilies, and orange birds of paradise. Ocean water bisects the boardwalk, with arched bridges allowing guests to wander back and forth, and it's all so inviting, I find myself not knowing where to start.

"Isn't this amazing?" Madison asks breathlessly.

"Consider me amazed," I say, sounding more sarcastic than I intend. Because honestly, you'd have to be completely dead inside not to appreciate the level of detail and care taken here.

Val and Jared work together to corral the group, fighting for our attention against the beautiful backdrop.

"Okay, everyone!" Jared finally shouts, so loud that several people jump back in surprise. "Now that you're all checked in, we'll start our orientation tour! This is the Boardwalk, where you can shop and dine throughout your trip. This is the most casual area of the island, because as you can see, it is not tied to any one particular Disney story. There will be live entertainment and activities here daily. Let's take a stroll down the Boardwalk now!"

As we walk, I can't help but ask Madison, "Does Jared's voice sound like—"

"Somebody broke the knob on his volume level? Hopefully, Val takes over delivering the rest of the details because he is seriously ruining these chill beachy vibes."

We stop in front of Tiana's Palace, a grand two-story eatery with upbeat jazz floating out of every window. The smell of simmering gumbo gets my stomach grumbling, and I realize I haven't eaten in hours. Hopefully there will be food on this tour.

"This is Tiana's Palace, the finest restaurant on Happily Ever Island," Val says proudly. "I highly recommend the beignet-making class we do here each morning, and yes, I'll happily take any samples you're willing to share!" After some polite laughter, she continues. "There are classes and activities offered throughout the island, most of which are themed to a specific character or story. While you're each already signed up for a week's worth of activities, please see me —"

"Or me!" Jared yelps.

" —if you need help adjusting your schedule. Classes and group activities are planned throughout the day, but you'll always have designated time in your area of the island to participate in scheduled story scenes if you would like. Your itinerary details which scenes will be performed each day, with wardrobe and blocking suggestions. You'll also find screenplays from your movie, if you're interested in using exact dialogue for your character."

Madison shimmies her shoulders in anticipation, while I feel mine droop in dread.

"Each night you're scheduled for dinner at a different location." Val looks down at her clipboard, then eyes the crowd with a mischievous look. "But, the best part, in my opinion, are the hero moments."

"What's a hero moment?" Jared asks, scratching his chin in exaggerated wonder.

Val seems to hold back a sigh. "Thanks for asking, Jared. Hero moments are the biggest, most memorable sequences from each princess's story, and because they're so special, the entire island is welcome to attend. Think Belle dancing with the Beast, or Rapunzel seeing the floating lights: iconic scenes that until now could only be experienced on the screen. There are one or two hero moments scheduled every day, and while

the starring roles have already been set, you can still participate by being a villager or other background character. I can
help you with costuming options if you're interested; I definitely recommend attending at least one hero moment that isn't
your own to give you the most magical experience possible."

"She's cute, don't you think?" Madison whispers in my ear.

"Hmm? Who?"

"Val, obviously. She's like this sparkly queen of Disney
nerdom."

"Just your type," I say, although I'm not really paying
attention. I don't want to miss any of these instructions.

"Speaking of magic . . ." Val pauses for dramatic effect.
"In order to help you all have the most fantasy-filled stay, we
do have a couple of recommendations and rules. First, staying
in character as much as possible will certainly help heighten
your connection to your story, which can be achieved through
wearing the provided costumes and avoiding using your real
names. It may take a little getting used to, but the longer you
can respond to Anna or Elsa instead of your actual name will
help make everything feel more real. And about those costumes: Everything has been fitted to your exact measurements
with every stitch and button carefully considered. While the
wardrobes are incredible—I'd personally love to wear Tiana's
lily dress—please only wear your costumes in your area of the
island. Mismatched costumes can break the illusion; imagine
Moana getting lost in Arandelle! Disney bounding is okay, and
I can assist with costume changes if desired."

Disney bounding? It takes me a second, but I remember

Madison using this term to talk about wearing everyday clothes that subtly nod toward particular characters—mostly to justify all the plaid she'd packed for me. I tune back into Val's speech.

"Second, we have cast members playing several of the roles throughout the island to help keep the make-believe going. See if you can guess who's a professional and who's just really good at Disney role-play."

Madison points to herself assuredly and mouths, "Me." I'm honestly surprised she hasn't already slipped into one of the many Cinderella outfits I know she packed for herself.

"Finally—and you may not like this part—there are no cell phones allowed on the island."

The crowd groans, and Madison gasps in horror.

"I know," Val says. "But, as this is our inaugural run, we want to ensure everything runs smoothly before it's all committed to the cloud. Plus, there's no cell service here anyway, and if Mulan can save China without a smartphone, you can make it through your vacation without one."

Rules, scripts: What kind of spring break is this? Val and Jared start collecting everyone's phones, but before I hand mine over, I notice a stream of texts from Mom.

Lanie, please call me.

I'm sorry about our fight—I just want what's best for you.

I'm worried. Please call.

While I did text her to say I was going on this trip no

matter what, I never checked back for her response. I didn't want to find some long-winded diatribe about me not living up to my potential; I have enough to worry about with this bulging Merida study guide under my arm. But I didn't expect to receive an apology. Mom and I have never gone longer than twenty-four hours without a call or text, so this next week will be interesting for us both. I text her a quick:

> We made it here safely but no phones allowed. I'll be okay.

"Why are they doing this to me?" Madison whines as the bag of phones comes our way. "How am I supposed to prove I pulled off the perfect Cinderella role-play without my phone?"

"Paint a picture?" I suggest. "I think I saw a Rapunzel-themed art studio down the Boardwalk. . . ."

She scowls at me, huffing dramatically as she places her phone in Jared's sack of smartphones. "I don't like this."

Honestly, though it will be weird to go a week without technology, it doesn't bother me much. If no one has a camera, no one can document what a fool I'm bound to make of myself.

Once all the phones have been confiscated, Val announces, "Follow me to the Lighthouse, and then you'll each be off on your way!"

The Boardwalk ends with a giant lighthouse, precariously placed on a small mountain of man-made rocks rising out of a very large circular pool of sea water. Fountain jets dance along the base, while the blue and white lighthouse stripes alternate up toward the sky. A small bridge makes me think someone could actually climb up to the top; I bet the entire island is visible from up there.

"The Lighthouse is the island's hub: It's visible from almost everywhere, so if you ever get lost, just follow the light and you'll be okay!" Jared shouts, gesturing to the rotating light above.

Val nods. "Now, if you'll notice, there is a separate path leading to each of the thirteen different story areas on the island. This is where we leave you! Follow your path to get familiar with your designated area, and don't worry, your bags have already been delivered to your character's dwelling. Tonight, there is a special Be Our Guest dinner for all guests in the Beast's castle, but until then, go! Explore! Your itineraries don't start until tomorrow, so use this time to play and delve into everything the island has to offer. Have fun!"

The group breaks apart, guests eagerly checking signs and quickly scurrying away to start their role-plays. Cinderella's and Merida's paths are on completely opposite sides of the Lighthouse, and for the first time since we got here, Madison lets go of my arm.

"So . . . meet back here before dinner?" she suggests, tip-toeing away ever so slightly.

Oh no. I thought we'd be exploring our two stories together. "You're leaving me?"

She grimaces. "I mean, yes? But not like, *leaving* leaving.

Just . . . engaging. But separately! And only for a little while. I want to meet my evil stepsisters and kick-start their hatred for me." Her blonde eyebrows wiggle playfully.

"But . . ."

"Don't worry," she calls out, skipping away. "You'll be great. I believe in you! Let the will o' the wisps guide the way!"

Will o' the *what*? What are wisps? "I don't know what that means!" I yell after her. But she's already gone, leaving me alone with only the sound of splashing fountains and heart-pounding nerves.

I head over to a heavily wooded path on the far right side of the Lighthouse, an intentionally faded sign reading DUNBROCH. As I start down the dirt trail to Scotland, I feel anything but brave.

MADISON

"ONCE UPON A DREAM"

I would feel bad about leaving Lanie if it wasn't for the drumbeat in my heart absolutely compelling me to explore every inch of this island as quickly as possible. It was great to get the official vacation rundown, but it's taken every speck of self-control not to just take off running, flooding my senses with this Disney paradise. This place is INCREDIBLE, and I haven't even seen the princess-themed areas yet. If they're anything like that beautiful boardwalk, I may wring myself dry on day one. I've already cried once, and I wouldn't doubt it happening again.

I find Cinderella's path, a cobblestone walkway with neatly trimmed trees and topiaries behind the sign reading FRANCE.

But just before I take my fairy-tale journey, I spot Val hurrying back down the Boardwalk, legs moving at a furious pace. I didn't really get to introduce myself, what with the group tour and Jared ruining any potential vibe with his incessant loudness, and I'd prefer to be on her radar in case I need extra towels, dinner reservations, or someone cute to make out with.

You know, casually.

Curious, I follow her, but she's moving really fast, like I'm not sure how a person moves at this speed without actually running. I catch her back at the Boathouse, calling out a breathless "Val! Wait up!" to prevent her from disappearing inside.

She twirls back my way, shoulder-length black-and-caramel hair shining in the sunlight. Slightly shorter than me, all curves under her fitted vest and skirt, she flashes an impossibly adorable customer service smile, daring me not to stare. "Yes? How can I help you?"

"Well, first of all, thank you for the very entertaining orientation," I say. "Looking forward to yours and Jared's 'Kill the Beast' duet where you throw him off a castle for being so obnoxious."

"I'm sorry?" says her voice, but the way her bottom lip bends to the right in a mischievous smirk, she knows exactly what I'm talking about.

"Also, I wanted to make sure you knew who I was." I extend my hand, which she grabs with a soft yet firm shake. "I'm Cinderella."

Dark brown eyes twinkle as she consults with her clipboard. "Ah, yes! Madison, correct?"

Hmm. Didn't she just say we should avoid using real names to heighten the Disney experience? There's no way cast members are exempt from this. "I prefer Cinderella," I reply with a smile.

Val touches her hand to her chest. "Apologies, fair maiden. I hope you can forgive my error."

"Of course." I dip into a shallow curtsy, because after all, Cinderella is nothing if not patient and kind.

She nods. "What else can I do for you, then, Princess?"

"I wanted to thank you for returning my shoe," I say, pointing to my silver ballet flat.

"Losing footwear already, I see." She grins.

"Always gotta be on theme!" I say with a flourish. "And also, I'm interested in your self-anointed Disney expert status. I'm a bit of a master myself, actually. Some might even say a Disney queen."

"Really?" One eyebrow arches in curiosity. "I'm always ready to defend my crown."

My heart picks up its pace. "Okay, then, tell me: Who is the youngest Disney princess?"

She answers without hesitation. "If you're talking about age, it's Snow White. She's technically only fourteen in the story. Though, as the star of the very first full-length Disney animated film from 1937, she's simultaneously the youngest *and* oldest Disney princess."

I swallow down a smile. I see someone's not here to play.

"My turn," Val interjects before I can ask a follow-up. She tilts her chin up, ready to best me, which only makes me want to prove myself more. "Which princess has the fewest speaking lines?"

"Many might guess Ariel," I say, "since she literally loses her voice, but actually it's Aurora, who spends over half of the movie asleep."

"Correct," she says with surprise, giving me a blink-and-you-missed-it head-to-toe glance, as if she originally misjudged her opponent. Which I'm used to: Most people write me off immediately. But I'm proud to still be in the game for once.

"And did you know," I add, "Aurora has the least amount of lines *and* screen time compared to the other leading ladies? Even though she's the title character of *Sleeping Beauty*, she's only present for eighteen minutes of the seventy-six-minute film."

Val laughs to herself, letting her clipboard fall to her side. She pushes her hair back off her face as she says, "You seriously know your stuff."

I shrug. "Yeah, well, this is kind of my thing. I feel like I was born to win this trip, you know? To be here for this opening week?"

"I do, actually. It's not every day you get to be a part of Disney history."

A calypso version of "A Whole New World" plays from the Boathouse, and yeah, this certainly is a dazzling place. Not the least because usually when I flirt with a girl for more than five seconds I immediately start envisioning our wedding, but right now I'm more invested in how I can impress Val with my vast knowledge of our shared interest.

"Yeah, I've always loved those windows on Main Street with the names of badass Imagineers like Mary Blair and Tony Baxter. Can you imagine doing something so monumental that your name would live in the parks for all eternity?" I spread my arms out wide, smiling up at the Florida sun.

"I can," Val says. Her tone is dry yet endearing, not the sugary sweet you'd expect from a Disney employee. She's keeping her enthusiasm close to the chest, whereas I can't help but vomit pixie dust everywhere I go. "But I'll admit I used to think the pinnacle of being was becoming a Jungle Cruise skipper."

I snort. "Isn't it, though?"

She bobs her head from side to side. "I mean, there are worse things than looking at the backside of water all day."

My cheeks flush, and I have to look down at the pavement to prevent myself from full-on fangirling. Outside of texts with Grandma Jean, I've never met anyone who would just casually drop a Schweitzer Falls reference, and it is deeply different coming from a cute girl than it is from a grandparent. I kind of want to ask Val her star sign next, but before I can, Jared comes bounding up our way, all spaghetti arms and legs.

"Hey, Val," he practically yells, even though we're standing a few feet apart. "I need help with prepping the Be Our Guest dinner. I'm not sure if I set up the audio correctly."

She turns her head slowly, facial features working overtime to suppress annoyance. "I'm helping a guest at the moment." She gestures to me. "I'll be right with you."

I know that voice. It's the I-would-rather-eat-fire-than-deal-with-you-right-now-but-I'm-financially-obligated-to-assist tone of a customer service professional. But Jared doesn't seem to notice, bounding away like a puppy chasing a butterfly.

"Sorry," Val says.

"It's okay. You have work to do." I smile, but in truth, I don't want her to go. I want to keep swimming in this pool where I'm somehow an equal with this smart, sassy woman. She starts to turn and my heart pinches, desperate to keep her near. "Before you go," I blurt out, to which she stops in her tracks. "Last question: How many times does Cinderella lose a shoe in the movie?" I fold my arms smugly, as this question always trips people up.

"Three," she says confidently.

"Ha! Wrong!" I dangle a finger in her face, but she doesn't even blink. "It's twice: once when she's running down the steps at the ball, and again at her wedding to Prince Charming."

Val's lips press into a thin smile. "But don't forget, she also loses a shoe walking upstairs to deliver her stepfamily's breakfast. Her spinning around to retrieve it is what makes Lucifer look for Gus under the wrong teacup."

My jaw drops.

Oh. My. God.

She's right. She's absolutely right. I didn't even *think* of that movie moment, but I can't let her know that. I have to remind myself that I'm no longer playing the fool.

"Obviously!" I exclaim, rolling my eyes to save face. "That was a test and you totally passed, so good job. Anyway—"

"Forgive me, Your Grace," Val interrupts. "This has been a real treat, but I need to see what my . . . partner needs help with." She says *partner* like it's a bad taste in her mouth. "Perhaps you can study up on your facts and try to best me another time?"

Study up on my . . . "Hey—"

"Don't worry. I won't reveal the Disney queen regime change." She steps closer, leaning in to whisper, "Your secret is safe with me."

Her words tickle my eardrums, sending a pleasing shiver down my spine as she winks and spins away. Despite the Florida heat my arms break out in goose bumps, and I have to remind myself to *slow down*. It's only been a few days since I almost threw myself in front of Tessa; I need to tighten the reins on this wild heart of mine and breathe.

I twist my hair up off my neck, letting myself cool down as I replay the conversation with Val in my head. On the plane, I daydreamed about taking romantic midnight boat rides with Moana or snuggling up with snow cones with Elsa, but sparring with Val was something totally different. I'm not even sure what it was, though I do know I wouldn't mind doing it again. But trying to start something with a cast member seems way too complicated: not at all the easy, breezy fling I had in mind. Cozying up to someone when they're at work feels like a scheduling nightmare, our priorities on opposite ends of the spectrum. I want to escape into the fantasy; she's behind the curtain *making* said fantasy.

Okay, it's decided: I will not let myself go off the deep end. I will only interact with Val on a strictly friendly basis. I'm supposed to be here for *me* anyway. I take a deep breath, refocusing my energy where it really counts: stepping into a pair of glass slippers.

I return to Cinderella's cobblestone path, clearing my head so I can be present for the theming all around me. After a few steps, the island vibes of the boardwalk fade away, and I'm transported to rural France, where Disney soundtracks are replaced with chirping birds and a bubbling stream in the distance. For a minute, I forget I'm even at a theme park, the trail is so remote and enclosed by trees that it really does feel like walking into a different world. Eventually, the secluded path opens up to a clearing, and there, nestled in the hillside is Cinderella's château, a gothic stone house covered in moss and creeping vines, shadows hinting at the sad family dynamics within. Thoughts of Val slip away as I'm struck by the scene; it looks exactly like the animated movie, down to the last detail. There's Cinderella's tower curving up on the left, while a garden, small barn, and a meandering pumpkin patch dot the rest of the property, a few stray chickens pecking for seed on the crushed limestone. I kneel over one of the biggest pumpkins innocently lazing in the sun.

I'll be seeing you soon, I think, tapping its glossy orange rind.

After taking a lap around the perimeter, I walk in through

the main door, which opens to a grand entry with an ornate winding staircase. Black-and-green tiles, carved white pillars, wall-mounted candelabras, and velvet-lined furniture — it's all here, and it's all perfect. At the base of the stairs, I run my fingers over a wrought iron fleur-de-lis detail, which gently swings open, revealing a hole just big enough for a mouse.

Well played, Disney. Well played.

I spin around a few times, my heart light and free. I can't believe I'm here. I can't believe this is real! I'm about to bolt up the stairs to see my room, when I hear a female voice call, "Cinderella?"

A tall, matronly white woman walks toward me, gray hair swept up in a voluminous bun. With a high-necked frilly collar and chin that could cut glass, her look is so severe, so frighteningly on point as Lady Tremaine that I gasp, unsure if the presence before me is human or animatronic.

"Holy shit," I gulp, clutching my chest. "You are —"

But my out-of-character reaction displeases her, red lips pursing in disgust.

I bow my head. "Yes, Stepmother," I say, resetting my tone to Cinderella's soft cadence.

Her green eyes run over me slowly, bony hands tightening around her wooden cane. I can only assume this woman is a cast member, because only a professional could have me both shaking and giggling over this spot-on interaction.

"Finally, you're home," she says, voice low and controlled. "Your sisters and I have been waiting."

"I'm sorry. I got here as fast as I could."

She squints, unconvinced. "It's a long journey. I'm sure you did your best. Though there is always room for improvement, hmm?"

I nod, cheeks filled with a nervous laugh begging to break free. I love that we're just jumping in like this. "Yes, Stepmother."

A loud bang sounds in the other room followed by muffled bickering. Anastasia and Drizella burst in, already dressed in their terrible mauve and pea-green gowns. While not as eerie as Lady Tremaine, the two are still instantly recognizable, screeching at each other over who knows what.

"This her?" asks Anastasia, a Black woman in her early thirties, big curls piled on top of her head.

"Doesn't look like much," retorts Drizella, a similarly aged Latina woman with a buzz cut. They fold their arms in sync. It's pretty clear everyone already memorized their character packets, their Tremaine trio energy strong. If everyone is going to be this committed to the fantasy, I'm here for it. I better bring my A game as well.

"Girls, girls," Lady Tremaine coos, taking place beside her daughters. "Perhaps we should let Cinderella settle in. Get acquainted with everything."

Anastasia picks at her cuticles. "Sure, have fun sleeping in the tower, sis."

"Yeah," Drizella chimes in. "Hope the rodents keep you warm."

"I'm sure it will be lovely," I say with a smile. No matter

what, I have to stay sweet. "The view from up there must be incredible."

They exchanged annoyed looks, until Drizella shouts, "Incredibly pathetic!" causing them all to laugh.

"Well then, it was a pleasure meeting all of you," I say. "Perhaps I'll see you all at dinner tonight?"

"Ugh, we don't eat with *you*," groans Anastasia.

Drizella mocks gagging. "Yeah, there's some extra chicken feed out back if you're hungry."

The stepsisters face each other and shriek, "Ewwwwww!"

I. LOVE. THEM.

"Now, now, let Cinderella have her daydreams, as unfathomable as they may be," Stepmother says to her daughters' delight. "We have our sights set on more important things, to be sure. In fact, girls, I believe we have an etiquette lesson to attend?"

They frown, posture slumping in protest, but Lady Tremaine shoos them away, leaving me to explore the rest of the château on my own. In my excitement to check out the tower, I trip over a fat black cat sitting on the main staircase. He hisses at me, flexing his claws before curling back up in a ball.

Ha! "Oh, Lucifer."

On the second floor, I marvel at the elegant hallway, draped in rich fabrics and metallic blue wallpaper. But when I cross the tower threshold, I'm greeted with a less than dreamy sight: a spiraling wooden staircase that's so tall, I can't even see where it ends. Shoot. This is for real. I'm all about authenticity, but I guess I didn't think about what this climb would be like.

I sweat all the way up, up, up to the top of the tower, chest heaving and thighs aching by the time I reach Cinderella's wooden door. Pulling my long hair up off my neck, I take a deep breath, swinging the door open into my princess's tiny abode.

It's perfect. A cozy space filled with more dreams than furnishings, curved stone walls and a perched wooden ceiling working together like the coziest of hugs. There's a small sewing table, nightstand, and not much else, a single bed topped with a threadbare pink comforter taking up most of the floor space. I peek into the closet, thumbing through a collection of Cinderella's aprons and work dresses; no ball gown yet, but of course, why would there be? The ball is the final hero moment of the week according to the itinerary, so I'll be wearing more brown and periwinkle than sparkles until then.

"Jacques? Gus Gus?" I ask into the quiet, hoping my little mouse friends will appear. I'm so curious about how my animal companions will come to life. Animatronics? Highly trained mice wearing pint-size T-shirts and booties? I'm not super down with rodents on the regular, but I guess I can make an exception in this case. But no furry friends appear, the cracks in the wood and stone left vacant for now. Maybe they'll pop up when we officially start role-playing tomorrow; just because my stepfamily is already game doesn't mean it all has to click into place.

I cross the room to the one window, thoughtfully placed

with a panoramic view of Prince Charming's castle far away in the distance. It shimmers in the sunlight, silver turrets beckoning onlookers with promises of romance and royalty. Leaning against the windowsill, I envision it all: me, dazzling everyone at the ball with my mysterious presence. I'm so captivating, no one can look away, as if the Fairy Godmother's spell included a side dose of group hypnosis. I dance the night away, practically floating around the ballroom, until I'm forced to make a dramatic exit, leaving behind only a hint of the magic I hold within.

As for the prince? Eh, that's not really my scene anyway. What matters is the experience, an escape from everything that's been bothering me lately. When I'm in that gown, I won't have to worry about The Future because that moment is all about the present. No pressure to pick a major or map out a major life plan: just pure, unadulterated fantasy that no one can take away from me.

"Thank god," I whisper, wiping away a stray tear. I really needed this. The freedom to be myself without judgment, a moment of whimsy before the clutches of adulthood pull me down forever. I have to make every second of this trip count, to let this dream carry me forward once the real world sets back in.

I sigh, the chorus of Cinderella's theme song swirling around my heart.

I wish Grandma Jean could see this. She loved this fairy tale even more than I do and had a replica jewel-encrusted

Cinderella storybook displayed on her nightstand as if she were trying to evoke the dreams our heroine was always singing about. Grandma Jean found a way to grow old while still being young at heart, and I want to do the same.

I have to make her proud.

LANIE

"A WHOLE NEW WORLD"

The path to DunBroch is lush and green, soaring pine trees leading me deeper and deeper into make-believe Scotland. I want to enjoy the forest landscape, but with every step, my anxiety spreads, worry worming through my nervous system as I question what's about to happen next.

How am I supposed to transform into a Disney princess? Will I ruin the other guests' experiences if I'm not "Merida" enough? What if I say the wrong thing? Oh god, am I expected to talk in a Scottish accent? Ahh!

Spiraling, I plop down on a flat boulder, focusing on my breathing until it hits a more manageable pace. I wish Madison and I didn't have to go our separate ways. Why couldn't I be Cinderella Extra #12 or something equally innocuous instead of this starring role? Taking this spot feels wrong; it's someone else's fantasy, not mine. I know I'm only here because Tessa backed out, but the pressure of doing this character justice is definitely not my idea of a happily-ever-after. Madison's probably singing with birds right now, and good for her; I wish I could steal even a slice of that carefree, when-you-wish-upon-a-star attitude.

But that's just not me.

A minute later, a tiny blue blob of light pops up in front of me, like a mystical jellyfish lost from the sea. It hovers expectantly, undulating at eye level, its misty tendrils inviting me to follow. How is this . . . ? What is this? A hologram? A panic-induced fever dream? But before I can figure it out, it vanishes in thin air.

"Um . . . hello?" I question, curious if the blob is voice acti-vated. "Am I supposed to do something . . . Merida-ish?"

It reappears, again hovering in smoky cerulean light. I reach out to touch it, but it jumps back, a duplicate blob appearing directly behind.

"Oh!" I gasp. As I stand, another one materializes, then another, creating a trail of phosphorescent blue light. "So I should . . . follow you, then?" They quiver in agreement.

As we continue down the path, I find myself distracted by how these incredibly realistic, seemingly three-dimensional spirits are bouncing along before me. I search the trees for a light projection source, but they're either not there or extremely well camouflaged, adding to the magical sensation.

Then it hits me—the wisps! This is what Madison was talking about! Fuzzy *Brave* memories filter in: Merida lost in a spooky place, encircled by blue spirits. I can't remember if they're friend or foe, but since they're not causing me any harm, I assume it must be the former. Before I know it, the forest opens to reveal an ancient stone castle sprawling against a mountain backdrop. A curtain of mist blankets the scene, and I have to remind myself that I'm in Florida, not medieval Scotland. So far today I've traveled from freezing Chicago, to a sunny boardwalk, and now to the hills of Scotland: I wouldn't believe it if it wasn't right in front of my face.

Is this why people are into Disney?

"Thank you for your—" I try to tell my wispy friends, but they're already gone, having done their duty. Slowly, I approach the sloping castle walls, mouth agape as I take in the stone walk of its arched entryway. Having actually been to a European castle, I'm stunned at the accuracy of this fortress; I can't speak to how well it depicts Merida's residence, but it would definitely be at home on the Scottish Highlands.

Once inside the castle's perimeter, I'm greeted with an entire cast of DunBroch villagers: people playing with swords, shooting arrows, and setting up stalls to sell a variety of wares. Many of them are already in costume, with lots of fur-accented robes, metal helmets, and, of course, tartan kilts. I pull off my hot-pink visor, feeling incredibly out of place in my street clothes, but no one really seems to notice, everyone happily engaged in their vacation setting of choice.

Do they know I'm their Merida? Can they already tell I have no idea what to do?

I wish that Val—or even Jared, at this point—was here to guide me. With so many towers spanning my sightline, I have no idea where Merida's room would be or where I should go. I duck inside an open castle door, pressing myself into the stone. Voices carry up the torch-lit hallway, a pair of shadows heading my way. I tense, but before I can even think about running away, a Latinx couple in their late fifties barrels toward me, the woman pulling me in for a surprisingly tight hug.

"You must be Merida!" she cries, pressing me harder into her ample chest. Once she's squeezed all the air out of my lungs, she lets go, round cheeks flushed with excitement. She wears a beautiful medieval-style emerald-green gown paired with a golden crown atop her flowing brunette waves. I don't know much, but this has to be Merida's mom. "We are so excited!"

"Ah, yes. Our daughter at last!" the man chimes in, equally decked out with a brown-and-blue tartan swathed across his chest and potbelly. They stand very close to me, faces plastered with exaggerated grins. Madison warned me how Merida's parents (her mom in particular) are overbearing, but I didn't think this is what she meant. "How was your trip, lassie?"

"Good. Fine." My voice cracks. "A little overwhelming."

My new mom nods. "Oh I know. The island is so much more than we expected, but in a good way! Sal and I were looking for a fun way to kick off our retirement, and while we were originally planning an Alaskan cruise, when we won that giveaway we thought, *Perfect!*"

"Although I still want to see those whales, Dorothy," Sal says pointedly, rubbing a weathered hand over his bald head.

She breathes heavily. "Yes, yes, enough about the whales. Can't you see our fake daughter is not interested in Pacific coast sea life right now? We're in Scotland, for heaven's sake!"

He grumbles something under his breath, but then kisses her on the cheek in apology. "Of course, *mi amor.*"

"Maybe you can go grab her a bite from the kitchen?" she asks her husband before turning to me. "They just put out a cheese board that is nothing like you've ever seen. Are you hungry, dear?"

My stomach grumbles loudly in response. I never did get any of that gumbo from Tiana's Palace.

Dorothy continues. "Good. Sal, grab us both one of everything. Wait—make that two of everything. I'll take her up to her room."

"Two of everything, two of everything," he repeats quietly to himself as he shuffles away, stiff legs making slow and steady progress. Dorothy puts her arm around my shoulder and gives it a quick squeeze. Despite my general aversion to being touched by strangers, I relax a little, settling into the warm welcome from these two. I was so nervous to meet them, but so far, they seem okay.

"So what's your name, dear?" Dorothy asks as we start up a winding stone staircase.

My heart clenches. Wait, aren't we not supposed to say?

HAPPILY EVER ISLAND

"Of course you don't have to tell me if you don't want. That's perfectly okay," she adds with a wink.

But I want to tell her, especially since they already shared about themselves so freely. "It's Lanie."

"Lanie," she repeats with a smile. "And where are you from?"

"Chicago."

She scrunches up her face as if she bit into a lemon. "Ooh! It must be cold there. I hate snow. Sal and I just moved back to Puerto Rico to be closer to my parents. When our daughter got accepted to Yale, we moved to Connecticut, but I couldn't deal with that awful northeastern weather. I'd rather have a sweaty backside than freezing fingers, you know?"

I grin, though not necessarily in agreement. As someone who's constantly doubling up on deodorant just to make it through stress sweats, I can't exactly say it's a feeling I relish. "And you're big Disney fans?"

Dorothy dreamily tugs at her long hair, and I spot golden ribbon woven through. "I'd say so. Maybe not the biggest fans ever, but we've been to the parks a bunch, seen all the movies. It's always a nice escape. You?"

"Oh, um." My face burns with guilt, but the lighting is so low in these hallways, I hope she can't see. "I'm . . . newer to the fandom."

Comforting crinkles form around her warm brown eyes. "Well, don't you worry, Lanie. We're going to have lots of fun this week. We got here very early this morning and already did

98

a lap around the entire island, so if there's anything you need, just let us know."

"Thank you." I continue to blush.

"And, don't tell him I told you . . ." Dorothy leans in conspiratorially. "But Sal is actually the bigger Disney fan. He *loves* this stuff and watched *Brave* fifteen times before we left."

"Fifteen? I think I've only seen it a couple of times."

"He's your go-to. He may play it cool, but I'm pretty sure he has all of King Fergus's dialogue memorized. Probably Merida's, too. He made me run lines with him the whole plane ride here."

I laugh, picturing Sal standing at his bathroom mirror, bald head shining as he mouths words belonging to a teenage Scottish princess. So cute.

"Anyway, here we are!" she announces, gesturing to my wooden door with a flourish of her long-sleeved gown. She pushes it open, revealing a cozy medieval space with stone walls and heavy fabrics layered throughout. In the corner, a wood-burning fireplace crackles with redundant heat, while directly across hangs a massive tapestry, intricately sewn with figures resembling Merida's entire family. I run my fingers over their woven faces—the king, queen, and Merida's three little brothers staring back at me with blank expressions. This family looks so much different from my own, and not just because they are tenth-century Scottish royalty. My mom and I only have each other, our bond so tight it's often strangling. I wonder how she's doing, not being able to contact me. Hopefully, she hasn't hired a bounty hunter to come drag my rebellious butt home. I don't want some beefed-up dude lugging me away while I'm playing make-believe.

"Are the little brothers going to be here?" I worry aloud. I didn't know how to be around kids when I *was* a kid, let alone now.

"No, no, the island is adults only," she confirms. "I'm also not planning on turning into a bear anytime soon; wearing a full-length gown in Florida is one thing, but a full fur suit?" She shakes her head. "Out of the question."

A bear? Oh god, I forgot about that part. I really should've forced myself awake during Madison's mandatory *Brave* rewatch. What other unsettling surprises are waiting for me? Witchcraft? Evil spells? I shudder with nerves, focusing on the room itself before my concerns carry me away.

"Remarkable, isn't it?" Dorothy asks, having no problem rummaging through my closet to pull out what can only be a Merida costume. She drapes it over her arm, presenting it to me in all its velvet glory. "All the details in these dresses. I couldn't wait to put mine on. Should I leave you to get changed?"

I rub the heavy fabric between my fingers. I'm going to sweat to death in this. "Oh, well, I didn't think we were officially starting until tomorrow."

Her mouth pinches in a tight line. "Of course, no pressure!" she says briskly, whisking the dress away in a hurry. She scurries about the room, nervously touching the curving bow propped up on a shelf. "This is your vacation;

you should enjoy it as you like. Maybe I should go . . . Let you get settled, mm?"

Worried that I've upset her, I walk toward the closet, grabbing the gown once again. "I guess it wouldn't hurt to try it on. . . ."

But she shakes her head, readjusting her crown so it sits just right. "No, no. Don't mind me. I'll check in on you later, okay? I should go find out what happened to Sal. . . ."

I nod as she scampers away, closing the door behind her. Should I get changed? I wasn't planning on it, but apparently I'm behind all of DunBroch. I'm sure Madison would love it, although I guess I'm not supposed to wear any of this outside of Scotland. I shuffle through my wardrobe options. They're all so heavy: full-length sleeves and weighty fabrics that'd be great for Scottish winters but not Florida springs. A bead of sweat rolls down my back just touching the woven brocades. Gah. I pop open my suitcase waiting on the bed and rummage through Madison's handiwork, settling on a full-length dark blue gown made of cotton, not velvet. While it doesn't have the same intricate flourishes around the hem or neckline, the dress hits the right medieval vibe, with an empire waist and fluttering sleeves. At least it will be breathable?

Once dressed, I look in the mirror, not impressed at what I find. I haven't worn a dress since middle school graduation, and since my mom always made me choose female scientists and political leaders as Halloween costumes, I'm not exactly used to seeing myself look this way. The fabric swishes around my bare legs, loose long sleeves allowing for some air circulation as well. But even though I'm wearing the outfit, I don't feel like Merida at all, some key component missing from the total look.

And that's when I spot—the wig.

Sitting on a form in a dark corner of the room is a tangled orange-red hairball, massive ringlets of varying curl size and shape spinning out in every direction. Like three heads of hair combined onto one unfortunate scalp, the wig taunts me with its ridiculous volume, knowing full well what horror awaits the wearer.

I approach it slowly, scared it could come to life at any second. It's so heavy it falls over at my slightest touch, leaving a fiery splat of hair on the stone.

No. No way! My neck will snap off if I wear this or I'll sweat straight through my cosplay! There's a reason I cut my own hair into a pixie.

Instead, I ruffle my fingers through my own dark strands, hoping to give my short and spiky style a little bit of Merida's magnitude. Although the result makes it seem like I don't know how to use a hairbrush, I figure that's close enough.

Dressed for the part, I set out to explore the rest of the castle, killing time before I have to meet Madison. I do my best to keep a low profile, but now that I'm in my princess's clothes, it's hard not to draw the occasional smile or knowing nod from the guests playing villagers. I wave politely, keeping a quick pace to avoid conversation starters, until I find myself at the stables, rows of massive horses quietly chewing hay and whipping their tails.

They're beautiful, with dark coats trailing into fluffy white hooves, but their enormous size and height suddenly reminds me: Merida rides horses. She shoots arrows *while riding* said horses. I've never even *been* on a horse, let alone performed impressive acts of archery while doing so. Between wearing that gargantuan wig and riding horses twice the size of regular steeds, I'm getting the feeling that being Merida involves a lot more skill than many of the other princesses. All Aurora has to do is fall asleep!

I stop before a steed named Angus, his named carved into the wooden gate. The top of my head barely clears his nose, his black tail probably longer than my entire body. Yet despite his commanding size, Angus nuzzles me gently, blowing warm air into the crook of my neck. It's nice—comforting, even—and I breathe deep, thinking maybe this part of Merida's life won't be so difficult after all.

That is, until an expected voice interrupts my one moment of calm.

"Want a ride?" purrs a smooth tenor from behind. I whip around in surprise, Angus rearing up in tandem. His front legs lash out in alarm, a deafening bray freezing me in place. Even as his hooves hover above, I can't move, trapped as I watch him about to squash me like a bug. The owner of the voice pulls me away just before Angus slams back to the ground, his powerful force knocking us all into the dirt.

"Oh my god, I'm so, so sorry!" cries the mystery man. He props himself up over my chest, and I gasp, distrusting my vision. I either hit my head way too hard or this person hovering over me is the single most attractive human I've ever seen in real life. Black skin with a small dimple in his left cheek, full lips open in worry, he panics from above, warm brown eyes scanning my body for injuries. We're so close I catch a hint of his cologne, fresh and clean notes drawing me in. It could be my angle, but his shoulders appear very broad and strong, like he could throw me up over them with no problem. *That's a weird thought to have*, I catch myself thinking, but I can't help it; with only inches between us, it's hard not to be hyperaware of all the subtle ways our bodies are brushing up against each other right now.

He raises a hand cautiously, about to turn my head to make sure it's not bleeding. Part of me wants to lean into it, to let this vision of a man run his fingers through my hair, but the bigger part of me—the skittish, not-good-at-these-kinds-of-things part—jerks away before we touch. In my very limited experience with boys, I always find ways to awkwardly excuse myself before any meaningful interaction begins, but now I'm trapped, inches away from not only a boy but THE CUTEST boy imaginable. I tuck my head into my shoulder, unsure of what to do with my face while encountering someone so beautiful.

"Are you okay?" he asks hopefully.

"I'm . . . I'm fine," I manage, unable to meet his gaze.

He sighs. "What was I even thinking? *Want a ride?* C'mon,

man. That came out so much creepier than it sounded in my head."

From the safety of my shoulder tuck, I ask, "What did you think it would sound like?"

He sits back on his heels. "I don't know. Like, hey! Want a ride, nice person standing next to a horse? Can I help you with that?"

I snort out a small laugh.

"What I should have said was 'Pardon me, fair maiden. May I assist you with that gallant steed?'"

Now there's a sentence that hasn't been uttered this century. I laugh again. "No."

"Well, it would have been better than scaring you, at least." He throws both arms up. "And nearly getting trampled to death by this monster horse. Why is it so big anyway?"

I sit up, lightly brushing dirt off my sleeves. Suddenly, I realize my long skirt flew up almost to my underwear during the fall, so I pull it down quickly, wishing I could burrow my entire reddening body under its fabric. "Um, I think it's a specific breed. Feels very . . . fantastical."

He nods. "True. Everything here is larger than life. But turns out I am oh for one on happily-ever-afters so far."

"You're not alone," I admit, and he cocks his head in interest. Oh no, do I tell him more? Admit my Disney ineptitude to this total stranger? Madison would be so disappointed, but then again, this is a big resort with hundreds of guests; the odds that she'll ever cross paths with this guy are slim. "It's just . . . I didn't expect everything to be so lifelike."

"I know what you mean. It's a lot to take in. But it's good to know I'm not the only one still adjusting."

I blush, brushing dirt off my hands. He's nice. And cute. I don't know how to handle this.

"Here, let me help you up." He extends a hand, strong fingers covering mine as we rise to stand. I take him in, all the way from his closely cropped black curls to his . . . royal tunic? He must be playing a character from a different part of the island, since everyone around here is covered in plaid. But I can't quite place his story based on his outfit alone. "I still feel bad my jackass line knocked you off your feet in the worst possible way."

"I really am fine," I say, twisting my fingers nervously. Behind us, Angus continues chomping hay, as if he didn't just catapult me into this unprecedented situation.

The too-handsome-to-be-true man smiles in relief. "Thank god. Maybe I'll hide out in my castle to keep from possibly injuring anyone else."

"Castle?" I ask, remembering seeing several from the shoreline.

"Yes." He puts his chin out proudly before ducking in a bow. "Prince Charming, madam. At your not-very-helpful service."

Prince Charming. Ooooooooooof course. How could he be anything but? This guy *screams* Charming, coming to my rescue the second I fell (even if, okay, he caused me to capsize). He certainly looks the part, pulling off his fairy-tale tunic and tights like nobody's business. In fact, he's so likable and gentle and kindhearted that there's no way this is real. No guy puts off this intoxicating spell of princely perfection without being a professional; he has to be one of the planted cast members. Yet it's a relief, knowing that nothing happening now is real. He's part of the fantasy, and no matter what stupid thing I say or do, he'll still be pleasant and friendly and everything will be fine.

The pressure's off. Thank god.

"I'm Merida," I say, adding on a dorky wave. "Nice to meet you. My best friend is Cinderella, so maybe we'll be seeing more of each other."

He breaks into a dashing grin, all picture-perfect pearly whites. "I would like that. Actually, would you be willing to help me with something right now?"

More time with the prince? I guess it couldn't hurt to get to know Madison's future ballroom partner.

"As it turns out, this is the only stable on the island, and I wanted to sneak away for a quick jaunt—make sure I can pull off the whole prince-and-his-noble-steed thing." He gestures to Angus, who whinnies in dissent. "You seem to have a much more calming presence around the horses than me, or at least you did before I came along and ruined everything. Would you help me escort one back to France?"

Having zero experience with horse wrangling, I frown. "I'm not sure how I would do that."

"You could walk beside me, feed the horse sugar cubes. Or maybe ride it while I lead?"

Ride it? "Um, you should know, the last time I was on a

horse was at Melissa Sampson's sixth-grade birthday party, and I puked from nerves the moment my butt hit the saddle." I cringe, wondering why I felt it necessary to share that detail, and also why so many of my stories end in stress barfing.

But he just laughs, a goofy little chortle that sets me back at ease. "Don't worry. One time I peed my pants during a sleepover and none of my friends ever let it go. Besides, I bet you can handle yourself on horseback now."

He has to say that, it's his job, I tell myself. Still, I'll take the compliment, even if I'm unsure of the task at hand.

Charming chooses the one white horse from the stables, who is thankfully of regular size. After securing a saddle, he turns to me and asks, "Are you ready?"

No. "Okay."

"Allow me." From behind, he gently puts his hands on my waist and every inch of my skin burns beet red. "Is this okay?"

I choke out a garbled sound of consent, and he effortlessly lifts me onto the horse's back. I clutch the reins for dear life as he gives me a thumbs-up from below, and we're off, slowly trotting away from Scotland. I catch my reflection in a hanging shield and am surprised by what I see: wind in my hair, medieval gown, riding off into an adventure. Am I doing it? Is this Merida?

Once back on the forest path, I watch Charming lead the way, confidently striding forward as if he does this every day. Which, I guess, he does. "So, um, do you do this often?" I ask.

"Do what?"

"Take girls on horseback rides through fairy-tale settings?"

He grins, dimple deepening. "Actually this is a first for me."

Yeah, right. My face must betray me because he adds, "No, really! This isn't typically my speed. I mean, is it anyone's?"

"Not mine," I declare, still struggling to stay steady. "I haven't had a lot of practice with make-believe."

"It takes some getting used to. That being said, you won't catch me breaking into song or a choreographed dance while we're here."

A new fear kicks in. I don't remember seeing anything about singing on the itinerary! "Oh god, is that something we have to do?"

Charming shakes his head. "I hope not."

"Well, I will warn you. Once you meet Cinderella, she will drag you into every Disney moment she can."

"Interesting," he says like he's cracking a case. "Why do I get the feeling her fairy godmother forced you to join her here on Happily Ever Island?"

A pretty spot-on assessment, considering he just met me. I wonder if intro to psychology is part of cast member training. "*Forced* is a little strong. More like *strongly encouraged for the sanctity of our friendship*."

He bobs his head in time with the horse's steps. "Got it. She sounds fun."

"She is. She once helped me pull an all-nighter by reenacting scenes from *The Bachelor* every time I finished a chapter. Now I forever associate asexual reproduction with rose ceremonies." He laughs, accidentally hitting our horse's flank. "She's, uh, not into guys, though, just in case you were hoping for that fairy-tale ending."

"Nah, that's okay. I'm not usually into princess types." He sneaks a quick look my way over his shoulder before adding, "I already met Snow White, and within five minutes, she asked me if I'd want to share a poisoned apple sometime. I'm not even sure I know what that means."

I snort, grabbing the saddle to steady myself. "That's . . . Wow."

"It's going to be long week."

Before I know it, we're back at the center of the island, the Lighthouse welcoming our return. Funny how I was so terrified to get on this horse but suddenly don't want the ride to end.

"I appreciate your help with all this, Merida," Charming says, halting the horse just before the Boardwalk begins. "I can probably take it from here. I'm sure you have places to be."

I look up at sky, sunset turning the clouds a dusty rose. I'm supposed to meet Madison here any minute. "No problem. Royals gotta support royals, right?"

"Definitely." He grins, warm and inviting.

I take too long admiring his mouth to realize he's waiting for me to hop down. "Oh! Um, I actually have no idea how to get off a horse. Could you . . . uh . . . ?"

"Help you without making you tumble to the ground? Of course, Princess."

He reaches out just as I swing my leg way too violently over the horse's back, instantly tangling my limb in fabric and losing my center of gravity. On my way to a nose-breaking fall, Charming swoops in, wrapping his arms around my waist and pulling me into his chest.

"Thank you," I gasp, grabbing his bicep like it's a lifesaver, although in this case, it is.

"My pleasure," he whispers back, once again inches from my face. We stay there for a second, bodies close, eyes locked, before the horse brays in frustration. Stepping apart, Charming rubs the back of his neck while I pull on the ends of my long sleeves.

He clears his throat. "So, I'll be seeing you."

"Yes! Because we're here . . . on this island . . . together!" *OMG . . . WHY, LANIE?*

But my awkwardness doesn't faze him, his professionalism shining through. "Until then, Merida." He nods before climbing up on the horse himself, a prince literally riding off into the sunset on a white horse.

It doesn't get more rehearsed than that.

Still, something creeps through me, an electricity different from the usual anxious hum. It's warmer, lighter, covering my skin in goose bumps instead of hives. I know everything that just happened was all part of the fantasy; Charming probably has a daily quota of guests he has to charm. I'm sure he's trained to hone in on people's needs and dreams, and as an introverted, socially starved loner, I'm an easy target for fake romantic attention. But even if it's all part of the show, it still feels nice—exhilarating, even—to leave a social interaction feeling full instead of drained.

I spot Madison making her way up Cinderella's path, waving to me in one of her sparkly Disney bound ensembles. I wonder what she'll make of my time with Charming. Actually, I don't have to wonder: I know the second I tell her, she'll wring every drop of information out of me, instantly comparing our star charts and planning our honeymoon, which I do not want because this isn't even *a thing*. It was just one guy doing his job and me enjoying the ride. Right? Nothing to discuss, nothing to dissect. And on top of that, I've had so few positive experiences with guys, I want to keep this one to myself for a while.

Charming can be my secret for now.

MADISON

"BE OUR GUEST"

anie's face is so serene I almost do not recognize her. As she stands under the Lighthouse in a total daze, her usual tight-jaw-furrowed-brow expression has been swapped with surreal wonder, making me think Scotland must be killing it just like France. I need to get over there ASAP.

"Looks like someone is adjusting to island life!" I exclaim, skipping to my best friend's side. I smooth out the front of my shimmery blue baby-doll dress, a perfect vacation Cinderella look if I do say so myself.

She blinks rapidly, as if coming up out of a dream. "Hmm? What?"

"I haven't seen you this chill since the time we accidentally ate some of Wren's brownies."

She frowns, probably remembering how we ended up lying in the communal girls' bathroom looking for constellations on the tiled ceiling. "Ha. Good one."

"But seriously!" I continue. "Look at you, Ms. Merida! You look amazing in that dress I got you! Do a twirl for me."

"What? I'm not five years old."

"TWIRL, DAMN IT."

"Jeez, okay." She spreads her arms and spins around quickly, kicking up her dress's ruffled hem. I'm surprised she actually chose this look; I also packed a bunch of shorts and tanks since I know she's not a dress lover. Still, she looks so comfortable and carefree, I really wish I had my phone. There's no way I'll be able to prove this ever happened.

"Good. Now, tell me every single thing about DunBroch," I instruct, threading my arm through hers. We turn away from the bubbling fountains and start on the Beast's castle's path, a surprisingly dark trail with tree branches twisting together to shield against the sunlight. "Is it beautiful there? Did you get a bow and arrow? Are there giant murderous bears that were actually princes cursed by a woodworking witch?"

Lanie takes a deep breath, her mouth twisting into that concerned expression when Java Jam! customers order drinks with way too much sugar and espresso for one sitting.

"What? What's wrong?" I ask. "Wait, don't tell me: You hate it here."

"Actually, I—"

"You gotta give it a chance, okay? We've only been here a few hours! I know flying carpets and singing teapots aren't your thing, but there has to be something here for you. Something magical and fun that will stir up that cynical little heart of yours? Please?" I hear the desperation in my voice, yet I can't stop. "I can't do this by myself."

She jerks her head back, frowning. "First of all, what does that even mean? I know for a fact you'd be fine here without me, or anyone, for that matter. You know every single thing there is to know about Disney; they'll probably make you a cast member before the week is through."

My heart squeezes, pinching into a shape I know from Lanie's biology flash cards is not anatomically possible. Working for Disney? I don't think so. I may be a dreamer, but even I know that's not within the realm of possibility.

I've never been The Best at anything: average student, decent employee, dutiful child and friend. I write papers that meet—but never exceed—expectations; I come up with ideas that are fine—but not groundbreaking. All through school, I watched as the people around me developed into exceptional writers, musicians, athletes, and whatnot, all while I hovered in mediocrity, never finding That Thing to perfectly match my skills and interests.

Except, of course, for Disney. I learned about Imagineering in elementary school, when Grandma Jean and I watched a documentary about how theme parks are made. The film talked about how these Disney-devoted engineers dreamed up the technology and tools to push the boundaries of immersive experiences; they turned swashbuckling buccaneer stories into Pirates of the Caribbean and runaway trains into Big Thunder Mountain Railroad. Any dream could be brought to life, and a small, curious bulb flickered inside me, as I wondered if I could ever do something so amazing. Where would I start? What would I do? I thought those questions would be answered by the time I got to college, but as it turns out, I'm just as clueless, lacking the talents for the one place I'd want to go.

Because really, even if I did somehow manage to wrangle up a magical career at a place like Disney, what skills would I bring to the table? An exhaustive list of obscure trivia and facts? A collection of mouse ears and pins curated after years of careful trading? No. The fiery passion in my heart is not enough to do this world justice; loving something is not the same as helping to make it great.

But I can't talk to Lanie about stuff like this. She'd never understand, which sucks. Even when she's stressed, she's never aimless, somehow always landing on her feet. I'd love to open up to her, but I couldn't stand my best friend giving me those sad, pitiful eyes that almost everyone else greets me with. Lanie's on the bullet train to success, while I'm stuck at What Am I Even Doing with My Life station.

"You're sweet," I tell her, putting my life dilemmas back in their box. "I just want us both to have fun while we're here. Don't make up your mind about the island yet, okay? Let's stuff our faces while candlesticks and clocks dance around us."

Lanie presses her lips together. "Are there going to be spoons and napkins flying around our heads?"

"God, I hope so."

The trek toward the Beast's castle is spooky as hell, complete with barren trees, thickening fog, and the occasional wolf howl threatening from a distance. While I'm all for savoring the details, I wouldn't exactly put Belle's terrifying race through the woods on top of my must list, so we scurry through the creepfest as quickly as possible.

The castle is equally moody, set in the pre-Belle era when its inhabitants have lost all hope. Somehow, the sun has completely stopped shining on this section of the island, and although the temperature holds steady, a chill runs through me. Covered in a collection of shadows and spiderwebs that would make the Haunted Mansion jealous, the fortress is truly committed to its emo vibe, gargoyles silently screaming at us to stay away.

"Well, this is . . . inviting," Lanie jokes as we tiptoe through the creaking gates.

"Yeah, the Beast reeeeeeeeally steered into the skid after his spell. Like, WE GET IT, you're upset. Maybe instead of trashing your house you could invest in some mood-boosting decor? Not just one slowly dying red rose constantly reminding you of your impending fate."

Her fingers dig into my forearm. "But it will be cuter inside, right?"

My nose crinkles in doubt. "Mm, probably not *cuter*. But less foreboding, probably?"

She grumbles but marches through the castle doors, death grip tightening. Inside, the Beast's home is still pretty decrepit, a layer of dust blanketing every fabric and flooring. Our footsteps echo through the soaring main hall, lined with more screeching statues straight from my nightmares. Yikes! This is a lot. I spot a sign hidden in a dark corner that reads THIS WAY TO BE OUR GUEST, so before I lose Lanie completely, I charge forward, following a dusty red carpet down a hallway lined with candles.

Thankfully, reaching the dining room puts an end to our treacherous journey. While the room itself is still dimly lit and in need of brighter accents, the space is brimming with life, packed with guests excited for their theatrical meal. Some dressed in street clothes and some rocking seriously clever Disney bounds, our dining group is fired up, laughter and happy chitchat keeping the macabre vibe at bay. In a quick sweep, I spot Moana and Maui joking in a corner, while across the room Tiana and Naveen have already found each other, flirting it up as they sip something sweet.

And, oh, there's Ariel, wearing a subtle variation of her mermaid's land-bound rope-and-canvas dress, accented with a pink hibiscus pinned in her dark brown hair. Damn, the girl looks good, and I'm pretty sure she knows it. She winks at me, lifting her fingers in a subtle hello, and I wave back, giving a quick nod (*so* casual) before turning toward a group of wintry Arendelle villagers chatting away.

This is going to be awesome.

Just then, the lights flash on and off, signaling us that the show is about to begin. Jared and Val appear in the doorway, and my heart does a little backflip. She chitchats with a few guests, eyebrows high in excitement as she answers questions with friendly professionalism. With so many bodies in here, it's hard to get a good view, so I stand on my tiptoes hoping to catch her attention. After she guides a man to his seat, her eyes find mine, mouth bending in a smirk before she turns back to her responsibilities.

A spark runs through me, lighting up my insides. What should I do? Go over there? Ask for menu recommendations? My instinct is to shimmy up next to her and say something dorky yet charming, but I have to remember she's at her job while I'm on vacation. A spring fling sounds fun but may be challenging with someone who's on the clock. I hold myself back and instead search for Ariel, thinking maybe we can sit close enough for a little footsie action, but she's on the opposite side of the room and looks distracted by a surprisingly sultry Mother Gothel.

Jared puts his hands on his hips to take up space, while Val steps aside so as not to brush against him, using her clipboard as a barrier. I know I'm minutes away from a once-in-a-lifetime theatrical experience, but I'd love to see our island ambassadors' behind the scenes. I feel like there's a lot of eye rolling involved.

"Good evening, everyone!" shouts Jared, his voice way too loud for a confined space. "Please, take your seats! Your dining experience is about to begin!"

"Where do we sit?" Lanie asks, gesturing to the longer-than-long table stretching the entire length of the room. Everyone scrambles as I lunge for two seats next to each other.

"This is good!" I say. Lanie and I plop down as the lights completely dim, a hush falling over the dining room. A spotlight beams on the center of the table: Though he wasn't there seconds ago, an animatronic Lumiere has appeared, soaking in the admiration of all our bewildered faces. He bows, candle-tipped hands sparkling with light. Jerry Orbach's voice fills the room over the opening notes of an accordion, welcoming us to enjoy the show and our fantastical dinner.

❖

Oh shit, *OH SHIT*! This is HAPPENING! I grab Lanie's hand.

Lumiere flips a matchstick out of its case, coyly twirling a candle-stopper on top of his head as he sings out the iconic opening notes to "Be Our Guest," taking a measured beat between each word.

My heart *stops*. I'm instantly six years old, dancing around the kitchen with Grandma Jean as we pretend to whip up a meal fit for a princess. There's flour and salt everywhere, but we don't care, kicking and dancing as we stir and sauté.

The bouncing melody picks up the pace and a squad of serving carts steers into the room, each carrying tray after tray of soup du jour, hot hors d'oeuvres, and countless other French dishes that smell so good I want to cry. How the carts easily careen without hitting one another or spilling a single drop is a mystery, but I can barely concentrate on their controls since the table is now alive with spinning plates, twirling napkins, and singing spoons all dancing under blue and pink swaying lights.

Lanie's face glows, mouth agape as a chafing dish filled with beef ragout proudly trots before her.

"Is this for real?" she cries over the chorus.

"Yes! I don't know how but yes!" I wipe my cheeks free of tears as a mouth-watering cheese soufflé hops by my plate, tempting me with its warm gruyère scent. I scoop out a bite, the fluffy center melting on my tongue. It's all so good, so right, I decide I'll never be able to eat anything that wasn't served by magical dancing cutlery ever again.

An Eiffel Tower made out of dishes and flatware elicits applause. I turn to Lanie; she's happily bopping in her chair as she eats her pie and pudding en flambé. "This is the happiest I've ever been in my entire life," I declare as Lumiere juggles his waxy palms.

"I'm glad." She beams back. "This is incredible!"

It really is. The only thing pulling my attention away from spoons diving into a pink punch pool is Val, sneakily clearing plates and refilling water glasses when everyone's eyes are on the show. Her hip grazes my shoulder as she replenishes the rolls, trading one spell for another. Instead of watching pots of porridge promise to be in good taste, I think about what it'd be like to vibe with her again, our heads inching closer and—

STOP IT, MADISON. God. The real show is right in front of you! Don't split your brain into two fantasies at once!

A rainbow of spotlights dance around the table as the song hits its triumphant final verse, towers of cakes and pastries rising up from the floor. They spin in a dizzying array of swirling frosting and sugar as a massive golden chandelier descends from the ceiling, tiny forks synced in a perfect kick line. Lumiere hits the ending crescendo, belting out the final note as champagne bottles pop streams of frothy pink bubbles everywhere.

The entire table breaks into thunderous applause as a river gushes from my eyes, my heart so full of love and light that I may actually float away in glee. Even Lanie, who hadn't watched *Beauty and the Beast* until I met her, has her jaw on the table.

"I . . . I've never seen anything like that in my entire life!" She laughs.

"I know, right?" I fan myself in hopes of reducing puffiness. "No Disney experience is complete without a little water works."

With both hands on her chest she sighs. "There was so much to see, I only got a few bites."

I look at the motionless platters and bowls overflowing with food, finally done with their dance. "Same. And it all smelled so good, too. At least now we can focus and eat." I reach for a tray of boeuf bourguignon, its savory onion and red wine aroma calling to me, when the opening notes of "Be Our Guest" begin playing again.

Lanie freezes mid-bite of her coq au vin. "Oh. We're doing this again?"

I shrug. "Maybe they'll play the instrumental track?"

They do not. Lumiere takes the stage once again, and the second he starts singing the serving dishes spring back to life, my beef stew bopping away before I can get a spoonful.

"Hey!" I call out as a parade of appetizers flies past, each so wiggly it's hard to grab a bite before they're gone. My stomach growls in protest as dish after dish taunts me with its deliciousness, only to dance away in spite.

"Please stop!" I shout against the music. "I want to eat! *That's* my request!"

Lanie props her head in her hands, sadly eyeing a stack of croque monsieur that trots by. "I'm so hungry," she groans. She's not alone; everyone at the table has gone from entranced to befuddled in seconds.

"I got this." Fork in hand, I'm ready to stab whatever edible prances my way next. But with all the flashing lights and twirling linens, it's harder than it looks, my peripherals constantly distracted by a new teacup or feather duster flinging itself free. Defeated, I slouch back in my chair, arms crossed, waiting for the nearly four-minute song to end.

My best friend and I share a crestfallen glance right before she closes her eyes, her chest rising and falling in slow, concentrated breaths. Though the lighting is all over the place, I can tell she's turning a little green; all this blaring music and forced socialization must be wearing on her. The last thing I want her to do is stress-puke all over Cogsworth and company, so as the final notes echo through the room—again—I stand up, gently nudging her arm.

"C'mon," I say. "Let's go somewhere a little less panic-attack inducing. Where our food won't run away."

She resists, worry splashed across her pale face. "No. I don't want you to miss this. You didn't even get to try the gray stuff, to see if it's really—"

"Delicious? Eh, whatever. I mean, how good can gray-colored food be anyway? I'm starving. Come on, up you go."

Our dinner party offers half-hearted applause. No one really seems to know what to do or how to react, though there is quite the scramble to grab food just in case it happens again. We wobble out of the dining room, ears ringing and bellies aching, but just as we turn the corner, we run straight into Val, her vision obstructed by a massive stack of plates. A few shatter on the ground, and she mutters something under her breath, head tilted back like she's looking for answers from above.

"Are you okay?" Val and I ask each other simultaneously. She sets down the rest of her tower before it completely topples, and we both bend down to pick up a few broken shards. Reaching for the same cracked dish, our fingers brush up against each other: It's only a quick pass of her soft skin on mine, but it's enough to turn my ears pink. I shake my hair forward to hide my excitement.

"Um, so sorry about this, and all that back there," Val says, scooping up the last piece and straightening to stand. She brushes down the front of her navy skirt and is clearly flustered, shoulders slumped. "You two leaving already?"

"Kind of, yeah, we're starving," I admit but immediately feel bad, struck by her downfallen aura. "Is everything okay? We didn't expect fast food at a sit-down dinner."

"Apologies." Val sighs, cheeks flushed. She looks like she just ran a 5K but in saddle shoes instead of Nikes. "Having the song repeat was obviously not planned, I'm not sure how to explain. . . ."

"Maybe the Beast was having a meltdown or something," I say off the top of my head. "That dude has serious anger management issues."

Val's mouth opens, then closes, head tilting in recognition. "Yes, that . . . that's a good line. Do you mind if I steal that?"

I shake my head, blonde waves bouncing. "Not at all. Happy to help smooth things over."

She breathes a little easier, brown eyes tired and defeated. I lost track of how many times she weaved around the table, trying to keep things running even as the show spun out of control. As weird as it was for us to sit through back-to-back dinner theater, it must have been extra hectic for her, especially since this is a test run and they're still working out all the bugs. "I appreciate it," she says before adding, "You're smart, you know? Really quick on your feet."

I freeze, lips parted in surprise. I don't think I've ever had someone tell me I'm smart. Silly? Yes. Hot? Sure. But smart? I think the closest I've ever gotten is Grandma Jean telling me I'm a go-getter. But that is definitely not the same.

I struggle to find a response. "I . . ." I scratch my head, blinking rapidly. "Thank you."

Val eyes me for a moment, a curious expression splashed across her face. But before I can read it, she moves on. "Everything should be fixed now if you'd like to sit back down and eat."

I look over at Lanie, whose paler-than-usual complexion tells me we're not out of the woods yet. "We would, but Merida here needs some fresh air." Lanie gives a sad little wave in agreement.

"Okay, well, thanks for your help," Val says with a smile. "I'm going to go use that Beast line."

"Anytime," I respond, meeting her gaze. We hold steady, neither of us willing to look away first. Despite my best efforts to remind myself that's she's on the clock, that I'm here to focus on *myself* and the *magic*, there's something about her that's drawing me in, a pull much different from what I usually experience. At this point in any other relationship, I'd already be scheming how to chase my new crush and entrap her with my glittery nonsense. All I want to do is get to know Val better— her likes, dislikes, what she's thinking. And I'm doing everything I can to fight those urges.

To my right, I sense Lanie watching us both, twisting her fingers amid the tension. When we finally turn to walk away, Val calls after us, "Oh! One more thing. You're free to move about the castle, except—"

"For the West Wing, right?" I say, winking over my shoulder. She waves with approval before spinning in the opposite direction.

Once we're back in the dark castle hallway, Lanie looks at me and says, "So . . . what was that?"

"What?"

"That spark between you and Val. I was waiting for you both to break into song."

"Ugh, how great would that be." I exhale dreamily. "Too bad it'll never work."

She grimaces. "Um, why is that?"

"Because she works here. You saw, she's busy! Clearing plates and solving backstage mysteries or whatever."

"Since when have you ever let work stand in the way?"

"Since now!" I declare. "Besides I want to work on *me* for once." I think about my last failed attempt at a romantic gesture with Tessa and cringe. Nope, I do not need a repeat of something like *that* clouding memories of the ultimate Disney trip.

Lanie shakes her head. "I don't get you sometimes."

I stop in front of a very angry-looking gargoyle. "Okay, maybe it's the starvation talking, but you seem really sassy right now, Merida."

She laughs, apparently feeling a little better now that we're out of the enchanted rave. "I'm just saying, you're always so good at following your heart, so don't count this girl out."

I'm not against what she's saying, but I'm nervous to truly entertain the idea. I'm the queen of Getting My Hopes Up, and during my limited stay here I'd rather dive into something fun and easy, like a hookup with Ariel to fuel me through the rest of the semester. It takes considerable effort, but I push Val out of my mind for the second time today and focus on our beastly surroundings.

"You know what?" I say, changing the subject. "I was going to find us food, but now we're taking a detour."

Lanie's face falls. "Madison! Look, I'm sorry. I'm delirious. Can we please get dinner?"

I turn my cheek. "Nope. Follow me first." I stomp away, and since she has no frame of reference for anything in this castle, Lanie has no choice but to follow. We walk in silence, and after a couple of wrong turns, I find our destination.

"What is this?" she asks, staring at the arched doorway in doubt.

I wiggle my eyebrows in excitement. "You will love it, trust me." I swing the doors open, revealing the most dazzling library of all time. A three-story room with floor-to-ceiling shelves, multiple swirling stairways and ladders reaching to dizzying heights. Lanie's hands fly up to her face as we step onto the gold-inlaid tile, sunlight streaming in from impossibly high windows. I don't even read much, but this is pretty freaking amazing.

"Wow!" she gasps, eyes dancing around the room. "I've never seen so many books in all my life!"

"Well, look at you." I wrap my arm around her. "Maybe you should've played Belle instead."

"If it means I could have this library, then yes." She walks toward a shelf, hesitant to touch the spines. "Are these . . . real?"

"Grab one and see!"

Ever the overachiever, Lanie grabs armfuls of books, giggling at each individual tome. We take turns riding on the ladders, flinging our arms free in literary adventure. Whereas moments ago Lanie was crumbling from overwhelm, she's now full of light, totally in her element.

I'm gonna make her a Disney convert if it's the last thing I do.

LANIE

"UNDER THE SEA"

I s everyone ready?"

It's 7:00 a.m. and I'm chest deep in the ocean, my legs snuggled inside a shimmering green neoprene mermaid tail. Madison signed us up for Under the Sea snorkeling, saying she wanted to see if there's more green seaweed in someone else's ocean or something, but now she's not even here, leaving me alone to awkwardly flip my legs in a very unnatural motion just to stay afloat. Well, not *alone* alone—there are at least twenty other guests in the group for this early morning swim, including my fake parents, who moments ago offered their SPF 100 for my freckled shoulders.

"You can never be too careful!" Dorothy chimed, smearing sunscreen on her husband's bald head.

"Yeah, don't let your youth fool you: Someday you'll be covered in wrinkles and sunspots just like me," Sal added, pulling down his droopy under eyes for dramatic effect.

I look back at the shore, hoping to see Madison running toward the coast. She's never been known for her punctuality, but I figured she'd be on time for something like this. Where could she be? What could possibly be keeping her? Should I skip mermaid snorkeling in solidarity? This was her idea; it's kind of frustrating to be bobbing here without my best friend. She begged me to come on this trip so we could have all these extraordinary adventures together; if it were up to me, I'd be sitting safely on the shore, tucked under an umbrella with a book.

But what can I do? I'm already strapped into this fitted tail that feels like a wetsuit but moves like flippers, my upper half strapped into a life vest. A lot of the other girls opted for bikini tops to get the full Ariel effect, but me and my one piece are going for comfort and safety, especially since I've never even swum in Lake Michigan, let alone the open sea. Madison scheduled us for other classes and activities every morning this week, so if I want to find Nemo, this is my only chance.

"All right, everyone, snorkels on!" calls out our instructor from the front of the group. I didn't catch her name, but she's very committed to the *Little Mermaid* theme, with starfish and seaweed braided into her flowing hair. I'm glad it's not Jared leading this activity, though I guess he'd be easily heard over the ocean waves.

Again I glance over my shoulder, Madison nowhere to be seen. I can't decide if she'd be more upset with me for going without her or missing a Disney activity, so I go with the latter, stretching my goggles over my face. The plastic suctions to my skin as I breathe into the hose, really wishing my friend was here.

"Now, my mer-friends, let's practice using those tails, shall we? Take a couple practice laps around the bay," our instructor insists, lying on her back to showcase some advanced mermaid moves. The way she effortlessly glides her fins through the waves makes me feel like it's her actual appendage.

The group pushes forward, tails clumsily slapping the surface, but I hang back, not ready to take a tail to the face. After a minute of awkward undulating I start to find my rhythm; even the smallest tail kick propels like super flippers. I guess I should've played mermaid during all those pool field trip days at STEM summer camp; maybe then I wouldn't have been left behind to hang out with the camp counselors.

Swimming slightly off course I spot a castle rising out of the ocean, looking like it was carved from the cliffs above. Guests stroll along a suspended pier as a sailing ship sits parked nearby. If I didn't know better (and really, I don't), I'd guess this is Prince Eric's castle, the third royal manor I've seen in twenty-four hours. How many more does this island hold?

"All right, then, it's time to look for sunken treasure!" our instructor calls. "Gently place your faces under water and see what the ocean has in store!"

Tentatively, I lower myself, tipping my mask into the sea. And then—silence. One world fades away as another comes into focus, sunlight skating against the sandy ocean floor. My tail glimmers against the turquoise water, bits of seaweed innocently rolling by. I should be nervous—I've never been good at adapting to new experiences—but the slow, familiar sound of my breath eases me into a calming rhythm. *In, out. In, out.* My arms and legs relax as the ocean floor erupts with a rainbow of life.

I lose myself in the reef, fish freestyling between bright pink, orange, and yellow coral formations. A herd of seahorses twirls all around me, playfully tickling my skin and swirling through my hair before swimming away. At one point, I catch up with Dorothy and Sal, who give me a pair of underwater thumbs-up, which I enthusiastically return. *I love it so much!* I don't even know how long we're been swimming before our instructor gathers us all together at the edge of a deep drop-off.

Above water, we all pull off our masks, waiting for direction. "Now, rumor has it that King Triton's kingdom is not far from here," our guide teases. "Finding his castle is not for the faint of heart, but if you take a deep breath and dive low, you may catch a glimpse of his under the sea empire." She gracefully gestures to her left, hinting at the castle's hiding place.

Guests squeal into their snorkels, several plunging off the side almost immediately. I'm not one to jump into uncharted waters, but I feel strangely safe within Disney's protective net, knowing they wouldn't put us in any real danger. So before my anxiety can talk me out of it, I pull on my goggles, fill up my lungs, and dive, kicking as hard as I can.

The water darkens from turquoise to midnight. The pressure change challenges my breath and I'm just about to turn back when I see it: far, far away is Triton's castle, a glittering masterpiece of cascading golden towers spiraling together toward the surface. It beams from within, spreading rays of light throughout the ocean floor, beckoning its residents home.

How? *HOW?* Did Disney really build a castle and then plunge it into the sea? I'm suddenly wondering if the girl playing Ariel and all her sorority sisters had to be scuba certified just to get to their rooms. I want a closer inspection, but I'm out of air, so I swim to the surface where other divers are talking excitedly about their shared discovery.

I can't believe Madison missed this.

"Wasn't it beautiful?" Dorothy gasps, droplets shimmering on her light brown cheeks.

"Yes! I've never seen anything like it!" I exclaim. I turn to Sal, who's rubbing his eyes and sniffling. "You okay?"

"Oh, I'm fine. Just got a little salt water in my mask," he says, voice cracking. Dorothy gives me a knowing look, mouthing, "He's crying," behind his back. My heart pinches at his reaction; if only Madison were here, they could take comfort in each other's gooey Disney affection.

But she's not.

We swim back to the bay, the grand finale of our snorkeling adventure complete. Sal helps me shimmy out of my tail, which is easier said than done.

"Where's a sea witch when you need one?" Sal groans as he yanks on my fins. "Talk about poor unfortunate souls!"

"Oh for goodness' sakes, Sal," Dorothy chides. "Here, let me help." She adds her muscle and the tail slips free, sparkling against the sand.

She gives her husband a triumphant grin, but he shrugs, answering with "What? I loosened it for you."

Dorothy shakes her head but can't hide a smile. "Would you like to join us for brunch, Lanie? There's a spot steaming crab legs down the beach."

As good as that sounds, I need to find Madison. Something bigger than sleeping through her alarm must be keeping her. "Thanks, but I'm meeting a friend," I reply. "Have fun, though!" They nod and link hands, Dorothy resting her head on Sal's shoulder as they walk against the sea. As I watch them dreamily saunter away I think about the adventure we just had: I swam. In the ocean. For fun! Madison will be so proud of me.

If I ever find her. I throw on a cover-up over my one piece and scan the sand for my best friend. *Where is she?* Looks like I'll have to visit France to find an answer.

I'm on my way to her château when I spot Prince Charming surrounded by the next round of snorkeling voyagers. Guys and girls crowd around him, flaunting their beach bodies as he squirms in the middle, smiling and nodding politely at every blatant flirtation attempt. He looks like how I feel during lab presentations: like I'd rather be engulfed by the sun than have so many eyes on me.

The instructor summons the group to grab their tails, and Charming's admirers slowly peel away. I watch as they reluctantly head over to the rows of empty mermaid fins lying on the beach (a morbid sight if I ever saw one). Finally alone, Charming rubs his face with his hands, fingers scraping through his tight black curls before he spots me, a flood of relief washing over him.

"Hey!" he calls, trotting over in a pair of flip-flops and pineapple swim trunks. "Someone normal!"

I look around. "Where?"

He laughs, boyishly cute with his dimple. "I meant you, but you're right, I take it back."

"As you should. Normal is boring."

"Fair. Although, I wouldn't mind a little boring right now," he says. "I didn't realize, but apparently being Prince Charming is a big deal."

My jaw drops in fake surprise. "You don't say!"

"I'm serious! I don't get it. Of all the Disney leading males, Charming is the most nondescript. Eric sails ships, Li Shang trains armies. What does Charming do? Dress nice? Throw parties? Tell me one distinguishing characteristic about him." He folds his arms, an eyebrow raised in challenge.

I'm not exactly the one to ask, but I rack my brain anyway, trying to pull up a visual. All I can manage is a man-shape haze in a crown, though to be fair, a lot of the less prominent Disney characters look like that to me. "Um . . . he's rich?"

Charming cocks his head, face squished in doubt. "Yeah, he lives in a castle, but so does practically everyone here. Those other dudes have cool backstories, you know? Like Flynn Rider carving out a new identity for himself. What is Charming's deal?"

I snort in agreement. "Sounds like you're due for an origin story. *Prince Charming: Forgettable Face, Unforgettable Story*. Or something."

His arms drop, head dipping back in laughter. "Hey, I'd watch it. It'd give me something more to go on here other than being male, royal, and desperate for a wife."

Our eyes lock, a jolt of excitement running through me. I've never been able to talk so easily with a guy like this before; I'm usually the queen of dreaming up clever comebacks hours after a conversation, but here I am! Making quippy jokes! And not wanting to shed my skin in embarrassment every time I speak! I don't even care if he's being paid to pretend he enjoys my company; being with him makes me feel like I could theoretically re-create this kind of interaction in the real world, and isn't that what we're here for? Living out our fantasies?

"I think you're missing the whole appeal of Prince Charming, though," I continue, riding this wave of uncharacteristic confidence.

"What do you mean?"

"Well, it's not really about *who* he is but what he represents. He's an ideal: a level of happiness. When people talk about finding their Prince Charming, they're not talking about the actual character. You embody the fantasy of being loved and cared for, of never having to worry about companionship again."

His chin retreats into his neck, taken aback. "Wow, that's . . . Wow. Thank you, that actually helps a lot. Are you into film studies or something? Because that was fire."

Film studies? Oh no, even the most tangential reference to anything school or academia-related is off-limits here. I can already feel my insides squeezing over heading back to DePaul, where a pile of tests and classes I'm not even sure I want await. No, the second either of us reveals any personal details the spell will be broken, and if I'm only going to know him for a couple of days anyway, I'd rather them float on the frothy plane of make-believe.

I kick at the sand. "Film studies? What's film? I don't think we have films in Scotland," I say.

"Right, how silly of me, Princess," he says in a more aristocratic affectation. "I'm not sure what I was thinking." Still, he winks at me, chestnut eyes dazzling in the midmorning sun. He's so beautiful I have to look away, my body betraying me with red flushing up my neck and cheeks. He may pretend not to know much about his character just to make me laugh, but he's definitely got the whole make-people-weak-in-the-knees trick down.

As I look down the beach, the second group is already in the water, mermaid tails intact. "Were you going to snorkel?"

"I was supposed to but . . . I don't know." He shrugs. "What are you up to now?"

"Me? Oh, my Merida itinerary calls for me 'enjoying the forest on horseback,' but I kind of did that yesterday."

"Want to ditch? Explore the rest of the island?" He pauses, rubbing the back of his neck. "With me?"

I bite my lip as my heart does cartwheels. Should he be focusing so much attention on one guest like this? Doesn't he have other princely matters at hand? I've never had anyone ditch their responsibilities to hang out with me, except for Madison, who would drop any class or Java Jam! shift without thinking twice. *Madison.* I have to find her. What if she fell down a wishing well, or pricked her finger on a spinning wheel?

"Maybe first you could help me find Cinderella?" I suggest. "She was supposed to meet me here. . . . I'm a little worried." And annoyed, if I'm being honest.

"It would be my honor to escort you," he says, rolling his wrist before bending in a bow.

We head to a row of changing rooms to get out of our swimsuits. I left my full Merida getup back in DunBroch, opting instead for a pair of plaid shorts and an emerald tank: another Disney-bound combo courtesy of Madison. But a quick look in the mirror reveals weirdly dried hair and a faint goggle imprint around my eyes. Great, I looked like a drowned raccoon the whole time we were talking? Sigh. I didn't bring any grooming tools to the beach, so I do my best to smooth my wayward strands and hope the snorkel shape will fade soon.

Charming has also changed into a bound: red shorts with a white polo tucked in, revealing a golden hued belt. The polo is fitted just right, sleeves hugging his biceps. I think about yesterday when he caught me with those arms, bodies humming with adrenaline.

Damn, Lanie, be cool! I tell myself. Stop fangirling over the prince; he already has enough admirers.

We make our way from Ariel's beach back to the Lighthouse, making random small talk that in any other dynamic would be excruciating, but with Charming, flows naturally. He tells me about boring castle life (Prince Charming has next to zero screen time, so there's not a lot for him to do except stroll around the island being . . . charming), and I describe my Happily Ever Island experience as a Disney outsider, how everything is amazing but it always feels like I'm missing that deep, almost-spiritual connection everyone else around me is having. Like how the Be Our Guest dinner was cool, but mine were the only dry eyes at the table. And if there were hidden references during snorkeling this morning, I missed them all. It doesn't mean I'm having a bad time, I'm just on a different, less entrenched level.

He nods, listening to my predicament. "Is there anything I can do to help? I wouldn't call myself an expert either, but uh . . . I know some things."

As a cast member, I assume he knows all the things, but modesty must be one of his few defining character traits. "I don't know." I shrug. "I don't want to miss out just because I'm a newbie, you know? My natural state is to hide in a hole, but I'm already here, so if there are cool things to see and do, I want to give them a shot. Provided they don't involve me being put under a spell or endangering my life or generally embarrassing myself on a massive scale."

"So, you want death-defying, publicly humiliating magic?" he says with a smirk. "Got it."

"Yes. Perfect. Please give me exactly that." I roll my eyes but can't contain a smile.

"Hmm . . ." he wonders aloud. "What's on deck for hero moments today? Maybe we can start there." I didn't notice before, but at the Lighthouse's base there's a public information board, complete with an island map and daily schedule of events. There's a list of the morning's classes and activities, menu specials from the various themed restaurants, and details for the big hero moment productions that anyone can attend. Today there are two:

MOANA SETS SAIL FROM MOTUNUI ("HOW FAR I'LL GO")

PRINCE PHILLIP BATTLES MALEFICENT

Charming turns to me, brown eyes wide with adventure. "Oh, hell yes!" he cheers, pumping a fist in the air as he bites his lower lip. "We are so doing this!"

"What, sailing across the Pacific?"

"Fighting a dragon!"

I choke on a laugh. "No way . . . really?"

"Yes! Think of how awesome it'll be!" He must see how

my brain is spinning opportunity into disaster because he adds, "Didn't you just say you want to do all the cool things? What could be cooler than slaying a dragon? Literally NOTHING."

"But . . ." I protest, my autopilot response. *What if I get hurt? Is there going to be fire? Will I have to fight? What if Charming sees how completely uncoordinated I am? Oh god . . . Will he still want to hang out with me?* As the worries unravel, I fight to take stock of the world around me, grounding myself in what's real. The Lighthouse fountain bubbling; the smell of cotton candy down the Boardwalk. But most of all, the pure excitement emanating from this man before me. He claps his hands in prayer, eyes closed as he bobs back and forth awaiting my answer. A grown man desperate to strap on a sword and play pretend. Facing down a villain isn't exactly my idea of a perfect day, but watching Charming get lost in the fantasy? Now that could be entertaining.

"Okay," I relent, scrunching my nose up in doubt. "Let's do it. But we have to try and find Cinderella first. See if she wants to join."

His arms raise to the sky in victory. "Merida, you will not regret this."

✻

We do an island sweep, looking for Madison at Cinderella's Shoe Shop, Snow White's Dipped Apple Stand, and, of course, her château. But she's nowhere to be found. Without a phone, finding her across this vast storybook terrain proves impossible. Charming assures me she must be having her own adventure, so I give up, missing my best friend while also hoping she has a good reason for ditching me.

Before I know it, I find myself strapped into a brown body suit, designed to look like medieval rags but actually lined with protective padding. To be part of this hero moment, Charming and I will be playing some of Maleficent's goons, our goal to stop Prince Phillip before he reaches Aurora.

I have no idea what I'm doing.

Charming giggles as we're given foam pick axes and swords, painted to look like real steel. He bops me on the head with his club, so I poke his neck with the end of my mace, to which he gargles out a choking sound. He's loving every minute of this, treating our dark dungeon surroundings like a candy factory, not a crumbling chamber crawling with a sorceress's evil forces.

"Is this legal?" I ask, observing the disturbing number of hammers and bats all around me. Even if they have the weight of pool noodles, there's still a lot of weaponry in this scene, with about twenty guests huddled together in animated anticipation.

"I'm pretty sure we signed some sort of waiver before we got here," Charming says. "But really, who cares? This is going to be epic!"

A pair of island ambassadors who are not Jared and Val stand under a menacing green light, passing out helmets and talking through a safety spiel. It's hard to hear their warnings to "Fight fair" and "Have fun" against the thunder sound machine banging outside, the room growing darker by the second. Charming practically vibrates beside me, itching for the iron gate to let us into the action.

I scour the corners of my brain for cinematic memories of what's to come, but I've only seen *Sleeping Beauty* once, maybe twice in my life. Mom was pretty strict about TV time and usually chose documentaries over animated fairies, but I seem to recall a barricade made of thorns, with green fire all around? But that can't be possible. . . . They're not going to make us run through flames . . . right?

Suddenly, the gate screeches open and we're on, a bunch of idiots running down a chipped-stone spiral staircase, play weapons in the air as we growl and yell in panic. My feet fly down the steps as I fight to keep up with Charming, his face somehow even cuter in his attempt to look mean. At the bottom waits Prince Phillip, a beam of white light shining down on his heroic stance. We charge him, plowing straight into his massive shield, doing everything we can to prevent his escape.

Foam swords swing left and right as I cry out, "Are we winning?"

"No idea!" Charming yells back, his club clashing against Phillip's sword. With so many limbs flying and people grunting, it's impossible to know which end is up, until Phillip, tired of our shenanigans, makes a break for it, sprinting out of Maleficent's dungeon and onto his awaiting horse's back. We chase after him, watching him escape across a drawbridge and into a patch of dark, twisting bramble, three balls of red, green, and blue light blazing behind.

A bunch of our fellow goons collapse into a breathless pile, but not Charming, who's still laser focused on our target riding away. "Now *that's* a prince!" he pants, hands on his thighs. "Look at him! Colors flying, sword blazing! That's a man who's getting it done. He gets to charge a dragon, and what does Prince Charming do? Pick up a shoe?"

I pat his shoulder. "It's okay. . . . I still like you." I gasp, the words tumbling out without thought. I've never—ever—told a guy how I feel, romantic or otherwise. Yet here, dressed like some fairy-tale henchman carrying a mace, I'm able to freely share emotions I'm not even sure I've fully processed? Huh? Sure, I like Charming: He's funny, sweet, and damn easy on the eyes, but *liking* him is problematic. What would be the point? In a few days, I'll be back in Chicago and he'll still be here, charming the metaphorical and/or physical pants off another set of guests. Prince Charming's story is already written, our plot lines too far off to converge.

He looks at me, a shy smile across his lips, but before either of us can say more, a giant green fireball shoots through the sky demanding everyone's attention. On the horizon rises the threatening outline of a dragon, black wings stretching against the clouds. Excitement flashes in Charming's eyes.

"Should we go pay our respects?" he asks.

I follow his gaze across the inky-green sky to where Maleficent resides. "To . . . Maleficent?" I question. "Like get up close and personal with a straight-up evil sorceress?"

He grins, raising his eyebrows similar to when Madison is up to something sneaky. "Why not? We are her henchmen, after all."

His fingers interlace with mine, momentarily breaking down my defenses. "Sure, I guess," I hear myself saying. "It should be interesting to meet someone who opted for evil on vacation."

"Do you think that's bad?"

"No, no judgment. Actually, of all the villains, I always found Maleficent to be the most intriguing. I mean, isn't her whole thing that she's pissed off after not being invited to a baby princess's party?"

Charming chokes on a laugh. "Uh, I've never heard anyone phrase it like that."

"I'm probably wrong because I only saw that movie once, but I find her motives ridiculous and delightful."

"I'm sure she'll be happy to hear."

As we climb through thorny black bramble and bypass geysers of fire, the dragon terrorizing the sky reveals its true nature: It looked so real from far away, but up close it's only a video projection across a nearly transparent screen stretching miles high. That doesn't make it any less foreboding though; I almost drop my mace as the animated creature screeches in fury, bursts of real fire shooting up from a pit.

Finally, we reach Maleficent standing tall under the illustrated pointy wings flapping above, her face painted a sickly shade of green paired with a twisted horned headdress. Logically, I know it's all fake, but my nerves don't, arm hair standing on edge as the sorceress glares at us with bright yellow eyes. Those are some seriously fearsome colored contacts she rocking.

She rushes toward us, jaw clenched tight. "You let him get away!" she shrieks, pounding her staff on the broken cobblestone. "Prince Phillip will awaken Aurora!"

Charming drops to one knee, bowing his head in shame. I kneel beside him but keep my eyes up to follow his lead. Was this in the movie? I have no idea what we're doing, but Charming seems really invested.

"We tried, but we failed." He grovels. "Our lives are in your hands."

Um, what now? I scoot closer to him as she approaches, her jagged cape billowing behind like a cursed fog. This must be some sort of deleted scene.

Towering above us she sneers, "Yes. Well, I suppose I shall spare you. Just this once."

Charming jumps to his feet as the villainess's expression softens from pure disgust to delight as she drops her staff and grins.

O-kay?

"That was fun, wasn't it?" she says with a giggle. It's hard to tell her age with all that thick green face paint, but the crinkles around her eyes suggest older. Even with her black cape billowing against the flames, I'm not sure which is more unsettling: Maleficent in her natural evil state or dissolved into giddy joy. Charming doesn't seem to mind, so they clearly know each other; maybe Maleficent is a fellow cast member?

"Of course!" he exclaims. "That was awesome! All the fighting and fire—we loved it, didn't we?" He looks for my approval and I nod enthusiastically, not sure how to address a bubbly baddie. "Oh, this is Merida, by the way."

Her eyes dance playfully between Charming and me, like she wants to say more, but it'd be too out of character. Do villains make small talk? They have to, right? They are evil, after all.

"Good" is all she says despite the smirk on her lips. "Now, if you'll excuse me, it's time for me to make my dragon debut." With that, she makes a big show of waving her arms in good-bye, a raven swooping to her side as she glides off toward the crumbling castle, lightning striking the second she disappears.

"Damn! Now that's an exit!" Charming exclaims, fist pumping in the air.

I laugh to myself. He's so into this. "For sure. So, you two are friends?"

He rubs the back of his neck. "We're not *not* friends."

I wait for more details, but they don't come. It's fine; I guess cast members can't really talk about their coworkers. Don't want to break the illusion and all that.

"Thanks for coming with me," he finally adds. "I would've felt dumb doing this alone."

"Admittedly, I felt dumb the entire time," I say. "But, in a good way, I guess." Hero moment winding down, the area begins to clear, flames lowering and fellow goons returning their play weapons. "So what do we do now?"

"Hmm, I've got some ideas." He reaches for me and then we're off, running and laughing in the face of danger, hand in hand.

MADISON

"LET IT GO"

The morning sun streaks through my window, birds singing sweetly in the breeze. I crashed hard after last night's Be Our Guest blessing/disaster, especially after Lanie and I stuffed our faces at a Boardwalk hot dog stand (thankfully they had vegan options for my bestie). While I'm sure the French menu would've landed much better than multiple helpings of processed meat, I'm actually okay with how things went down, especially since I got Lanie to admit that Disney is "pretty okay." Progress!

Something scampers at the corner of my room, and I spring up in bed, wishing I had Rapunzel's frying pan to ward off any intruders. I know there aren't any ruffians in Cinderella's story, but hey, Lanie and I saw quite a few guests stumbling home from Gaston's tavern last night, so who knows where everyone ended up.

I throw off the covers, bare feet hitting the floorboards as I hunt for the scurrying sound. I kneel down, staring in a mouse hole cut into the wall, half excited and afraid that a pack of mice will come shooting at my face.

"Hello?" I whisper into the void. "It's me . . . Cinderelly." Holding my breath, I wait for my furry friends to arrive, but instead, I'm greeted by 2D images: animated drawings of Jaq and Gus Gus projected on the wall. I watch the cartoon critters run back and forth—Jaq bumping into Gus's belly, Gus stepping on Jaq's tail—all while their recorded voices chatter from a hidden speaker.

"Zuck zuck, Cinderelly! Zuck zuck!"

I sit back, slightly disappointed. Not that I wanted my room to be covered in rodent droppings or anything, but the mice and birds are Cinderella's only allies, and with my step-family so committed to their roles, I would've been nice to snuggle something soft and cuddly. Oh well.

In addition to the lack of animal friends, Cinderella's room has a few other alterations, including a much welcomed en-suite bathroom. No need to douse myself with a sponge behind some flimsy partition! I take my time getting dressed, layering a white apron and brown skirt over my swimsuit, my blonde waves pulled in a low pony with a blue bow. Even though I'm meeting Lanie at the beach for some under-the-sea snorkeling, I still want to look my best as I stroll through France to get there—it is the first official day of role-play, after all.

Just as I'm slipping on a pair of black ballet flats, a brass bell above my door chimes.

"Cinderella!"

Ooh, breakfast! I think, happily grabbing my swim bag before making my long descent down the tower staircase. I'm hoping there will be bagels or something equally portable to eat on the run; I can't wait to jump in the ocean and flip my fins!

But when I get to the kitchen, there's nothing, not even a pot of coffee. I spin around, nothing but an empty table and cold hearth to greet me. What in the actual heck? Where is the food? Our welcome packets specified that meals would be provided at every major island setting, so then why is my home empty?

A trio of wall-mounted bells rings impatiently throughout the room, followed by a shrieking chorus of "Cinderella!"

Ugh! This is so annoying! I didn't plan to stop before my snorkeling lesson, and I need coffee if I'm going to be exercising so early in the morning. I check the wooden cupboard, desperate for options. There's plenty of stuff, from loose-leaf teas, fruit, and baking ingredients, but none of it ready, none of it instantly edible. What am I going to do for breakfast?

"Cinderella!"

Unless . . .

"Cinderella!"

Oh god . . .

"CINDERELLA!"

I drop my swim bag, frozen in the realization. Wait a minute. Just . . . wait a minute. Am *I* supposed to make breakfast? I know Cinderella was responsible for all the cooking, but . . . I can't cook in here! There's no appliances—no stove! Only an unlit stone fireplace with a metal pot innocently dangling above. Even Java Jam! has more kitchen equipment than this, and it's, like, an eighth of the square footage. I can barely cook in normal circumstances, especially without a microwave. What am I supposed to do? Am I really expected to bring my pretend stepfamily breakfast?

"Cinderella!"

"Unbelievable." I sigh, palms pressed against my cheeks. The clock in the corner reads seven o'clock—no! Mermaid time! I picture Lanie alone on the beach, anxiously twisting her fingers. Okay, I just need to get through this, pretend it's the early morning coffee rush. Don't think, just do.

I grab a set of teacups, filling a pot with water (I should be grateful, I guess, that there even is running water). Starting a fire isn't as hard as I thought, if only because there was already a pile of wood in the room next to a thematically inappropriate yet much appreciated lighter. While the tea gets going, I rummage around to see what else I can find. A barrel of apples? Sure. A hunk of cheese? Whatever. I throw it all on three circular trays, balancing them across my arms but not my head—I don't care if that's cinematically accurate, that is just not happening—and shimmy up the stairs.

Knocking gently on Anastasia and Drizella's door, I crack

it open with my foot, darkness spilling out into the hallway. Wow, so everyone else gets to sleep in while I rush around delivering mediocre meals? Rude. I tiptoe in between their two canopy beds, light snoring bouncing between them. As I set down the first tray on the bedside table Anastasia stirs.

"Cinderella?" she croaks, wiping the sleep from her eyes. "What are you . . . ? Why are you up so early?"

"Your breakfast, stepsister." It's hard not to be annoyed; weren't these two shouting for me seconds ago? "You called?"

Anastasia sits up, eyes still closed but mouth in a frown, frilly nightgown wrinkled with sleep. "Huh?"

"That wasn't us," Drizella chimes in from underneath her pillow. "It was the movie actresses."

Shoot. She's right. Those high-pitched shrieks were so motivating because they were the original recordings. It makes me feel a little better, though, that actual humans weren't screaming at me just now.

"You made us breakfast?" Anastasia yawns, peeling her eyes open to observe my paltry offerings. "You didn't have to do—"

"Anastasia," Drizella interrupts, voice muffled under linens. "We're supposed to be evil."

"Oh, right." She rubs her face before switching back into character. "This looks terrible!" But she can't keep a straight face, immediately blowing out a laugh. "Sorry, I can't be mean without morning caffeine."

I exhale into a smile. "Well, you're in luck, because morning beverages are pretty much the only things I know how to make."

Anastasia reaches for her cup as Drizella peeks out from her blankets. "Thank you," Drizella says sweetly, before adding a rougher "Now get out of here!" The two of them spill into goofy giggles, far from the cruel cackles the stepsisters are known for. Maybe I will end up making some friends in this house after all.

My stepmother, though, is wide awake and upright in bed; apparently disdain is her I-woke-up-like-this face. Green eyes practically glow with anger against the heavy purple fabric draped above her bed. She says nothing as I enter, tracking me and my sad little tray as she strokes Lucifer's fur.

"Yeah, so . . ." I start, seeing how pathetic my breakfast of crumbled cheese and apple slices must look. "I didn't know we were doing this yet, or at all, to be honest, seeing as how our scenes aren't scheduled until the afternoon—"

"Quiet," Lady Tremaine commands, managing impressive volume despite barely moving her lips. Her nose turns up at the tray.

I grimace. "If we had an espresso machine, I could—"

A bony finger signals me to silence, so I zip my lip, equally impressed and frightened by this performance. She's too perfect, stirring her tea like she's plotting my death. I wonder how she and the other villains get in character; there must be some kind of official Disney villain training program on how to terrify guests with a single look. I'd be eating this up if I wasn't late for mermaid adventures.

"You'll find the laundry over there," she says with a nod. "I need a few things hemmed."

"Now?" I balk, looking at the absurdly tall pile of dirty clothes. We've only been here a day—what, did she grunge up her entire wardrobe in twenty-four hours?

She stares at me, wide eyes burning with indignation. "They're not going to clean themselves!"

"Right, of course, it's just that—"

"Just that what?" she snaps, she and Lucifer both sending massively combative energy my way.

I feel like I'm caught in the principal's office, every come-back sounding like a pathetic excuse. I doubt my evil step-mother, who has sentenced me to a life of indentured servitude, gives two craps about Under the Sea snorkeling, let alone the fact that I'm straight-up abandoning a friend who's probably too afraid to feel seaweed brush against her leg. So I hang my head, sighing, "Nothing," as I sulk over to the laundry basket, heaving the towering load. As I stumble down the hallway, a grandfather clocks reads 7:30 a.m.—I've officially missed it.

How Cinderella didn't murder her family in their sleep is a mystery I'll never understand.

❖

Once Lady Tremaine goes over all my work with a white glove (seriously, did she bring one from home?), I race out the door, hoping to catch Lanie at the beach. In my hurry, I take a wrong turn, finding myself in Snow White's forest, her wishing well echoing a wish for someone to love.

I stop, wondering how I got so turned around. Snow's sweet voice reminds me of Tessa, who used to break into high-pitched arias whenever I started acting like a *little doe in the woods* (her words). There were a lot of things I liked about her—the way she was always humming her latest solo to herself; her giggle whenever I snuck my hand into her back jeans pocket—but I didn't realize until the *grow up* comment that she'd been laughing at me, not with me, for my *frivolous, flighty* ways. I never teased her for dreaming about becoming a pop star; honestly I don't see how my fantasies were any less far-fetched. We both wanted love and admiration, to live incredible, out-of-this-world lives.

Yet somehow I was the immature one?

Leaving Snow (and Tessa) behind, I search the sky for the Lighthouse, letting its blue-and-white-striped beacon re-center my journey. But by the time I make it to the beach, the second snorkeling class of the day has already pushed off, their sparkly tails splashing against the sea.

Great. GREAT. I stomp out to the shore, angrily kicking the tide. I can't believe I missed this! All I wanted to do was swim up on a rock formation singing "Part of Your World" right as a wave crashed up behind me—is that so much to ask? Maybe I really messed up choosing Cinderella as my character. I only thought of glass slippers and royal balls, when in actuality her story is mostly scrubbing floors and hemming skirts. I hate both those things! My big hero moment isn't until the last night of our stay, so what, I'm just on cleaning duty until then? WHY. Why did I do this to myself?

I kick the waves again, sending salty spray right into my eye. "Argh!" I cry, using my apron to wipe away the sea. This is not my day. I flop down in the sand, claiming defeat. Let the water take me, I'm done.

I lie there for a while, listening to seagulls squawk and ragtime melodies play from the Boardwalk. I could get up and find Lanie, but sinking into the sand is oddly comforting, my body submerging into its warm embrace. Eventually, the ocean lulls me into a better mental space, quieting my frustrations while reminding me that at least I'm here: on a beautiful island away from dealing with reality and school. There's no way I'd be getting this substantial dose of vitamin D at home, and even if I missed my mermaid moment, there is still lots of magic on deck.

But right as my energy starts to shift, a shadow falls over my face. "Need something?" a familiar voice asks. It's Val, standing over me with her too-cute lopsided grin, which I have been working so hard not to obsess over. Oof. Her head turns like a little bird, trying to untangle why I'm collapsed on the beach in a pile of fail. "You look . . ."

"Like a shipwrecked sailor who's lost all hope?" I groan. I don't want her seeing me like this.

"Kind of." She cringes. "But hey, you're right on theme, being on Ariel's beach and all."

My fingers dig into the sand. Damn it, I *love* that that's her response.

"True," I say, propping myself up on my elbows. "Just thought I'd work on my tan. Gotta get that glow before the ball!" I kick up one foot, pointing my toe in fake enthusiasm. But Val's not buying it: She side-eyes my full-on Cinderella look, apron draped in the sand. Not exactly tanning attire. I hike up my skirt a little, revealing whiter-than-white legs.

"I thought maybe . . ." She pinches her lips, thinking better of what she was about to say. "Never mind. Enjoy your sun." I watch her hurry away, the hem of her navy-blue skirt hugging her just right, before she suddenly stops, conferring with her clipboard before she shakes her head and beelines back to me. She looks like she's having some kind of internal debate, and I'm not sure which side is winning.

"Can I help *you* with something?" I ask.

My question uncovers a smile, a visible wave of relief running through her. She takes a deep breath through her nose before confirming, "I wouldn't normally do this, but yes, if you're offering, I could use an extra set of expert eyes."

My heart leaps. Wait, for real? A legit cast member thinks I can be of assistance? "Oh, really?"

"Yeah," she exhales, cheeks a little flushed. "I liked your quick response to the Be Our Guest fiasco; if I'd had someone like you behind the scenes with me, maybe that dinner wouldn't have spun out of control the way it did." I sit up, astounded by this turn of events. Val's face is resolute yet soft, peeling back the thinnest possible layer of vulnerability. Even as she hovers above me, it's obvious that admitting she needs help is not easy, her brown eyes refusing to meet mine. She clears her throat, smoothing down the side of her hair. "Anyway, I'm in charge of a big hero moment today, and I thought you might be interested in seeing what's involved."

"Hold up—are you serious?" I ask, jumping to my feet. "You want to take me backstage?"

Her lips lean to the right mischievously. "Is that something you'd be interested in?"

Against my will, a geyser of excitement springs up inside me. While there's nothing I want more than being swept away in fantasy, part of me *is* curious about peeking behind the curtain to see how the magic gets made. Like riding Space Mountain with the lights on or learning how the Haunted Mansion's ghosts rise from the dead, the puppetry behind the tricks is interesting, though I've never really had the opportunity . . . until now.

"Isn't that, like, against the rules, though?" I ask. "I'm pretty sure guests aren't supposed to go backstage."

She considers this. "It's a little unconventional, but my job is to ensure every guest has a magical experience. Seeing you curled up seaside in the fetal position doesn't exactly scream 'having a great time,' so I'm taking emergency measures. Plus, it's really important I get today's scene right; I cannot handle another malfunction."

This defies everything I know to be true about Disney operations, though I guess Happily Ever Island plays by its own rules. My Cinderella itinerary calls for me getting acquainted with my household responsibilities, but I've pretty much already done that, and the idea of going back to wait on my overzealous stepmother right now makes me want to puke.

"Fine, I guess I can tag along." I sigh, downplaying my interest. "Though can we both agree that you asking for my help means that we're equals, and that maybe you're not the preeminent Disney scholar?"

She stops just short of rolling her eyes. "I'm pretty sure I never said that."

"Oh, I'm pretty sure you couldn't wait to say exactly that at orientation. 'Hi, I'm Val, and I know every Disney fact dating back to 1921!'" I mimic, balancing my chin on my fingers.

"And what should I say? 'Hi, I'm Val, I'm responsible for your waking happiness, but I don't know anything about these stories or this place'?"

Hmm, fair point. The only thing more infuriating than the brag is the undersell. "Still. You know how fired up fans can get. A lot of Disney people believe that they are the True Fans, and that no one else can love the parks and characters as deeply."

"You mean, like you?" Val snorts.

Yes. "No!" I knee-jerk say. But on second thought, "Okay. Maybe."

"It doesn't have to be a competition," she says. "We can all love Disney in our own ways."

"You're right." But I still love it most.

"Well, we should get going then," Val says, checking her

watch—a vintage Mickey Mouse timepiece. Nice. "It's a long walk to Arendelle."

Arendelle?! I look down at my thin dress; I'm going to freeze! "I didn't exactly bring a coat to the Keys."

She waves away my worry. "You'll be fine."

"Let me guess: The cold isn't real? It won't bother me?"

"Exactly."

We head off, and I find myself struggling to keep up with her hurried pace. Breezing around the Boardwalk and past the Lighthouse, we venture down the path to Arendelle, lined in white translucent stones that almost look like ice. The farther we go, the more the trees give way to rolling hillsides, until our trek becomes entirely uphill.

"So, how exactly are we going to be transported from Ariel's beach to Anna and Elsa's freezefest?" I ask, sprinting ahead to be at Val's side. "I don't doubt that Arendelle will be just as awesome as every other setting here, but I can't picture us suddenly being in snow."

Without missing a step, Val goes into full tour-guide mode. "If you look at a map, Happily Ever Island is roughly circular with two main story spheres. The inner sphere holds all the forest-based story settings: Snow White, Cinderella, Aurora, Belle, Merida. Each of these stories spends at least some time running around in trees, so these settings are grouped closely together. In fact, we're cutting through the forests of France and Scotland as we speak."

I look through the dense branches, hoping to catch a glimpse of Lanie. What is she doing right now? Archery?

Etiquette lessons? I can't picture her doing either, but I hope she's okay, and at the very least, not too pissed at me for bailing this morning. I'll make it up to her somehow. Now that I have a friend on the inside, maybe I can finagle a special surprise.

Val continues. "The outer coastal sphere holds all the settings with major water elements: Ariel, Moana, Tiana, Pocahontas, Rapunzel. But there are a few more stories that don't immediately fit on either sphere: Mulan, Jasmine, and Anna and Elsa. Because their homes are the most unique, they're also on the outer sphere, pushed far away from any of the others so we can play around with their environments more."

I love this, hearing the logic of how it all comes together. It's exactly how I'd lay everything out, too. Not that anyone's asking, but the validation still counts.

We must be getting closer now as the trees are dusted with white sparkles, a few flurries fluttering in the warm island breeze. I catch one in my palm, licking what is definitely not water. "What is this?" I ask.

"Soap flakes," she says. "Billions and billions of shaved soap flakes carried through a specially designed ventilation system. Imagineering really killed it over here, you'll see."

We hit a fork in the road, a wooden signpost guiding us either toward Arendelle proper or Elsa's ice castle. When Val turns toward the frozen palace, I can't help but squeal.

"Oh shiiit, are we doing 'Let It Go'?!" I shriek, nearly grabbing her in excitement. But I catch myself at the last moment, reminding myself I'm trying to keep things platonic. Besides it's not cool to be all over someone while they're at work.

She doesn't seem to notice my lapse in judgment. "Yes, but be chill," she instructs with confidence. (Ha! "Be chill.") "This is one of the only hero moments I'm running by myself and it has to go perfectly. Especially since Jared is across property running Mulan's 'Reflection' scene, which is way, way less technologically involved. All he has to do is release some cherry blossoms whereas I have to make an ice castle rise out of a mountain." Her jaw tightens, paired with a straight-up death grip on her clipboard.

"Wow, you really hate him." I laugh.

"What? Who?" I give her a look, prompting her to add, "Jared? No, of course not." But her body betrays her, stiff with frustration. "Let's just focus on the task at hand."

This feels like something to be unpacked, but I stay quiet while she checks and rechecks her to-do list, physically tapping the bullet points over and over. She mouths something to herself, like a performer running through lines backstage. I've seen Lanie do the same thing on the way to class, listing periodic table elements or whatever it is she has to memorize on a daily basis. I usually just show up to things and hope for the best.

I can tell Val is in deep concentration mode, and while I want to give her that space, my insides are screaming to get to know her better. This whole being-casual-around-a-crush thing is unbearable (how do people play hard to get? HOW?), and try as I might, this girl is a mystery I can't let go. "So, back on the beach, when you said you 'wouldn't normally do this,' what did you mean?" I ask.

162

She bristles, looking up from her list. "Did I say that?"

"You did. And I was just wondering if that meant you don't usually bring girls backstage, or . . ." I trail off, wanting her to fill in the blanks.

After a few silent steps, she quietly admits, "I don't like asking for help. I like doing things myself."

I nod, realizing these are probably words she doesn't say aloud too often. "A self-made woman, I respect that."

"I mean, there's nothing *wrong* with asking for help, I'm just not used to it. It wasn't really a thing for me growing up."

I want to understand, but it's hard to wrap my head around. I was always going to Grandma Jean with all my troubles, big and small. Val must see me struggling because she continues.

"See, I have two older brothers; I'm the only girl. They teased me relentlessly, always saying I wasn't as strong as them, that I couldn't do the things they could. But that didn't stop me from trying. I tagged along for all their dumb boy stuff—tricks at the skate park, setting toys on fire—but the second I asked them for help, or god forbid, went to my parents for something, they'd laugh."

"Boys are stupid." I sigh.

"That's what my grandma would say," Val adds, expression brightening. "I didn't get to see her much because she lived in Japan, but she always sent me letters, adding 'Don't let those boys underestimate your strength' at the end of every one." She smiles at the memory, brown eyes sparkling.

"She sounds awesome. Kind of like my grandma Jean."

"Yeah? You two are close?"

"The closest! She raised me." My heart pinches. "She passed two years ago, though."

Val stops in her tracks, lips pressed into a tight frown. Ever so gently, she rests her hand on my shoulder, warmth instantly flooding through me. "Mine too. I'm so sorry."

Carefully, I place a hand on top of hers, my fingers grazing her soft skin. We hold there for a moment—eyes locked, hearts beating as one—and it's so surprisingly intimate, I almost have to look away, my cheeks fully flushed. I've never felt like this before, never really even had the chance to share a moment this personal. I've always wanted to, but the girls I've dated have never really seemed interested. This is something new . . . something real.

I like it.

Ugh, but I'm supposed to avoid catching feelings! I should be singing to birds, sewing with mice: EASY BREEZY. So why do I feel so invested in this moment of reality?

I quickly let go, and we continue on our journey, my heart taking a minute to reset to its normal pace.

"So what made you choose Cinderella?" Val asks after a little while.

"I've always loved her," I admit. "She never stops believing in miracles, that she can get her own happily-ever-after, fairy-tale wedding and all." I feel my face flush. "Not that I want a *wedding*. I actually don't even want a relationship right now. Doing the solo thing for a while, you know. I've got no strings." *Smooth, Madison.* Why don't you just tell her about all your romantic failures next?

Val shoots me an unreadable glance but doesn't say anything. Luckily, the scenery changes again, ushering in a welcome distraction.

"Oh wow," I breathe. We're now walking through a snow globe, fake flakes swirling around a desolate mountainous landscape. Dark, windy, frozen: I'd be shivering if it wasn't still eighty degrees. It's too bad we bypassed the charming village where Anna and Elsa live, because the setting for Elsa's frozen self-discovery is not a very cozy place to hang out. Arendelle is in desperate need of a hot chocolate stand; maybe Barry can franchise them a Java Jam! cart. But before I get too bummed out by my blabbermouth or the bleak winter before us, Val leads us through a frozen cavern that's actually a cleverly disguised door, instantly taking us from a snow-swept cliff to what looks like a space shuttle control room.

Two cast members wearing headsets sit before a panel of buttons, levers, and screens, a massive one-way mirror illustrating the snowy scene we just left. Val greets them in hushed tones before taking her place behind them, slipping on her own headset.

"So, here's what's going to happen," she says to me, face stern. "As soon as we see Elsa walk up the edge of that cliff, we'll cue the music. I took her through a quick rehearsal yesterday of where she needs to stand and when, but most of the final effects will be a surprise."

"What do you need me to do?" I ask.

"Just let me know if anything feels off? I'm assuming you've seen this movie a hundred times."

I nod. Obviously.

"So if there's too much snow or not enough sparkle, tell me. Okay? Let's get as close to perfect as we can."

I give her a thumbs-up just as the woman playing Elsa, all moody in her billowing burgundy cape, appears on the frozen horizon. Val takes a deep breath, then whispers into her microphone, "Go."

One of the cast members turns a switch, and a tinkling piano plays, the opening notes of "Let It Go" echoing across the mountains. From a distance, Elsa hugs herself, closing her eyes as she sings about glowing snow and the absence of footprints.

But right away something is off. I look at Val with alarm—that's not Idina Menzel singing! But Val shakes her head sharply, covering her microphone as she explains, "Guests have the option of doing their own vocals if they want."

Oh dang. Respect.

As Elsa continues her first verse, the trio of cast members prepare for what's to come, fingers flying across an impossible combination of buttons. With the first chorus seconds away, Val commands, "Cue ice projections."

Elsa gestures left and right, pale blue snowflake swirls lighting up above each palm. It's amazing—a simple flick of a switch, and it really looks like ice is coming out of her hands. Elsa grins in delight, waving her arms as if she's actually creating the fluffy white Olaf rising out of an underground platform. The projections grow in size and shape, filling the sky with crystalized illuminations. It's all so seamless, so magical, I find myself being whisked away in the pageantry, holding my breath as Elsa unclips her cape to announce how she can't be troubled by temperature.

Yet Val is anything but enthralled, hyper focused on every note and step. "Verse two, get ready for staircase and castle reveal."

Elsa runs up the mountain as she sings, her voice ringing with pure joy. This woman has some serious pipes! My traitorous brain pulls up memories of Tessa, but I push them away; ex-girlfriends are not invited to this party. Just as Elsa reaches a dark cliff, the behind-the-scenes team clicks a series of controls and an icy staircase bursts from the shadows, causing both me and Elsa to gasp.

"This is incredible!" I sigh, drawing a quick wink from Val. But there's no time to enjoy her success just yet: Elsa stomps the floor as a giant snowflake pattern spreads across the snow, building the foundation for her ice palace.

Val grips the backs of her team's chairs. "Here we go, just like we practiced. Cue castle." Over the next several seconds I watch as a technological marvel takes place, an engineering masterpiece synchronized to song. Mirrored wall panels that I didn't even see before start to spin, reflecting purplish-blue ice shards climbing toward the sky. I see it happening, but I still can't believe it—the castle's structure was there the whole time but hidden in plain sight. Frozen fractals spin into place, shimmering in all their icy splendor. By the time Elsa pulls out her braid to let it all loose, I'm convinced that Val and her cohorts are actual wizards, performing a high-tech spell unlike any other.

Elsa tugs at her sleeves, ripping away her coronation dress to reveal the iconic ice queen gown underneath, sparkles bouncing from every surface. I gasp as she struts her dazzling stuff, working that victorious moment for all its worth. Now all she has to do is hit that last note. . . .

But no, Elsa's voice cracks at the exact wrong moment. The orchestration finishes without her as she scans the castle walls for help.

All three cast members groan. Val covers her face with her hands, head hanging heavy. She sits there, grieving a mistake she didn't make before uttering, "So close."

"But that is so not your fault!" I offer in sympathy. "That note is like, inhumanly hard to nail. The rest of it was perfect."

She peeks out from behind her fingers. "You think so?"

"Hello? You made a castle appear out of thin air!"

The corners of her mouth fight to smile, but her eyes are cloudy with doubt.

"Um, excuse me?" Elsa whimpers from inside her icy palace. "Can we, um, do it again? I know I can hit that note."

Val's face drains of color. "Do it again?" She scans the control panels as if she's never seen them before. "I'm not sure we . . . The technology takes a while to reset. . . ." Her coworkers agree, pulling off their headsets in defeat.

I bite my lip. I know how I'd feel if I fell up the stairs on my way to the ball or stepped on the prince's foot mid-dance.

These moments are special. Sacred. And doing them right is a sign of respect. "Can you just rewind the scene a bit? Let her do the last verse one more time?"

Val raises her eyebrows. "You want me to rebury an ice castle bursting from the snow?"

"Yes? I mean, no, not really. For the last verse, the castle is already there, everything's already in place. Could you set up a redo of the final thirty seconds only?"

Val's team shrugs with doubt, but she sits a little straighter, eyeing me with wonder. Wheels are turning in her head, but I can't tell if she thinks I'm brilliant or bonkers.

"Hello?" Elsa calls again from her fortress of solitude. "Is anyone there?"

Without permission I scoot my butt next to Val, brushing against her as I call into her microphone, "We got you, girl! Stand by!"

"What are you doing?" Val whispers, her lips dangerously close. She smells like honey, which is the absolute wrong detail to fixate on right now.

Focus, Madison. "Saving the day! We can't leave Elsa hanging. She's already rocking the dress, the scene is set: All we need to do is cue the music and let her shine!" I wiggle some jazz hands for effect.

With that, something in Val knocks free. Pulling her chair back up to the control panel, she springs back into action, twisting dials to cue up the triumphant finale.

Celebratory strings and brass ring through the ice once more, and Elsa is visually flooded with relief, taking a deep breath before she breaks back into song. Her voice rings clear as she saunters to the balcony, sunlight sparkling against the snow. I lean into Val as we reach the closing crescendo. *Come on, Elsa, you got this!* And she does, this time hitting the note with perfect vibrato as everyone in the control booth applauds.

"We did it!" I cheer, leaping out of Val's chair to do a happy dance. She jumps up beside me and stops just short of pulling me in for a hug, self-consciously nodding toward her fellow cast members instead. If they weren't here, would we be wrapped in each other's arms right now, bodies touching, hearts pounding? Would she want to after I basically told her I'm not looking for love?

"*You* did it," Val says, removing her headset. "I totally panicked back there, but you knew exactly what to do."

I swipe away her comment. "Don't be so hard on yourself. You were just . . . *Frozen*."

She snorts. "You did not just say that."

"I totally did."

"Well, dorky pun aside, I'm really glad you were here," she admits with a lopsided grin. "You have the Disney touch."

Her comment shoots straight through my heart, and I almost melt to the floor. Our eyes hold for moment, locked in shared excitement over everything that just went down. Elsa calls out a stream of appreciation, and I'm flooded with pride. I've never been personally responsible for making someone's dreams come true, but it feels good—intoxicating—to know that something I did made a difference. From the look on Val's face, I know she feels the same.

I stand there, letting this unfamiliar sense of accomplishment sink into my bones. Yes, I like it here—weirdly, the not so shiny, behind-the-curtain parts. The parts I definitely did *not* come here for.

What is going on with me?

LANIE

"DIG A LITTLE DEEPER"

I'm starting to feel ghosted by my own best friend.

Sitting alone in a garden just outside of Mulan's village, a hot cup of green tea and dim sum before me, I seem to be the only one following the Happily Ever Island Friendship Tour that Madison spent so much time making. The tables around me are filled with friends and family members eating breakfast and chatting away about the adventures ahead, but all I can do is sip my drink and take in the beautiful surroundings, cherry blossom trees gently rustling in the light breeze. Today's itinerary called for an early morning treat-up (a meet-up with treats) before our scheduled Disney activity for the day, but even though I pulled myself out of bed at sunrise to be here, Madison is once again nowhere to be found.

It's starting to really annoy me. I mean, what is happening with her? She begged me to come here, and now she can't be bothered to show up? Has she gotten so lost in make-believe that she's forgotten about her best friend? Because that would be really unfair. Maybe I need to do something dramatic, some kind of gesture to snap her out of her daydreams. I could send in Prince Phillip for another rescue. . . .

Or maybe . . . Prince Charming?

Heat licks my neck and cheeks at the thought of our *Sleeping Beauty* escapade, the two of us running through the thorny brambles hand in hand, laughing hysterically. From up close, I could see tiny flecks of gold in his warm brown eyes, his lips so close I could—

"Damn girl, you have got to tell me what you're thinking about right now." Madison plops down in front of me, cutting my fantasy short. Her hair is pulled up in a high pony without a trace of Cinderella blue; in fact, she's dressed all in black. Strange. "You look like you're having some very dirty daydreams, and I want details."

"Oh, look, you're here," I say sarcastically, tucking away my lustful thoughts. I do my best to reset my expression to neutral, but between being frustrated with her and caught up with Charming, it's hard to find a chill place to land. "I didn't think you were gonna make it."

"What? Why wouldn't I?" She looks genuinely surprised.

"Um, yesterday? The snorkeling? Which I did solo?"

She groans, leaning her head back. "I'm so sorry about that. Lady Tremaine is like a straight-up warden. She's taking this role-play way, *way* too literally. This morning I had to scrub her underwear!"

I frown. That does not sound right. "Are you serious?"

"Yes!" She throws her arms out in exasperation. "Yesterday I had to pull together breakfast in some medieval-style kitchen. You know how I can't cook; my only culinary success comes in liquid form."

That is true. I once saw her burn a muffin in the toaster oven. I push a bowl toward her. "Sounds like you could use some mango pudding."

She forces a smile. "I really, really could." Madison sadly reaches for a spoon, but her first bite doesn't seem to bring any joy.

"Hey, are you okay?" I ask softly.

She sighs, licking light orange sugar from her lips. "Well, it's just that things are not going like I expected. I mean, it's not like I'm having a horrible time or anything. Everything here is amazing, and I did have a very enlightening experience with our ambassador Val. . . ." Her blue eyes flash with something spicy before she slumps back into, "I'm . . . sort of confused. And with all the role-play stuff, I'm doing a lot of chores. Like, a lot."

Guilt courses through me, highlights from my adventures flashing before me like crime scene evidence. Here I am swimming like a mermaid and running through forests with a handsome prince, while my best friend—the person who actually loves this stuff—is stuck laundering a stranger's unmentionables. I feel awful and decide not to share any of my magical details until she experiences some of her own.

"There's still time," I offer. "And your big hero moment is still coming up. Nothing can mess with your being the belle of the ball."

"Yeah." She brightens, taking another big bite. "Mmm, this is good. What else did you order?" She looks over my collection of sweet cream buns and taro cake. "And you're right. Although I'd hoped to meet Prince Charming already. Practice our waltz a little. But I haven't seen him yet. Have you?"

My ears get hot. "Uh . . . nope. Nope, I haven't. It's a big island, so . . . nope." *OMG, Lanie, stop saying nope! She's going to see right through you!* Part of me really wants to tell her about these Charming developments, but the other part knows that the second I do, she'll blow everything out of proportion. She'll want me to reveal every last detail of our interactions: who reached for whom, what were the "vibes." And right now I'm still processing those moments; I'm not ready for them to be verbalized. Not until I figure out how I feel. Luckily, a group of musicians begins playing a song from what I can only imagine is the *Mulan* soundtrack, drawing cheers throughout the garden and distracting Madison from my very obvious lie.

She adds to the applause before turning back my way, ponytail flopping to the side. "Well, at this point, I'm just hoping he'll be a relief from my stepmother. But who knows. What kind of guy signs up to be Prince Charming anyway? He's either totally full of himself or here with a girlfriend."

I almost spit out my tea. A girlfriend? I didn't even consider that possibility, automatically assuming such a vital character could only be handled by a professional. "You don't think" — my throat catches — "you don't think he'd be a cast member?"

She shrugs. "Maybe. I guess. As long as he's not one of those himbos who thinks he's God's gift to women."

My insides scream but I force out a laugh. "Yeah. Princes . . . who needs 'em?"

"Not me!" Madison proudly declares. Clearly perking up, she sways dreamily to the music as she says, "Let's do something fun today."

"Don't we have Make a Man Out of You boot camp on the schedule?"

Her nose wrinkles, tongue sticking out in disgust. "Blech, who chose that?"

I stare at her blankly.

"Okay, well, I must have been feeling extra ambitious that day. But exercise? On vacation? No. What about . . . ?" She taps her chin. "Ooh! How about shopping? In New Orleans? I bet we could find some fun vintage pieces."

"Sure, whatever." I slouch back in my seat, weighed down by my evil brain that has already clipped together a nightmare reel of Charming and his alleged girlfriend kissing, laughing, and being all-round sweet together. I can see her now: amazingly beautiful just like him, all legs and lips and boobs. She's probably playing a princess, too, rocking that Jasmine midriff or Rapunzel hair. I bet she doesn't break out in hives during social situations, no; she'll be a people magnet, admirers flocking to her side. Argh! This is exactly why I told myself not to think about Charming romantically. . . . Well, maybe not *exactly* why, but what does it matter! I knew from the start that he was off-limits, but he suckered me into his fantasy and I am so frustrated with myself!

"Um, not the reaction I was looking for, but okay," Madison says, waving down our server.

"Ugh, I'm sorry," I groan. This is the first chance we've had to hang out, and I can't let this self-made drama drag me down. "Ignore me. Let's go to Louisiana!"

❈

Tiana's area of the island is an incredible re-creation of New Orleans, a place I've actually been and recognize. Cobblestone streets, Creole-style architecture, and countless little shops take us back to the 1920s. We peek into the colorful boutiques, grabbing beignets as we stroll along.

To the sound of upbeat jazz, Madison lays out all the details about her hyper-committed stepfamily and her Arendelle adventures, going back and forth on whether or not she should spend more time with Val. I want to conjure up the kind of supportive excitement my best friend deserves, but I'm stuck in a mental loop, spinning 'round and 'round with thoughts about Charming and how stupid I am for having thoughts about him.

I'm desperate to share this turmoil with her, because if anyone knows about romantic drama, it's Madison, but I can't reveal my secret now, not when I blatantly lied about never having met him. What is wrong with me?

By the time our morning together is over and I've trudged back to Scotland for scheduled archery lessons, my head is so heavy and unable to concentrate, I nearly shoot my instructor in the throat with my first arrow.

"Aack! Sorry!" I squeal, dropping my bow. My archer, a cast member named Greg, waves it off, but his reassuring smile doesn't mesh with the fear in his eyes.

"Not to worry, Princess. It happens all the time," he says while subtly pulling up the neck of his costume. "Now, let's try again."

He walks me through the archery basics, showing me how to properly hold a bow, position the arrow, and hit a target. Never in my life did I think I'd be learning this skill, but it's all in preparation for Merida's hero moment, when she shoots for her own hand. Madison made me watch that scene over and over before we left, insisting I pay extra attention to Merida's confidence and determination. *Merida doesn't care what other people think*, she told me. *She does what she wants*.

Unfortunately for me, I do care what other people think, most of the time giving their opinion more weight than my own, so it's nearly impossible to access that kind of self-assurance and tenacity. What would it feel like to know exactly what I want? And to have the backbone and courage to actually go and get it? It's much easier to convince myself I can't have something, to accept all the limitations and challenges around me as unconquerable truths not worth dismantling. I can't even let myself have a silly little crush without shriveling into a shame spiral, let alone declare my independence as bravely as Merida.

Even after nearly killing Greg multiple times and sacrificing countless arrows into a giant haystack, my head fails to clear, the storm inside me growing stronger and stronger. Shot after shot, miss after miss, I grow more and more agitated, to the point where I have to walk away, my eyes welling up with tears.

Why is it so hard for me to let myself want things? To daydream and see where things go? All of my goals have been based on need, not want. I *need* to get good grades; I *need* to get into medical school. Anything even remotely off the predetermined path is immediately squashed with wisdom and logic, the reasons for why it could never happen coming in fast and furious.

Like with Charming. The second my heart flipped, my brain came in hot and fast, deciding with no evidence at all that he's an unobtainable cast member. I slammed that door shut before it even opened, dead-bolting hope further with this whole girlfriend thing. I'm supposed to be here having fun, and what's more exciting than a spring break fling? I wouldn't know, because if my nose isn't buried in a book, my entire being assumes something must be wrong.

I know this is partially my mom's doing. Back in Chicago, she's probably working herself into a nervous breakdown, envisioning her only daughter as some irresponsible, unemployable miscreant all because I took my first ever break from school. *One* B on *one* test and I've fallen from grace; I wouldn't put it past her to call my professor and explain, citing excessive dehydration or exhaustion as the reason for my decline. Imagine his confusion. I'm still a top performer, just not The Top like I've always been.

Tired of crying, I find myself back at the castle courtyard, having plodded around the perimeter for god knows how long. A group of villagers tell stories around a fire, drinking from copper mugs and snuggling under tartan throws. I spot Dorothy in the circle, and she immediately hops to her feet and scurries over to walk with me.

"Good evening, Merida!" she chimes, all rosy cheeks and kind eyes.

"Hey" is all I can manage.

"Turkey leg?" she offers, holding up a half-eaten hunk of meat.

"Oh, um, no thanks. I'm a vegetarian."

She cringes. "How dreadful." But immediately after, her hand flies up to cover her mouth. "I mean, good for you! No judgment, of course! Taking care of your health is so important. Well, if not some juicy meat, how about a helpful ear? You look like you have something on your mind."

I shrug, not exactly comfortable sharing my feelings with anyone but Madison, and sometimes not even her.

"I'm a good listener," Dorothy singsongs. "And I promise to keep my opinions to myself. At least, I'll definitely try to."

She sits down on a wooden bench, patting the empty space beside her. I can see she's not letting me off the hook until I open up at least a little. Reluctantly, I sit cross-legged, gaze on the pink glow of sunset.

"I guess I was just . . . thinking about my mom," I start.

"That's sweet. Do you miss her?"

I snort. "The opposite, actually."

Her eyes widen. "Oh. I see. You two aren't close?"

"That's the thing—we're *too* close. Like sometimes it's hard to breathe."

She nods, looking down nervously at her lap. "My daughter, Kali, says I'm too much. Too nosy, too clingy. Too in her business." Her voice softens, face falling. "She's older now—in her thirties—but it's hard for me to step back. I want to be there for her, to help her. I try to respect her space, but . . . sometimes I fail."

I scoot closer, gently placing my hand on her knee. She sniffles at the gesture, clasping my hand with hers. "You don't seem like my mom, though. She's always pushing me, always making decisions and plans without asking."

Dorothy bites her lip. "Well, we did push. Sometimes. Like our annual family trip to Disney World. You know Sal—he counted down the days all year. But Kali never had fun. She complained it was our thing, not hers. Still, we kept going because we thought she'd learn to love it. I mean, what kind of a person doesn't love Disney?"

I clench my jaw.

"It's hard being a mom," she continues, lightly dabbing her

eyes with her sleeve. "You want what's best for your kid, but that doesn't always come out in the right way."

That's the thing: I know Mom wants the best for me. No one pushes their kid to be a doctor because they want them to have a crappy future. But with all the studying, planning, and résumé stacking, I honestly can't remember when or if I actively chose to be on the path I'm currently hurtling down. There was never a jumping-off point; no dreaming, no deciding, only drowning in the inevitable, carried by a current too strong to fight. And now it feels like it's too late to break free. Too much has happened, too many plans set into motion. Even if I wanted to change course, what would I do? Where would I go? I'm so unfamiliar with listening to my heart I wouldn't know where to start.

Madison would know. She's an expert dreamer. I tease her for having her head in the clouds, but at least she opens herself to what's possible. For better or worse, she willingly welcomes love and adventure in her life, even if she ends up brokenhearted. I've never taken that kind of risk, but there's a part of me that wonders what it would feel like to fail, to leap without a net. Would it be terrible? Exciting? Will I ever get the chance to find out?

"I just wish I could tell my mom . . ." I trail off, unable to comprehend an emotional conversation like this with her. "I don't even know."

Dorothy gives me a tight-lipped smile. "Well, I can tell you one thing, Ms. Merida: Moms aren't mind readers. I didn't know my Kali needed space until she told me. If you don't open up, things will never change."

My heart sinks, knowing she's right. I'm not sure what changes I want to make, but I do know I can't go on like this. Feeling like I'm in the passenger seat of my own life. Like even when I succeed, I'm somehow still behind. I need a little more wiggle room, a little more forgiveness . . . and yeah, maybe a little more magic in my life.

"I appreciate the advice," I say, to which she sits up a little straighter. "Are you supposed to be this nice to me? My friend told me Merida's mom is pretty overbearing."

"Oh, you're right!" She laughs. "I guess I'm not very good at staying in character. But I'm not interested in bossing you around; we're on vacation, for goodness' sakes!"

"Fine by me." I already have one demanding parent figure in my life; I don't need another.

"Our castle is hosting tonight's island dinner. . . . What do you say we go get cleaned up and dressed for the occasion?"

We head to our rooms, where I let Dorothy fuss over me just a bit. She begs me to try on Merida's wig, but I don't think I could keep my head on straight, let alone eat dinner, with so many curls bouncing around. She settles for picking out my gown and tying a gold cord around my head like a headband. It's something I'd never do with my own mom, and even though I'm very inexperienced with this kind of mother-daughter bonding, I force myself to be open.

Heading into the great hall, I feel much better than I did hours ago. Arm in arm with my pretend mother, we draw a small round of applause when we enter the room, with guests from all the different island kingdoms recognizing our royal stature. Dorothy bows, humbly placing her hand over her heart, whereas I give a quick curtsy, clinging to her and hoping my skin stays calm under pressure.

The room is lovely. Candlelight bouncing off stone, a massive fireplace crackling under walls draped with intricate tapestries. Everyone is packed in tight along heavy tables piled high with platters of roasted meat, fresh vegetables, and buttery rolls. As Dorothy breaks off to find her king, I scan the room for Madison, who agreed to meet me here tonight. But before I can find her, I lock eyes with someone else.

Charming. Looking like he just stepped out of a storybook, he lights up when he sees me, waving from across the room. But rather than return his enthusiastic greeting, I duck behind a stone pillar, unsure of what to do next. Now that both his employment and relationship status are up in the air, I don't know if I can be the same around him. It was so easy to be myself when I knew it didn't matter, but now I'm not so sure. If he's here with someone, why would he spend so much time with me? And if he's not a professional, then . . . again, why is he hanging around? Yes, I want love and adventures and all that, but it's not a switch I can easily flip. I can't go from total structure to total abandon in a day. Without the security of knowing what he's about, I don't know how to act.

So rather than face the unknown, I race back to my room, hiding from what could be and hating myself for it.

MADISON

"I SEE THE LIGHT"

For tonight's dinner in Scotland, I decide to up my fashion game. Wearing Cinderella's apron and headscarf was fun at first, but now I'm ready for something a little more glam, especially since my bibbidi-bobbidi makeover is still days away. While shopping in New Orleans I bought myself some beautiful pink silk fabric, knowing full well that my room is stocked with all the sewing essentials. Even though I'm sure a pink dress will eventually appear in my room after some rodent handiwork, I'm aching for something different now . . . anything to help me forget that I spent the afternoon sloughing the dead skin off Lady Tremaine's heels. She insisted the family have slipper-ready feet, and while Anastasia and Drizella cringed through the experience, shooting me apologetic eyes as I painted their toes, my stepmother clearly enjoyed finding yet another way to keep me in her service.

But whatever. It's my glass slipper, and she knows it; I'll have the last laugh.

I clear off Cinderella's sewing table, smoothing out the silk to cut into a skirt. I may not be a costume designer, but I do know the basics of a circle skirt. There was a brief moment in time where I thought being a fashionista seamstress could be My Thing, but after stitching the tip of my finger into nearly every fabric I touched, I took it as a sign from the stars that sewing was not my destiny.

I get to work, quietly cutting, pinning, and stitching alone in my tower. From my open window, I hear a familiar chorus from "Dig a Little Deeper" sounding for one of the *Princess and the Frog* hero moments. That must be a lively one, partying it up in Mama Odie's section of the bayou. I wonder if Val is there facilitating the fun.

I set down my needle as she waltzes through my thoughts. From the moment we got here, something about her major Disney energy pulled me in, a kindred soul equally hell-bent on jamming her heart with everything the fandom has to offer. But yesterday when we were letting it go, I witnessed her devotion on a deeper level: She worked so hard to make everything perfect. Every snowflake, every flourish: She obsessed over the details. When Elsa rocked that final note, Val shared in her joy, visibly relaxing and letting the magical moment wash over her. Elsa's happiness became her own.

I know that's how she felt, because I felt it, too.

Val didn't have to bring me backstage. In fact, I'm not even sure that was technically allowed. But her bending the rules in an attempt to give me something magical . . . to take my breath away . . . It's something I've always wanted. To have someone give me the kind of thoughtful gesture I've planned for others so freely. How many times have I sent flowers or left love notes only to walk away empty-handed? I know Val didn't light a roomful of candles or lay a path of rose petals or anything, but she instinctively knew what I'd love—an über-exclusive Disney moment—and made it happen, no strings attached. That in itself is enough to turn my insides to goo, but when she looks at me . . . it's like she's stumbled upon a treasure no one else has yet to find, something shiny and full of potential. When I'm with her, I feel all lit up inside, and not in the usual you-are-so-cute-let's-run-away-together kind of way. I mean, yes, that's there, too, but this is different, deeper. Instead of blindly falling, I feel myself wanting to rise up, to meet or exceed whatever it is she sees in me. I don't know if I can do it, but know I want to try.

That still counts as taking time for myself, right? Thinking about the (*shudder*) future and what I could be? Val's inspiring me to try, which is a gift even if she's not into me. Although . . . is she? It *seems* like she might be interested in more, but what if I've misread everything and she's just being nice? Or you know, the ultimate friendly cast member? I don't want to end up disappointed again, especially not by this perfect woman in the most perfect and magical of places. I want to be cautious, but it doesn't come naturally to me.

As I replay Val's hand touching my shoulder, my body instantly shuddering with delight at the thought alone, I poke myself removing a pin. "Oww!" I suck my finger, checking the clock: 8:30 p.m.! What! How? I'm late AGAIN. Argh! I pull on my new skirt, pairing it with a white tank top and a strand of blue beads I brought from home—a pretty killer Disney bound if I do say so myself.

After I run down the tower steps, it's clear my step-family left for dinner without me (real nice), and by the time I run across the island to DunBroch, cast members are already clearing dinner plates, the castle's main hall mostly empty. No! I frantically grab a few leftover scraps before they're taken away, sadly munching on a sausage while I look for Lanie.

She's not here, because of course she's not. She probably finished dinner a while ago and bailed, pissed at me ditching her once again. I hang my head, looking down at the skirt I just had to make. I wanted to be festive! Fun! Especially since I know my bestie is not feeling this vacation. Her mind was somewhere else during our tea and shopping spree this morning, and I'm not sure why I thought *my* dressing up would make *her* happy, but I don't know what else to do. She won't open up to me. While I didn't expect her to become a full-on Disney convert (well, okay, maybe a little), I'd hoped something would capture her imagination. If that's even what's bothering her! It's pretty obvious something's churning in that anxious little head of hers, and I don't understand why she won't just share. I'm her best friend after all, and if she can't reveal her worries to me, what does that say for our friendship? I'm always there for her, always cheering her on through study sessions and early morning caffeine rushes, but a lot of the time she keeps me at arm's length. I don't want to push her, but it does hurt my feelings sometimes.

I set off to find her, grabbing a handful of shortbread cookies as a peace offering, but before I hunt down her room, I spot Val trapped in a corner getting harassed by one of Ariel's sorority sisters. I tiptoe over, my heart practically propelling me in her direction.

"It's just that my fingers are like so pruney all the time. See?" The girl shoves her hands in Val's face, who jerks her head back into her neck. "I don't even really like swimming. Why can't we just lie on the beach?"

Val presses her lips together. "I can help you arrange more land-based activities. . . ."

"But then my sisters will get annoyed at me. Ugh! Being a mermaid is so hard!" The girl stomps away, leaving Val to angrily scribble on her clipboard, jaw clenched in rage.

"Trouble under the sea?" I ask sweetly, nibbling on one of the cookies.

Her pen stops, but her expression doesn't soften; I can almost smell smoke wafting from her ears. "You don't even

know. Yesterday I got chewed out by Jafar because apparently he's allergic to birds and having Iago follow him around
is causing problems."

"I mean, Iago *is* pretty annoying. . . ."

"And so I asked him, 'Sir, did you report this allergy on
your dietary restrictions and allergen form?' And he says,
'Well, it's less of an allergy and more of a reoccurring nightmare about being picked apart by birds.'"

"So, why did he willingly chose a role where his costar is
his biggest fear?"

"Beats me!" she nearly yells, flinging her arms out in exasperation. "But it's my job to make sure he's happy."

I know she's angry, but it's kind of cute how she's all puffed
up, fits of rage tucked neatly into her blue vest. Still, I want to
help. "What if . . . oh! What if you swapped out his Iago for a
tiki room bird? Didn't Magic Kingdom have an animatronic
Iago in their Under New Management version?"

Val's mouth falls open. "Oh my god. Why didn't they think
of that? Why didn't *I* think of that?"

I rock back and forth in my sparkly flats. "Don't be so hard
on yourself! You have A LOT on your plate right now."

"It's just . . . Jared is spending all his time acting like the
fun one, causing the guests to only bring their complaints to me.
I mean, look at him." She nods to the opposite side of the room,
where he's cartoonishly juggling beer steins for the "entertainment" of one guest who looks desperate for an escape. "What is
he even doing? He's a concierge, not a performer. He's always
showing off even if no one is looking. And for some reason, our

boss eats it up." She sighs, shaking her head. "He'll be the one who gets to stay."

Stay? "What do you mean?"

She looks around to see who's in earshot, gently taking my elbow and guiding me outside to the courtyard, where there's fewer echoing chambers. It's the second time she's touched me, and while I try to stay cool, a shiver runs up my spine. "I shouldn't even be saying any of this, but I'm tired and I need to vent. You know how this week is the island's trial run?" I nod. "Well, just like we're working out the kinks in operations, the entire staff is basically on an extended audition. Only the best and brightest will be permanently hired, so everyone—from the actors to the waitstaff—is going all out trying to prove they provide the best service, the best experience, and the best ideas on how to make Happily Ever Island a success. Jared never actually says anything of value, but he gets noticed because he's *so damn loud*. I'm not here to scream for attention: I want to be hired based on merit." She pauses, eyes glassy. Blinking rapidly to fight back tears, she adds, "I want this so badly I feel like my insides are screaming and my brain is melting under the pressure to think magically twenty-four/seven."

My heart goes out to her, and I instantly recognize that same yearning tangle I feel every time I set foot on Disney property. It's always the same. After months of planning and anticipation, that moment when I turn the corner on Main Street, U.S.A. to see a castle welcoming me home: It's heaven, endorphins taking over and flooding my body and soul with absolute certainty that this is where I'm meant to be. But in the back of my mind, I know that time is fleeting: Just like with Cinderella's slipper, the magic will come to an end. I feel this same complicated brew emanating from Val now, brown eyes burning wild with hope but also fear of waking up from her dream. I know how it feels to think you'll never be enough, that the one secret wish you have for yourself could never come true. I don't want that for her.

"Well, what if I helped you?" I ask, coyly curling my hair through my fingers.

Her brows furrow. "Help me what?"

"Think of ideas! Push out Jared! Be the best!"

She hesitates, head tilting to the side as she takes in my offer. And there's that look again: questioning but hopeful, intrigued but guarded. "How do you do that?" she asks once her assessment is complete.

"Do what?"

She waves her pen up and down my body. "That! Just . . . offering yourself up so freely, being so kind and help-ful like it's nothing."

I shrug. "I didn't realize that was anything special."

"Trust me, it is. Did you know you're the only guest who hasn't come up to me upset about trying to reschedule their hero moment or switch characters altogether?"

"Oh yeah, I've been meaning to talk to you about that," I joke. And she laughs, a delightful little chortle that sends my soul soaring. *Mental note: Make Val laugh more.*

"But seriously though: Disney girls have to stick together. After all . . ." I sing the opening line from *Toy Story*'s "You've

Got a Friend in Me," hiking my elbows like I'm a stuffed cowboy sheriff. I instantly regret it—not because it's not a totally classic song, but because it's the second time I've basically said I just want to be friends. Which I do. Don't I? Ugh.

Val's cheeks puff up, whistling on the exhale. "Wow. That was dorky. Maybe I don't want your help?"

"Please. This princess has a lot to give!"

"That I don't doubt." She holds my gaze, tucking her hair behind her ear. My heart pounds, and I force myself to take a breather, glancing around at our surroundings. The Scottish courtyard has taken on a new nighttime glow with a cast member playing bagpipes by the bonfire while guests cozy up together with steaming mugs of cider. It feels like everyone from *Brave* is out here enjoying the night, laughing and playing against the roaring fire. It's a much different vibe than at my château, where there's basically a sign on the door that reads GET OUT. I'm glad, though, that Lanie's kingdom is more inviting, even if she's probably up in her room reading a book about Marie Curie or some other female hero of science that she's destined to follow. You can take the girl out of academia, but you can't take the academia out of the girl; Lanie will have already changed the world by the time I've found my place in it. I only hope she hasn't gotten bored of me by then.

I search the perimeter of the castle, wondering which of the few lit rooms could be Merida's. I should go get her, force her out of her seclusion and into the warm night air, but before I can figure out where she's hiding, a different light catches my eye. Small and bright, almost like a star shooting through the inky dark sky. But it's faster, bigger, climbing with a mission. Silently, the single light is joined by another, and another, until it's clear these are not celestial bodies.

THE FLOATING LIGHTS!

"Oh my god!" Without another thought I take off running, dashing across the castle grounds straight into the shadowy forest. I hear Val call, "Wait! Where are you going?!" but I absolutely cannot stop. I may be here to play Cinderella, but I will give my voice to a sea witch before I miss Rapunzel's lanterns, easily one of the most gorgeous animated moments of all time.

Smashing through branches off the beaten path, I have no idea where I'm going, letting the sky be my guide. Val somehow catches up despite my early lead.

"If you're trying to see the lights, I have a quicker way!" she yells through the trees.

I come to a crashing halt, but not before stepping in a very inconveniently placed stream. "Why didn't you tell me?" I pant.

She shakes her head, fighting a smile. "You are so exhausting. Come with me." She guides me out of the water over to a huge boulder, the backside of which contains a hidden door that she knocks open with her shoulder.

"What?!" I exclaim, still breathing heavily.

"There's a tunnel system under the island," she explains as we race down a spiral staircase. "Makes it much easier to get around in a hurry."

"Like the utilidor tunnels at Disney World?"

"Exactly."

We find ourselves in a long concrete hallway, metal pipes and flickering fluorescent lighting overhead. It's like a department store back room that stretches on forever, but instead of sad boxes filled with overpriced designer jeans, there are storage racks displaying costumes and props from all the different kingdoms. Polynesian grass skirts, Chinese suits of armor, various ball gowns: I try to take them all in, but Val is not slowing down, dark hair flying back as she races ahead.

"Hurry!" she calls, voice echoing around the tunnel. "The lights won't last much longer!"

Finally, we reach a sign reading RAPUNZEL'S KINGDOM, so we fly up the stairs, instantly bathed in the radiance of thousands of glowing lanterns. They bob in the breeze: pale orange-and-yellow light filling every open space with their flickering warmth, purple floral prints blossoming against the creamy papyrus. A hidden orchestra swells as Mandy Moore and Zachary Levi sing their dreamy duet about finally seeing the light.

I stumble back, overwhelmed. It's too much, too beautiful, and we made it here just in time, the final chorus lifting everyone's hearts in sync. Offshore I see the guests playing Rapunzel and Flynn Rider, their canoe encircled by pastel petals and light. I picture myself in that boat: flowers in my hair, hand in hand with someone looking at me like I'm the most amazing creature to have ever graced her presence. How truly magical to have someone love you exactly as you are. To accept your roguish ways, your hair that glows when you sing . . . or, you know, actual struggles with punctuality, maturity, and all-around life planning. This is the kind of love I want; a hero moment in real life.

A wayward lantern dips down between Val and me. Instinctively, we both reach out to guide it back skyward. A spark ignites my skin, so fiery I worry I grazed the actual flame, but no. It was Val, her soft skin tingling my own. Together we release the lantern, my heart rising with it as she keeps hold of my hand a moment longer than necessary, then slowly moves it away. A sherbet swirl of orange, yellow, and pink dances all around us, pushing us closer to create our own secret world of light and warmth.

"Thank you for getting me here in time," I whisper breathlessly.

She smiles shyly, a golden glow shimmering across her cheeks. "I didn't want you to miss it."

We're so close I could easily bend down and kiss her, our chests rising and falling in tandem. But I don't want to move, don't want to blink. I need every detail committed to memory. The way her eyes are twinkling in the starlight; the way her body feels pressed up against mine. And then I realize: Why have I been fighting my feelings for Val? This smart, incredible woman who has done nothing but show me kindness and appreciation from the moment we met. I know I said I just wanted a fling, that I didn't want to fall head over heels for once, but this energy between us has awakened something new, inspiring me to dream bigger for myself. As she looks at me, I feel like Aurora finally waking up, like Anna unfrozen from the ice. There is more to my story than what has been written so far, and I'm ready for a different chapter.

Oh yes, Val. I see you.

And maybe I'm starting to see myself, too.

But this definitely wasn't covered in my Happily Ever Island itinerary.

So . . . what now?

LANIE

"JUST AROUND THE RIVERBEND"

The next morning, I knock on Cinderella's door bright and early, to-go coffee and apology bagels in hand. I acted like an actual child last night pouting in my room, abandoning my best friend at dinner in my own castle (wow, now there's a thought I'll never repeat for as long as I live). And for what? What did squirreling myself away prove? All I did was miss out on what I'm sure was an amazing meal; I'm no closer to understanding how I feel or what I want. I must be the only type-A super nerd walking around this fairy-tale paradise worrying about the future. The whole point of participating in a world like this is to escape your own.

Which is exactly what I'm going to do today: no Lanie

drama, just pure princess fun with Madison. Starting with actually attending our scheduled morning activity together: a Just Around the Riverbend canoe tour through Pocahontas's forest. That is, if I can get us there on time.

I knock again, knuckles rapping against the giant oak door, but when no one answers, I try the knob. Locked. Hmm, there are no signs of life inside, but she has to be here, right? No way she beat me to the river. I'd sooner believe in talking teacups than Madison arriving at an event early.

"Madi—er—Cinderella?" I call out. "Are you home?" I consider going around the back to sneak my way inside when I hear the lock click and Madison, covered in a light layer of dust, pokes her head outside.

"Hey! Good morning!" she whispers, all smiles despite the dirt smudges on her cheeks. "Ooh, that coffee smells good, can I have a sip?"

I pause, not sure how to respond to the sliver of face pressed through the door crack. "Uh, yeah, I brought it for you." She slinks out a hand, carefully consuming the caffeine on the outer threshold, as if coffee isn't allowed in the house. "Are you . . . ? Why are you so messy? It's not even eight a.m."

"Oh, you know. The tapestries needed a good beating," she says, as if it's the most normal thing in the world.

"I'm sorry, are you cleaning right now? Like actual Cinderella?"

"Yes, I told you . . ." Her voice lowers. "My stepmother is taking this very seriously up in here. And I can't leave."

"Because . . ."

"Because I'm not done with my chores yet."

I blink. Did I hear that correctly? "You're not serious."

But before she can answer her blue eyes go wide, gasping as she shoves the coffee back my way. The door behind her swings completely open, revealing the scariest woman I've ever seen in my life. Gray hair swept up in a severe bun, green eyes ringed with disapproval, she towers over Madison, laying a possessive palm on my best friend's shoulder. She's so frightening that I actually yelp and spill coffee down my shirt.

"Cinderella has work to do," the woman commands, in a tone that somehow makes me feel like *I* did something wrong. I can already feel my blood pressure rising. "She may join you when she's done."

Madison exhales pointedly, squirming out from her stepmother's grasp. "It's fine, Lanie. Trust me when I say it's just easier and faster to play along."

What is going on here? I know she told me her stepmother was committed, but this is a whole different level. Who does this? It feels like way too much, even for a cast member who's supposed to stay in character. I search Madison's face for signs of danger, but she makes a goofy grin, the same one she does behind Barry's back when he's nagging us about espresso-to-foam ratio. She may be okay with playing along, but I don't like this at all.

"This is ridiculous! I'm going to get help," I say, shooting daggers at Madison's captor. She doesn't even flinch, gripping the end of her cane with gross satisfaction. "Madison, I'll be back, okay?" Madison waves sadly as the door slams, trapping her inside.

Yikes. Now what? Do I go to the Boathouse, file a complaint? Where would I even begin? *Hi, excuse me, but my friend is being held prisoner in her kingdom. Can you please send in her fairy godmother early?* What is this reality?

I decide to find Val; she'll know what to do. She's usually around at our scheduled events, so I check the map and head toward the river that runs through many of the forest kingdoms. Even before I arrive I hear Jared barking a series of instructions, going on and on about the importance of avoiding rocks while paddling. I've never even been in a canoe and that feels like pretty obvious advice. A line of canoes waits on the riverbank as Val greets the guests, checking off attendance on her clipboard. I wait as she makes small talk with Kristoff and Hans, an unlikely though adorable pair holding hands as they chat about the wildlife we're about to see.

"Hey, um, Val?" I start once those two have snuggled into their boat. "Can I ask you something?"

"Of course, Princess!" she says brightly. "I have a canoe for you and Cinderella right over here." She stands on tiptoe, looking hopefully over my shoulder. "Will she be joining you?"

"Well, that's what I need help with. I think she's being held hostage."

Val touches her fingers to her temple like she's got a migraine coming on. "I'm sorry . . . what?"

"Yeah, I just went by her house and her stepmother won't

let her leave." I twist my fingers nervously, watching Val's expression fade from buoyant to boiling. "I don't think she's in danger or anything, but it was definitely . . . weird."

She hangs her head, black and caramel strands falling forward. I swear something very not-Disney comes out under her breath. "I had a feeling this would happen." She sighs. "When I first met Lady Tremaine, she struck me as rather—"

"Unhinged?" I suggest.

She holds back a laugh. "I was going to say 'overzealous about live action role-play.' But don't worry, I'll take care of it. Although that would mean leaving Jared to lead this tour on his own. . . ."

We turn his way, catching the tail end of his latest rant. "AND ANOTHER THING," he shouts, red curls bouncing as he barks. "THERE WILL BE TURTLES. SOMETIMES THEIR SHELLS LOOK LIKE ROCKS SO WATCH OUT."

"Does he ever tire himself out?" I ask.

"He really doesn't," she answers with a frown. "But let me partner you up with someone so you don't have to go alone."

"Oh, no. That's okay. I can go for a hike instead, or back to my room, or—"

"I can take her." Out of nowhere, Prince Charming is suddenly beside me, all smiling and valiant and—is he glistening? Yes, there's a distinct sheen on his dark brown skin, taunting me with its attractive glow. Why does he have to be so beautiful? It's not fair!

"Prince Charming!" Val exclaims, flipping through the

papers on her clipboard. "I don't see you scheduled for a canoe tour. . . ."

"I was out for a jog and heard someone yelling, but when I realized it was just Jared talking, I thought I'd see what Merida here was up to," he says, using the bottom of his tank to wipe some sweat from his brow. I can't help but sneak a quick peek at his torso, all sweaty and tight. My face flushes. Damn it. Of course he jogs.

"I don't need rescuing," I announce out of nervousness, surprising everyone including myself.

He tilts his head slightly, confused. "Um, that was not what I was implying."

"Okay, well, good!" My voice is much too loud. Who am I, Jared? And now I'm adding my hands on my hips. *Stop being so weird, Lanie!* "As long as we're clear. I am capable of doing this myself."

Charming rubs the back of his neck, eyeing me self-consciously. Why am I being so pseudo aggressive? He's done nothing wrong; I'm the one having this convoluted crisis about who he is, who I am, and how that all ties together. I should just ask him—talk to him like a normal person—but now I'm back to my usual self where I can't make words come out in a casual way. Great.

Val clears her throat. "I do recommend canoeing in pairs if possible. It makes for a less strenuous, more peaceful journey around the river bend."

"Fine," I relent in an exasperated tone, even though of all

the activities Madison planned, this was the one I was most looking forward to. For once I'm dressed for the part, wearing my sportiest shorts, a T-shirt, and my one and only sports bra. Dorothy caught me on my way out and insisted I add sunscreen to my admittedly very white legs, so I'm ready to do this, even if I'm lacking the proper upper body strength to actually paddle alone.

"Great!" Val chirps, guiding us toward the last empty canoe. Charming and I stand on opposite ends, avoiding eye contact. "Well . . ." she continues, trying her best to cut through the tension. "I'm going to make sure Cinderella isn't being forced to paint her stepmother's bedroom or whatever, so have a pleasant ride, you two!" She practically sprints away, leaving me with a very confused-looking Charming.

"Did I . . . do something to upset you?" he asks. "Last time I checked we were, I don't know . . ." He breaks into a shy smile. "I thought we were having fun."

His cute little grin is not helping, twisting my heart. Should I be honest with him? Tell him about all these complicated feelings swirling inside? It feels like a lot to unpack, especially if he is a cast member or here with his girlfriend. I told myself I'd keep it light and princessy today, but so far I'm failing on both accounts.

"It's just . . . I'm having a hard time keeping fantasy and reality separate," I admit.

"Is that something we're supposed to be doing? Because if so, I never got the memo," he jokes.

"TIME TO PUSH OFF, PEOPLE!" Jared calls from down the shore. "GET IN YOUR CANOES AND LET'S GOOOOOOOOOO!"

Charming gestures for me to climb in, and I take the seat near the front, clutching on to the sides. Effortlessly, he pushes the boat out into the water, hopping in the back without barely getting wet. We dip our paddles into the river, letting the other canoes pull ahead as we try to get our rowing in sync. It's not as easy as it looks, especially since I'm not very coordinated, but after a few minutes, we fall into a slow rhythm.

"But seriously," Charming says from behind me, "are you mad at me? You ran in the other direction last night at dinner."

Oh god, he *did* see that? I look around, seeking calm in the tall, thin trees covering most of the sky; the occasional fish swimming its way upstream. Maybe I can do this. Since we aren't face-to-face, maybe I can rip the Band-Aid off and tell him what I'm thinking. And if it goes terribly? I'll jump out of this boat and overanalyze this moment at 3:00 a.m. for the rest of my life. No big, right?

"No, I'm not mad," I start.

He exhales deeply. "Well, that's a relief."

"But I do have some questions. Some personal questions, if that's okay."

"It's okay by me. You were the one who didn't want to get personal."

"And I still don't. I mean, maybe. I don't know!" OMG,

why is it so hard to release the words tumbling around my head! At least I can't see his face. I can only imagine his expression right now. "Okay, first question: Are you here with someone?"

"You mean, besides you? I don't think anyone else would fit in this canoe. . . ."

"No, like on Happily Ever Island. Are you *with* someone?"

He paddles a few strokes before answering, "Yes."

I knew it. I KNEW it. My heart was right in holding me back. There's no way someone this cute and funny and sweet and—

"But not in a romantic way, if that's what you mean," he adds on, interrupting my mental spiral.

A goofy grin spreads across my face, cheeks lighting up in glee. I'm so relieved I nearly reach out to hug a squiggly pair of otters passing by. "Oh yeah, no, I was just curious," I sputter, tamping down my excitement. "So then, if you're here with a friend or family member or other person free of romantic entanglement, does that mean you're not a cast member?"

Charming snorts before breaking out into a full laugh. "You think I work here?"

There's no way to get out of this now, but still I say, "Ha, no. That was . . . a joke."

"No, no, no, it's too late now! Tell me more about this theory."

What am I supposed to say? That I think he's Prince Charming personified? That there's no way Disney could find someone better for the role? Thank god he can't see my face right now because I can feel it burning up, though it's possible the back of my neck is just as red. "I . . . I'm not an expert at Disney filmography or anything, but you strike me as very . . . princely." I cringe. Princely? Is that even a word?

He gives a quick sound of approval before saying, "I'm flattered, Merida. Although, maybe I should be offended, seeing as how we've already established that Prince Charming is the blandest of the bland?"

"No, I meant is as a compliment." I squeeze my paddle so hard it's a miracle I don't get a splinter.

"Well, thank you." He extends his right leg, the toe of his sneaker lightly tapping my heel. Slowly, I slide my foot back in line with his, the side of his shoe gently stroking mine. I look down without moving my head, watching him play footsie with me. The rest of the forest fades away as I focus all my energy into my right foot, nerve endings tingling under leather. Part of me wants to turn around, to see that sweet dimple in his cheek, but I stay steady, letting the exhilaration of this new sensation be enough.

We row in silence for a minute, arms synchronized, feet entwined, hearts soaring. I allowed myself to swim in emotional waters and didn't drown. It's nice, comforting even, just to feel his presence. Our canoe glides under a small waterfall and Charming runs his fingers through the spray, flicking me playfully. I try to get him back but end up rocking the boat so much we almost topple over. Smooth.

"So, are you looking forward to your big hero moment

coming up?" he asks once our canoe has righted itself. "That's tomorrow, right?"

Shoot. Is it? I've been so preoccupied that this big event I should theoretically be looking forward to has barely crossed my mind. "I guess? Honestly the thought of so many people looking at me makes me want to vomit. And what if while I'm shooting for my own hand, I miss? Will that be like an affront to feminism?"

"I'm pretty sure Disney magic will guarantee you don't miss. Unless every other guest here has spent years cultivating their character's exact skill set in preparation for their visit."

"Don't even joke about that. You don't know: Prince Phillip may actually slay dragons in his spare time."

"You're probably right," he says. "In which case, you're screwed. Unless you've been taking archery lessons for the past decade?"

"Archery isn't exactly a prereq for premed, so no."

"Whoa. You're going to be a doctor?"

Crap. I didn't mean to let that slip. The babbling river and footsie game lulled me into complacency. Although, we already started blurring the lines between reality and fantasy; is it okay to keep going? "Yeah but let's talk about something else."

"Okay . . . but why?" he asks.

Because it's complicated. Because I don't know what I'm doing. Because he's too cute and too perfect to muck up with all my real world drama.

When I don't respond, he adds, "You know, someone once

told me I was princely, and a prince is sworn to protect his people. Your kingdom may not fall under my jurisdiction, but I am here for you, if you need me."

His kind words break down my last barrier, opening the floodgates. "I'm not sure I want to be a doctor," I admit. It's so weird to hear the words outside my head; I'm not sure I ever have.

"What's holding you back? Too many years of school?"

I shake my head. "No, nothing like that. I mastered the school scene years ago."

"So the problem is . . ."

For once, I answer without thinking, the words flowing out of me. "I can't picture myself being a doctor, doing the actual job. Working with patients, diagnosing illnesses: I don't see myself doing any of that. The path getting there is clear — the classes, the residency — but after I get my doctorate, it all goes blank." *Whoa.* I stop rowing, paddle frozen by surprise. I've never consciously had this thought before, but I know it's the truth. This has been my problem all along. I've spent so much time obsessing about the journey but none considering the destination, blindly checking off boxes. Never once have I envisioned my life as a doctor, not even what it would feel like to slip on a stethoscope. Can this really be my aspiration if I've never once dreamed about it?

I dip my oar back in the river, but my arms have lost all strength. Luckily, Charming keeps us moving through the winding forest.

"If it helps, I can't exactly picture my future either," he says after a beat.

"Besides your eventual rise to the throne?" I joke.

"Well, right, besides that."

Since I'm already on a roll, I press it further. "But even if I wanted to switch paths—which I'm not sure if I do—where would I go? What would I do?"

"Do you have to have it all figured out right now?"

"According to my mom, yes."

"Moms are good at that. Mine is, anyway," he says. "Even with all the stuff we've been through in the past year, she somehow still finds time to worry about what I'll be doing after college. It's like, Mom, I got this. I don't want her to worry."

I'm about to ask his advice on how to talk to moms more honestly when I notice we're gliding toward a fork in the river. To the left is a wide-open channel, free of turns or obstructions, while the right winds back and forth, rapids bubbling over jutting rocks. At this point, the rest of the group has paddled out of sight, leaving us on our own to choose the correct direction. Where's Jared and his big mouth when you need him?

"So, which way?" Charming asks.

I look back and forth, considering our options. My overly cautious brainy Lanie self says steer left, but I told myself I'd be a princess today, and Merida would definitely choose the challenge on the right. "Let's go right," I say before I can talk myself out of it.

"You sure?" he asks with a laugh.

"Not at all." I look back over my shoulder just in time to see his face light up with a grin.

"Then let's go!"

We paddle toward the twisty turning path, and it's instantly clear this section of the river is way beyond my athletic ability. Charming does his best to keep our canoe pointing forward, but we keep knocking into rocks, water pouring into the boat. At one point, we're completely backward, and by the time we spin back around, the tall trees have disappeared behind us, leaving nothing but clear open sky and an abrupt river's end.

"Uhhh," I worry. "Is it just me or does the river just stop up ahead."

"No, I . . . I think we're approaching a waterfall," he says, voice shaky.

"WHAT?!"

"But how steep could it be, really? It's not like Disney would let us die out here."

"NOT FUNNY!" I shriek over the rushing water all around us. We try to steer away from the cliff, but the current is too strong, ready and willing to pull us over. I drop my paddle in a panic, looking for something else to grab on to. But the canoe is soaked, every surface slippery. Suddenly, Charming's arms wrap around my waist, and he pulls me close in between his legs. I clutch his forearms, squeezing myself as close to him as I can as the canoe dangles over the cliff.

"Hold on!" he yells, and I close my eyes, waiting for my stomach to drop as we topple over the abyss.

Only that never happens, because while the top of the waterfall made it look like we were about to plunge over Niagara Falls, the cliff was so small we barely even noticed the elevation change, our canoe gently gliding down into calmer waters.

Well, that was ridiculous.

We hang there for a second, lingering in the closeness between us. Our wet shirts stick together as I become acutely aware of his breath, warm against my damp neck. Surely I'm turning red as I admire his strong arms holding me tight, but I don't care; I don't want to move, even though there's no reason to stay.

Out of nowhere a stray seagull swoops down, breaking us apart. I spin around in my seat to finally face him, our thighs brushing up against each other.

"Um, sorry I—"

"No, I was—"

"Just wanted to—"

"Oh, no, totally—"

Awkward laughter fills the air, but neither of us looks away. I'm already missing being in his arms, feeling his body against mine. I let my leg rest against his just to be close to him again, and he reciprocates by scooting closer, his shins bumping up against my seat. Slowly, he reaches for my hand resting on my knee, lightly tracing my wet skin with his fingers. He bites his bottom lip as I clutch on to his wrist, sliding myself even closer. Our faces only inches apart, I watch as passing shadows dance across his handsome face, the river's surrounding topography changing from a dense forest to marshy swamp. We pass through a curtain of green vines, engulfing us in a dimly lit blue lagoon. No matter the lighting, all I can see is him.

"Charming?" I say softly, his brown eyes on my lips.

"Yeah?" he breathes.

Heart racing, I lean in, eyes fluttering closed. But before our lips touch, a chorus of sha-la-la's joyfully bounces across the water, breaking me from my trance. Gone are the pine trees and raccoons, replaced with lily pads, cattails, and . . . flamingos? The seagull from earlier circles overhead, while frogs happily hop between rocks. Something tells me we're no longer in Pocahontas's bend of the river.

And did I just hear a crab encourage someone to kiss a girl?

Yes. Yes, I did.

Charming and I lock eyes in alarm. Oh no! This is a hero moment! And we're very much interrupting!

"Shoot, shoot, shoooooooooot!" I yell-whisper, my nails digging into his arm. "We're not supposed to be here!" To my right, the people playing Ariel and Eric struggle to keep their eyes on each other, sneaking curious glances at our boat as the dancing avian and aquatic characters continue their vocal pleas to just hurry up and make out already.

"What do we do?" Charming panics as a glittering trail of fireflies swirls around our heads. This intimate circle of water and vines is too small for four people, but there's no way out. We both dropped our paddles during the waterfall fiasco, leaving us completely at the river's mercy. A barricade of jumping tadpoles and turtles has all but collided our boat with Ariel and Eric's, and they are doing their best to stay in the moment despite the fact that their romantic moment has been party crashed.

Ariel, sporting a truly ginormous blue bow in her flowing mermaid wig, stares at me with so much confusion I consider plunging into the water and never coming up for air. But despite our ruining the scene, the music plays on; Ariel digs deep and bats her long lashes at Eric, whose nostrils flare with frustration.

"Oh my god, we are RUINING THIS!" I sob, burying my face in my hands. I'm completely mortified as a team of rainbow-colored fish encircles both boats, elegantly shooting streams of water up from their mouths like little bobbing fountains. We're so close I could lean over and kiss Eric myself, much to his annoyance.

Flamingos wave their pink feathers; playful fish pop out from pelicans' mouths; but no matter how hard they try the spell has been broken. As the song comes to a close, the wildlife inches closer, critters puckering their gills or beaks as whispers of "Kiss her! Kiss her!" linger in the lily pads and vines.

Charming gives an awkward wave; Ariel shrugs.

I have never been more embarrassed in my entire life.

The last note sounds and right on cue, Ariel and Eric's boat topples over, knocking us into the water as well. The lagoon is surprisingly deep, but Charming quickly scoops me up under my arms, helping me swim to shore.

"You okay?" he says, coughing once we're safe on the sand.

"Yeah," I say, peeling a lily pad off my leg. But I'm not the one to be worried about: Eric stews on the shore, curled in a tight ball with water pooling all around him. Ariel pats his back a couple of times as her once perky blue bow sags into her tangled hair. A pair of island ambassadors exchange exasperated looks, and wow, we seriously ruined everyone's day. The crooning fireflies and fish have all sunk back into the sea leaving us with only Eric's huffing and puffing.

I twist my fingers into a knot as anxiety spikes through my veins. It floods my system and paired with the cold water dripping down my legs, I'm shaking, despite the warm Florida air. I almost hate confrontations more than public speaking. I know I should say something, but what? *Sorry for destroying your dream? Apologies for tarnishing a treasured moment?*

Practically vibrating with guilt, I tiptoe to Ariel and Eric's soggy moat of disappointment. "Um, hey." My throat catches as Eric looks up.

"Why did you do that?" he asks. "'Kiss the Girl' is a private hero moment!"

I take a step back, wondering how I can make this right; I can just imagine how Madison would feel if someone stole away her Disney spotlight. "We're so sorry," I say, my voice like a mouse. "It was an accident."

Eric wipes his nose on his saturated sleeve as he scoffs, "You accidently traveled by canoe directly into our scene?"

Charming and I exchange a glance. "Yes?"

"Right." He's jumping up and starts rolling his sleeves.

Ariel intervenes. "Eric, relax. it's fine. The scene still ended like it should. Maybe with an even bigger splash." She lets out a little laugh, clearly trying to lighten the mood.

But this does nothing. "It wasn't the same, all right?" Eric's aggro energy stirs me up even more.

Like the true prince that he is, Charming attempts a peace offering with, "Listen, man, how about I talk to the ambassadors? See if they can run the scene again for you?"

"No, it's too late," Eric pouts. "I wouldn't be able to do it again right now even if they could. Just . . . forget it." He storms off, leaving his land-bound mermaid behind.

She turns to us. "Don't worry about him. I think he just likes to be mad. When I sang the 'Part of Your World' reprise to him on the beach, he made us redo it three times because he said the scene didn't have the right *ethereal essence*."

"Sounds intense," Charming says.

"Honestly, don't worry about it," she continues.

"We truly are sorry, though," he says with a sympathetic smile. Ariel gives a little wave and heads off, following Eric's footprints in the sand. Once they're gone my last bit of resolve breaks down. Ariel's efforts to smooth things over weren't enough to tackle the pent-up nervous energy just waiting to burst free, and against my will I start crying, the water droplets from my hair mixing in with tears.

I turn away from Charming, pointlessly rubbing the end of my wet tank top over my eyes, feeling dumb. I'm no stranger to crying, but I usually hold it in until I'm alone; I've never even cried like this in front of Madison, not even after the time I accidentally scalded a student with spilled espresso. Charming shouldn't have to deal with this. In fact, it'd be better if he left so he wouldn't have to see me this way. Puffy, red, all wrung out. Not exactly the look of a princess. As my sobbing slows, I nervously peek over my shoulder. I half expect him to be gone but no, he's still there.

"I'm sorry," I say, my autopilot response for anytime my anxiety gets the best of me. But he's not having it, mouth twisted in dissent.

"You have nothing to be sorry for." He steps closer, head tilted as he bends over slightly to meet my eyeline. "Are you . . . ? Can I hug you? Is that okay?"

I nod, desperately wanting to feel something other than this, the jittery hum that has kidnapped my body.

Charming wraps his bare arms around me and gently lays my head onto his chest with one palm. Although his shirt is wet, I feel the warmth from the other side, taking comfort in a heartbeat that isn't consumed by an imaginary threat. We breathe together on the sand as the sun dips toward the sea; the misery in my veins slowly retreats back to its dark hiding place. Charming doesn't press me on why I broke down or how to make it better. Instead he just holds me, offering support without saying a word.

"I feel bad," I finally whisper. His fingers softly stroke my hair, sending a good kind of tingle down my spine. "We ruined that for them."

"Well, it wouldn't have worked out anyway," he says. "And it seems like the two of them have a lot going on. Especially

Ariel: I mean, she only has before the sun sets on the third day to get her voice back. That's a lot of pressure."

I pop back, looking up at him incredulously. "What? Are you serious right now?"

"I'm always serious about contractual agreements with sea witches."

With nowhere else to go, my remaining adrenaline devolves into laughter, taking a different hold over me. Shoulders shaking, stomach aching, I start cracking up, somehow conjuring up a second round of tears.

"What's so funny?" Charming asks, unable to keep from giggling himself.

"It's just . . . she's . . . a mermaid . . . but with legs!"

He snorts. "You okay there?"

Now I'm laughing even harder, clutching my stomach. "And she . . ." But I can't even finish my thought, my face frozen in a silent laugh. Charming reaches for me, gently wiping my cheeks with his thumbs. I stare up at him, trying to catch my breath as I lean my face into his strong hands. The setting sun casts a halo of light around his head, and my speechlessness continues, although now for a different reason. How did I get here? Standing inches away from this incredibly sweet, impossibly cute guy? Back at home, I never could've guessed that in a few short days I'd be falling for a prince, yet here I am, captivated by this character before me. The chorus from our mishap plays on repeat in my head, and I can't help myself from looking at his mouth.

Kiss the girl, my heart sings.

As if he hears my silent song, Charming leans in, lips parting ever so slightly. My heartbeat blares so loud in my skull I almost miss him say, "I'm so glad I met you, Princess."

Eyes closed, I wait for my first fairy-tale kiss, but seconds before that moment comes true, we're interrupted by something loud.

"There you are, Charming!" Jared storms up behind us as we spring apart. "I have been looking for you everywhere."

Charming walks in a tight circle, pressing a fist against his mouth. "Jared, what's up?" he asks, words clipped in frustration.

Jared flails his lanky arms about. "Weren't you on the river bend tour? What happened to you?"

"We got . . . sidetracked."

"How is that even possible? Don't you know we have a scene with the king today?"

I've never actually stood this close to Jared, but it really is a marvel at how much sound can come out of such a slight body. He's like a string bean with a microphone. Spit collects on the crease of his mouth, probably from excessive force of volume.

"I don't know, man. I guess I forgot." Charming shakes his head.

"Well, come on, then. Let's go!" Jared all but shoves Charming along, circling his arms up the shore. We don't get to finish our moment; we barely get to say good-bye.

Charming turns, walking backward as Jared nudges him in the shoulder to keep going. "See you tomorrow?" he asks, shooting an imaginary arrow into the sky.

I nod, waving sadly. I don't want tomorrow to come; I want to exist in the reality of one minute ago. We almost kissed; I know it would've happened if Jared hadn't appeared. *That* could've been my hero moment: getting kissed by a great guy and for once not worrying about everything else in the world.

Still dripping, I walk alone on the tropical trail back toward the Lighthouse. I know I have to shoot for my own hand, but I also really enjoyed the feeling of his in mine.

MADISON

"FOR THE FIRST TIME IN FOREVER"

Pearlescent bubbles fill the room, the song of a nightingale singing sweetly all around me. It would be beautiful—hell, downright magical—if I were in the bathtub, face mask and cucumber slices in tow. But no. I'm on my hands and knees, scrubbing a seemingly endless tiled floor with a stiff brush. I don't even clean the carpets in my dorm room, so this is pretty cumbersome. Still, at least Lady Tremaine isn't breathing down my neck for once; she's upstairs conducting a music lesson for Anastasia and Drizella. They too seem to be tiring of our stepmother's rigid ways. They both helped me make some truly delicious pancakes for breakfast this morning and told me all about their plan to sneak away and spend the day on the beach. I guess they got caught, though, since every so often one of their intentionally off-key notes clashes with the peaceful melody playing on the first floor. Not that I'm singing, of course. I would never dare tarnish the perfection of Ilene Woods.

I sigh, fingers wrinkly from the soapy water. Even if I hate the actual physical labor, this is an iconic scene, and I know I'm nailing it. Each time I dip my brush back in its sudsy bucket, I wipe the floor with sweeping circular movements, keeping my face dreamy and serene. A particularly pearly orb floats by, and I catch it on the tip of my finger, admiring my kerchief-covered reflection in its shiny surface. Man, this is totally a missed opportunity for a cute social post: "Never stop dreaming, even when you're cleaning! #DisneyLife"

Happily Ever Island desperately needs some kind of photography or filmography package for guests, because this whole "no phones" thing is not working for me. I know they don't want technology around during their test run, but what's the point of looking so cute and living out this once-in-a-lifetime experience if you can't show it off to the world, made even better by professional, Disney-fied footage? Half the reason for going on vacation is to make other people jealous, but besides that, I won't have anything tangible to look back on when this is over. My upcoming pumpkin coach ride, ballroom dance, and glass slipper escape will all be quick blips in time, living only in my heart. I would pay serious coin to replay these yet-to-be-realized moments for the rest of my life.

I need to tell Val this idea.

Especially because I can't stop thinking about our time together under the floating lights. A moment so perfectly romantic it's dethroned my Cinderella daydreaming. There's no denying my feelings for her now, so what do I do? Confess to what's burning in my heart? Ask her out for coffee and beignets at Tiana's Palace? The island is bursting with idyllic backdrops for a first date, each of them so perfect it makes me want to cry. But no matter the whimsical setting, the fact still remains: Val is here to work. And while we've had basically the most romantic almost-kisses ever, I've also brushed her off more times than not. Even if she did accept a date offer, we probably couldn't even do it here, not when she's on the clock. So that would mean what, exactly? Waiting until this trip is over? My heart shudders at the thought. I don't want to wait, and I don't want both of us to scatter back to our individual ends of the earth. I've only had a glimpse of what we could be, how I could be more than someone's make-out partner. It feels so good to be seen, understood . . . respected. I want her to know who I am inside and out, and I want to soak in everything about her, too. Last night standing under the lanterns was so magical, I can still feel the electricity in my veins from Val's fingertips on mine, candlelight warming her eyes, her hair, her lips. . . .

The lullaby stops, and I reluctantly pull myself away from my *Tangled* encounter back to the château, only to find Lucifer scattering dusty cat prints all over the foyer, effectively erasing the past hour of scrubbing.

"Lucifer!" I scream, slamming my brush against the tile

as I climb to a stand. I knew this was coming, but my frustration is amplified after having actually done all that work. How Cinderella kept it together all those years is beyond me. "You've got to be freaking kidding me!"

The cat, somehow perfectly inhabiting his animated counterpart, sits at the base of the stairs glaring at me. He licks his now-dust-free paw before snuggling himself into a ball. His feline smugness is so strong I would almost be impressed if I wasn't totally annoyed.

"That's it! I'm out!" I kick my soap bucket, sloshing water all over the place, but I don't care. I am not cleaning it up. Throwing my apron into the puddle with dramatic flair, I storm toward the front door, swinging it open to find Val poised to knock.

"Oh! Hey!" I cheer, brushing a stray hair off my face. Just seeing her lifts my mood into a less-murderous place. My heart skips a beat. "What are you doing here?"

She stands on tiptoe, looking over my shoulder as if there should be a monster behind me. "I'm here to rescue you," she answers in questioning tone. "Your friend Merida said you needed help with Lady Tremaine?"

Aww, Lanie. Good looking out. "Ugh, yes, my stepmother is the worst while also simultaneously the best. If there is some kind of Character Accuracy Award, she would win hands down. She's a cast member, right? I mean, no one could really be that consistently evil while on vacation."

Val leans in with a sly grin. I try not to be a weirdo and take a deep whiff of her vanilla perfume. "Actually no, she's a guest," she whispers. "The villain roles were in the high-est demand and filled up before all the princesses, if you can believe."

"Whoa, that's . . ." I pause. It clearly wouldn't be my choice, but getting to breathe fire or cast a spell on someone would be pretty sweet. "Actually that tracks."

"Honestly, if I were staying here, I'd probably choose a villain," Val admits. "Like the evil Queen, dipping apples in poison and filling jewelry boxes with beating hearts."

I picture her draped in a dramatic cape, pointy gold crown perched on her dark glossy hair. She's already doing such an amazing job smoothing over all the bumps and mishaps in the island's trial run, it's not a stretch to imagine her ruling over us all, plotting schemes while admiring herself in the mirror. Damn, that's actually something I'd love to see. I feel my cheeks redden; why is this totally working for me right now? "Oooh, interesting, I—"

"Cinderella!" Lady Tremaine beckons from upstairs.

All the hairs on my arm stand up, and not in a fun way. "Quick!" I yelp. "Let's get out of here!" Without hesitation, I grab Val's hand, yanking us away from a world of chores and laundry and into the fresh air and sunshine of Happily Ever Island. Fingers intertwined, we run up Cinderella's cobblestoned path giggling as we make our escape. She squeezes my hand, and when I look back over my shoulder, I catch her biting her lower lip. I can't help but think about biting it, too.

Oh man, I'm in deep. How do I not mess this up?

Just before we reach the Boardwalk, I jump a few steps off the trail, pulling Val behind the fronds of a stout palm tree. I'm sure she has other Very Important Things to attend to, but I don't want her to disappear, not yet; not when our hands are touching and minds are racing with hopefully similar smoochy thoughts. Brown eyes questioning but not resisting, she finds her footing in the mess of rocks and roots I've led us to and waits for me to say . . . what, exactly? *Hey, Val, I really like you. You're unlike any other girl I've ever met. I know I said I wasn't looking for anything serious, but that was before I met you. It's probably way too soon to say this, but I feel like we could be great together. What do you say?* Gah, too much! My heart swells up like a balloon cutting off oxygen to my brain. Oh, this impulsive Gemini soul of mine: I always feel too big, too fast, my words unable to catch up with the desire burning within.

"I, umm . . ." I stammer. Her eyebrows raise expectantly, mouth bending to the right in amusement. If I don't say something coherent soon, this is going to get stupid awkward. "I have some island improvement ideas for you."

"And you wanted to share under the secretive shield of this tropical tree?" She all but laughs.

"Um, everyone knows the best ideas are exchanged in the most unexpected places."

"Uh-huh."

"Plus, I don't want Jared overhearing and stealing your thunder! He could be anywhere!"

She blows a raspberry in disagreement. "Uh, no. Jared's about as sneaky as Kronk from *The Emperor's New Groove*. You

226

can hear him from a mile away! Besides, I know exactly where he is." She ruffles through the papers on her clipboard and frowns. "Shoot."

"What?"

"He should be finishing up the Just Around the River Bend tour any minute now, which means we're due at the Royal Court rendezvous next."

"Ooh, what's that?"

"Just a quick rehearsal for Prince Charming, the king, and the duke regarding the royal ball."

Prince Charming actually exists? I was beginning to think he wasn't real. "Wait, how come I'm not invited? I'm the star of the ball, after all." I shimmy my shoulders for added emphasis.

"Because technically you're not royal yet." She lightly bops my arm with her finger. I can't help but blush. "And anyway, don't you want there to be some surprises that night? You've already met Charming and—"

"What? No I haven't," I interrupt defensively.

She scrunches her head back in confusion. "Seriously? But I thought . . ." Something tumbles through her head, but she shakes it away just as fast. "Hmm. Well, it's fine. Even better, actually."

"No, c'mon! Let me crash the meeting. Please?" I step closer, batting my eyelashes innocently. "I want to see what he looks like and practice our waltz so he doesn't accidently step on my feet."

"Trust me, you're both so perfect it's almost gross," she

deadpans. "Like if I didn't know you, I would actively hate you both."

"Aww, that's sweet. But stop distracting me with compliments and let me come with you."

She toys with the idea, rocking her head from side to side. "Mmmmmm, no, not happening." I stomp my foot impatiently, making her snort. "It'll be better this way. Remember, Cinderella didn't even know she was dancing with the prince, so let him be part of the big reveal."

Damn it. Why does she have to be right all the time? "Fine," I pout.

"But here." Val rips off a fresh sheet of paper from her clipboard. "Why don't you write down all your ideas for me, and we can meet up after dinner to discuss."

Tonight's dinner is a Motunui seafood buffet. My skin hums as I picture Val on the beach in the moonlight, a pink hibiscus tucked behind her ear. I wonder if I can find whoever is playing Moana and borrow some cute shell accessories because I want to look just as dreamy to Val. "I don't know," I tease. "My ideas are pret-ty amazing. Are you sure you want to wait that long?"

She steps even closer, our bodies almost touching if it wasn't for the clipboard between us. "No . . ." she breathes, looking up at me. Slowly, her arm slinks up her side, and for a second, I think she's going to wrap her hand around my neck and pull me in for a kiss. Everything fades away as I hyper focus on her next move, but instead of her tangling her fingers in my hair like I want, she rests her chin on the back of her hand, flashing me her vintage Mickey Mouse watch. "But the mouse waits for no one." With that, she gives me one last smile before scurrying away, leaving me all hot and bothered under the blazing Florida sun.

That's it — I can't keep all these feelings boiling inside anymore. I need to find Lanie for some serious girl talk.

Somehow, my wish upon a star instantly comes true, because the second I step foot on the Boardwalk I spot my best friend, soaking wet under the shade of the Lighthouse. What in the world? Merida doesn't have any swimming scenes that I can remember.

"Lanieeeeeee!" I jog over her way. "Just the person I wanted to see!"

"Hey," she replies, self-consciously wiping away the droplets trickling from her short brown hair.

"I have sooooo much I want to tell you, but first of all, why are you all wet?"

She twists her fingers round and round, breathing picking up. I honestly can't tell if she's going to cry or what. "I . . . I think . . . I'm in over my head."

I bend down to her eye level, but she refuses to meet my gaze. "Lanie, what is it? You're freaking me out." The fact that she's soaked to the bone only adds to the uncertainty.

"I . . . I need to tell you something, but I'm afraid you'll be upset."

What could she possibly say that would upset me? That she hates it here? As much as it sucks I already figured that out myself. I'd rather her just be honest with me at this point

229

instead of holding in this guilt balloon. "You can tell me any-thing. I can help!"

She shakes her head. "I'm not sure you can."

"Is this about your hero moment tomorrow? Because if so, excuse you, but I am the expert here." I playfully pose my hands on my hips.

"No, it's not a Disney thing. Actually, it kind of is, but only because we're here, and after we're gone, it may not even matter, except it will matter because it has me thinking about my life and my choices and my dreams and lack thereof and—"

"Whoa, babe. Slow down," I interrupt, gently rubbing small circles on her back. She takes several deep breaths with her eyes closed, and when they flutter back open, her focus slowly returns. "Okay, now start from the beginning," I say. "What's going on?"

Lanie looks down at her sneakers, socks sloshing around inside. "I just . . ." She shakes her head again, stopping her-self. I wait for a nugget of truth to fall out, even a glimmer of what she's going through, but rather than free herself from whatever's tumbling inside, she holds it all in. Turns out she'd rather suffer in silence than confide in her best friend.

I take my hand off her back, audibly sighing. I know it's harder for her to open up, but I can't deny that this hurts, that after all this time she doesn't feel like I'm a true confidante she can rely on. Haven't I always been there for her? When have I ever judged her or turned her away? What else do I have to do at this point to prove that I love her no matter what?

I walk toward the Lighthouse and take a seat on a stone bench. The bubbling fountains fill the void between us but do nothing to soothe the frustration building in my chest. Lanie creeps over to me, leaving a trail of droplets in her wake, and sits on the opposite side. She looks down at her lap, biting her lip as she struggles to find the words. I'm not going to be the first to talk this time.

After an extended pause, she finally cracks. "I'm sorry," she whispers.

I turn in the opposite direction. "Sorry for what?"

"Sorry for . . . being bad at this."

I rub my face with my hands. "Lanie, no one is really *good* at this. It's not easy for people to be honest with each other."

She looks at me for the first time. "It seems like it's easy for you."

"Okay, well, it's not. I mean, yeah, I've opened up to a lot of people, but look where it's gotten me. Dumped. Heartbroken. Feeling like a total loser. It's not easy, it's just that sometimes you have to take a risk." Lanie nods, eyes glassy. "I wish you would take that risk with me," I add quietly.

She sits up straight, staring off at the ring of pathways leading to the worlds of Belle, Aurora, Pocahontas, and more. I don't know if she suddenly finds strength in their stories or what, but she eventually begins, "This morning . . . when I couldn't tear you away from your Cinderella life . . . Val partnered me up with someone else."

Just the mention of Val makes my heart flip. I'm glad she

was looking out for Lanie; none of my past love interests have ever really cared about my friends. "Well, she is really good at her job."

"Was she able to help you escape?" Lanie asks, visibly brightening as we shift the focus off her. "I was really worried about you, but I figured if anyone could come to your rescue, it would be Val."

I flash back to our near kiss behind the palm tree, Val tempting me with her cuteness. I don't know if I can go much longer without sharing these increasingly steamy feelings with someone, but I need to see if Lanie is taking this anywhere.

"She did," I confirm. "But then what happened?"

"Well, our canoe accidentally drifted into someone else's hero moment—"

"Oh my god, which one?"

"Kiss the Girl."

I tilt my head back, Sebastian's sha-la-las instantly ringing in my ears. "Classic."

"Yeah, well, Prince Eric was not too happy about it. Both our boats toppled over, and he made a big scene."

"And that's why you're all wet? Oh, Lanie, you have nothing to worry about. That's how that scene's supposed to end!"

She sighs. "I guess."

"I'm sure it was embarrassing in the moment, but hey, you made it through! Dr. Lanie always figures it out." Lanie cracks a weak smile. "Was there anything else?"

I wait for more details, a clearer picture on why she was so nervous to share. Was it because she messed up someone's hero moment and thought I'd be upset on their behalf? That doesn't feel right: Sure, I care about Disney accuracy, but I'm not going to berate my best friend on an honest mistake. There has to be something else. But if there is, she's still unwilling to reveal her secret, because all she does is shake her head no.

Fine. Whatever. I'll just sweep this aside like I always do. As annoying as it is, I'm not going to let her reluctance to open up keep me from doing the same. "Okay, then, well, I have some news to share with you."

"Oh yeah?" Lanie perks up.

"Yes." I turn in toward her, flinging my hair over my shoulder before I clasp my hands in my lap. "I'm officially into Val now."

She smirks, as if this isn't news at all. "Finally."

"Right?" I cheer, looping my arm through hers. "Lanie, I like her soooooo much!" We get up and start making our way to Scotland, giggling over my dramatic retellings of my and Val's near romantic encounters. Lanie's always been better at listening than gossiping, and since my storytelling has freed her from releasing whatever dark secret she was too nervous to share, she happily claps and squeals over my recent developments. I give her several opportunities to open up about whatever is bothering her, but she keeps swinging the conversation back my way. It's nice, I guess, to be able to gush as much as I want; I could talk forever about how Val is lighting me up in entirely new ways. But as good as it feels to get my crush out into the open, it would be that much better if my best friend could be just as open with me.

Once we get to DunBroch castle, we pore over the details of Merida's hero moment; together we rehearse her suggested dialogue while I reenact the entire scene, showing her how to project the right Merida attitude in every pose and shot. In return, she helps me fill up my idea page for Val, adding her outsider perspective on ways to make Happily Ever Island even better.

My heart feels very conflicted heading off to dinner. Lanie opts out of the Motunui meet-up in order to save her energy for tomorrow, and as I make my way to the beach, I can't stop thinking about her refusal to share what was on her mind. What is she hiding? Or more importantly, what am I doing that's making her think she has to keep secrets? It was fun playing make-believe Merida in her room, but I could tell something was humming in her veins, a knot of worries she won't let me help untangle. Will she ever get to that point in our friendship, or will she always keep me at arm's length?

Steps from the beach, I scan the sand for Val, heart pounding at the thought of being near her again. I may not be able to figure out Lanie right now, but that doesn't mean my heart has to hit pause altogether.

Time to knock the socks off a certain island ambassador . . .

And pray to all the Disney gods it doesn't backfire.

LANIE

"GO THE DISTANCE"

I feel sick. Not only is my hero moment a mere hour away, but I feel terrible for not being completely honest with Madison last night. There she was, trying to help me and sharing all her amazing news about Val, and what did I do? Join in the fun and dish about my own crush? Reveal the identity of Prince Charming? Finally admit that I've been having second thoughts about my future career path, the one thing I'm supposed to be confident in and have pushed her to figure out, too? No. I deflected attention as much as possible, further burying everything churning up inside me. I just can't handle the prospect of disappointing her like my mom.

Besides, at this point, if I ever do come clean about my

romantic and professional doubts, she'll probably be so hurt by my keeping her at arm's length, she may not even want the full story. I wouldn't blame her. All I want is for her to live her best Disney life, with birds and fairies and whatever else flying around in a magical halo. But I can't help but feel like I'm getting in the way, my weird energy messing up her free spirited flow. If I could have one wish, it would be to steal a fraction of her beautiful, openhearted soul so we could both just relax and not have to deal with my constant tangle of worry.

I read through today's itinerary over and over, repeating the lines Madison and I rehearsed last night.

I am Merida, first-born descendant of clan DunBroch, and I'll be shooting for my own hand!

But can I really do this? I had one very unsuccessful archery lesson, but even if an arrow does manage to hit the target, public speaking has never been my strong suit, let alone acting like a beloved character. I chickened out of an uncomfortable conversation with my own best friend last night. Can I really become Princess Merida in front of all those people? My performance will surely be scrutinized by my fellow guests, and it will be a huge disappointment for all if my arrows sadly flop to the ground.

I pace around Merida's room, side-eyeing today's costume neatly laid out on the bed. It's definitely the fanciest dress all week, with long sky-blue satin sleeves and intricate gold trim around the neck, wrists, and waist. A corset taunts me at its side—my ribs ache just looking at it—along with some kind of white silk headpiece thing that I can't quite figure out.

And then I glance at the thing I've been avoiding the entire time—the wig. There's no escape; I can't really be Merida without that outrageous head of hair. Reluctantly, I approach the wig form, pulling on one giant orange curl to watch it bounce back to a completely different place. Good god, this synthetic hair has a life of its own! And a personality much bolder and brighter than mine. Still, I'm sure no one in Scotland wants to see a pixie-cut weakling be *Brave* . . . maybe this curtain of curls comes with a confidence boost?

I pick up the hairball and fight to adjust the sudden load and length on my head. First the wig falls forward, blocking my vision with fiery determination, but when I pull it down, I almost fall backward, waves weighing me down with their expectations. How did Merida ever walk straight, let alone shoot straight? Red-and-orange coils block my peripherals as I wobble back and forth, knocking into a chair before I catch my reflection in a full-length mirror.

I can't even grasp what I'm looking at. Standing in only my underwear and Merida's unruly mop, I look completely wrong, like a bad princess knock-off who's seen one too many rough nights. This is not right. . . . This is not me. . . . What am I even doing?

Red splotches blossom across my chest as my nerves fire up. Soon the hives are up and down my arms, practically screaming to the world that I'm an overthinking loser who can't even enjoy a simple game of make-believe.

My eyes well up as there's a knock at the door, followed by a chipper "Are you decent?" call from Dorothy.

"Uh, no, actually!" I shout back, but the door swings open anyway, Dorothy sauntering in like she owns the place.

"Don't worry, it's nothing I haven't seen before." Already decked out in her Queen Eleanor regalia, Dorothy proudly strikes a pose, her emerald-green dress hugging her ample curves, long hair pulled back in an elegant set of woven gold braids. How does she do it? Slip on this other persona like it's a favorite pair of leggings? If anything, she seems even more empowered by her transformation, whereas I want to crawl in a hole and hide.

Tears flow out of nowhere and Dorothy startles, rushing to my side. "Sweetie, what's wrong?"

I feel so stupid. Why am I crying?! Others would kill to be in my shoes right now, and here I am sobbing about it. "I'm sorry" is all I can manage.

"Shh, shh, shh." Dorothy pulls me into her chest, patting my synthetic hair. "Are you nervous?"

I nod, resisting the urge to blow my nose on her beautiful gown.

"I am, too," she confides. "Sal and I have had such a good time all week, but now it's like being shoved under a spotlight. It's exciting, sure, but also a little scary."

"Just a little?"

She giggles. "Okay, maybe more than a little. But what has me most out of sorts is that as your fictional mom, I have to pretend to be mad at you today!"

Oh no, she's right. Madison warned me about this from the start, but I got so used to sweet, nurturing Dorothy that

I forgot how shooting for my own hand enrages Merida's parents!

"This is my nightmare," I groan, my head hanging so heavy I'm afraid it could fall off.

"Hey." Dorothy lifts my chin back up, wiping my tears. "Let me ask: Why did you come to Happily Ever Island?"

A very good question. I never would've ventured here on my own. If it weren't for Madison, I'd have spent all of spring break alone in my room, reading and studying for classes I'm not even sure I want to take anymore. Staying on that path is easy; I can ace classes in my sleep. But even though there's comfort in that familiarity, isn't this what I was secretly hoping for? Maybe not this role-play in particular, but a chance to break away and do something different? I needed a shove to shake things up, and my best friend answered the call. "For Madison," I say.

Dorothy smiles, round cheeks glowing. "Now I haven't met this friend of yours, but from what I can tell, you two care about each other very much."

I certainly wouldn't wear this wig for anyone else.

"I'm sure she'll be out there today rooting for you," Dorothy continues, "so if you're unsure about making it through yourself, think about doing it for her. How much it will mean to her. And who knows? Maybe you'll end up getting something out of it, too." She winks.

She's right. Madison will love this, even if my heart feels like it's being turbocharged by a hamster running on its wheel. She's done so much for me; I can dig down and be brave for her.

✿

After a rather comedic scene of squeezing me into Merida's tighter-than-tight betrothal gown and headpiece, I find myself sitting on an actual throne, looking out at my Scottish counterparts cheering and congregating on a wide open field. A sea of tartan dots against the lush green landscape; there's so many people, it feels like everyone on the island is here to witness my rise against societal norms.

Sal sits between Dorothy and me, proudly donning his black fur cape, leather-and-chain-mail armor, and a steel crown perfectly fitted to his bald head. He makes an exceptional King Fergus, happily waving to his subjects as a trio of fiddles accompanies his joyful movements.

"Isn't this great?" he cheers, bouncing in his royal seat. "I'm the king!"

I laugh, his enthusiasm tempering my nerves. At least one of us is having a great time.

Dorothy nods as my suitors file in, acknowledging their presence with stately regard. Going full Queen Eleanor, not once does she look my way, but I know she's still rooting for me, even if her character is not.

I scan the scene for Madison, hoping her Cinderella blues will stand out against the wash of brown and green. But knowing her, she probably packed a Disney bound for this very moment, leaving me unable to find her before the show begins.

I wonder if Charming is out there, too.

My heart clicks up to a speed I didn't think was humanly possible. I wipe my slick palms against my silky dress, but they slide right off. Will I even be able to hold my bow?

Dorothy and Sal stand, eliciting more applause. Hand in hand, they deliver their opening lines in unison. "Archers, to your marks! And may the lucky arrow find its target."

Okay, here we go. As my proposed suitors grab their bows and walk across the field, I run through my mental list of everything that's about to happen. *Watch suitors fail, declare my independence, shoot three perfect bull's-eyes.* Piece of cake. Except not really.

At least the first part is easy.

Step 1: Watch suitors fail.

The first one, a man who looks to be my mom's age, fires his arrow into the outermost circle of his target. The crowd boos, but I'm secretly jealous someone was able to hit it at all.

King Fergus leans over to me expectantly. Shoot. Am I supposed to say something? I focused so much on my one big line, I kind of forgot to memorize the rest. "Wow that was . . . not great?" I say, making an attempt. He chuckles, patting me warmly on the shoulder.

The next suitor queues up, a shirtless dude bro who reminds me of the idiots who ask for coffee with a "shot of tequila" because they think they're hilarious. I wish I could serve that at Java Jam! because it would taste god-awful and shut them up. He makes a huge show of setting up his shot, pushing out his pecs as he slowly pulls back his bowstring, pausing to kiss his flexed bicep for whatever reason.

"Now that's attractive," I groan.

"Don't skip ahead!" Sal laughs.

"Wait, was that an actual line?" I ask. He nods. "Sorry!"

And with that I've missed seeing the shot. Not that it matters, because for all his preening, pretty boy is whining in the dirt.

As the last suitor takes his mark, I slip off my throne, ducking behind the wooden stage where I find Val waiting, props in hand. Just seeing my bow triggers a fresh wave of nerves, but Val, undoubtedly sensing my panic, doesn't let me melt into a puddle of worry.

"You've got this, Merida," she cheers, yanking off my headpiece and adjusting my wig. "You literally cannot miss, okay?"

"Really?" My voice shakes as she drapes a gray hooded shawl over my head and shoulders.

"Really." She winks, handing me a sheaf of arrows and then squeezing my shoulder. It's so comforting and sweet; I can see why Madison likes her so much. "Now take this and go be your own hero!"

Be your own hero, be your own hero . . . Her words bounce around my head as I sneak through the crowd, everyone's attention focused on target number three, where an arrow just pierced the bull's-eye. Cheers flood the field as I creep to my spot undetected, fighting to keep my blazing-bright curls from popping out from under the hood.

Merida is a hero because she fights for her future. When her predetermined path doesn't align with her vision, she stands up, declaring resistance and demanding her wishes be acknowledged. She's not afraid to defy expectation and tradition, somehow knowing that the cost of disappointing her family is not as high as disappointing herself. It's a fire I've never felt, but there's no more time to obsess about it. I have to become Merida and all she represents—right here, right now—to the best of my ability.

Step 2: Declare my independence.

Trembling hands find a banner left for me on the field; I raise it high, Merida's family crest standing tall beside the other clans. I step forward from the crowd, my entire body shaking as I slide back my hood, orange curls blowing wildly to match my rebellious intentions.

"I am Merida," I begin, my voice surprisingly loud despite the waves of gasps behind me. Is there a microphone tangled up in one of these curls? I'm carrying so much weight up there it honestly wouldn't surprise me. "First-born descendant of clan DunBroch, and I'll be shooting for my own hand!"

Queen Elinor and King Fergus jump out of their seats, shocked yelps echoing throughout Scotland. I have to act fast. Bow in hand, I line up at the first target, which feels impossibly far from where I'm standing. *How am I supposed to do this? What if I—*

No. Don't go down that rabbit hole. Val said I can't miss, right? Just do it.

Step 3: Shoot three perfect bull's-eyes.

Positioning the bow like I was taught, I realize my dress is so ridiculously tight, I can't fully raise my arms. *Gah!* I strain against the silk, forcing my arms to pull the seams until they pop, ripping the arms free from the bodice. The guests behind me cry out, but with my full range of motion acquired, I pull back the bowstring, doing my best to line the tip of my arrow to the target. *Please work, please work!*

I let go, closing my eyes for the split-second flight, my ears greeted with cheers of approval.

I did it. I hit the bull's-eye! I don't know if it's pixie dust or magic lamps or what, but I successfully nailed the first target. I exhale in shock, a smile spreading across my lips. I may be able to pull this off after all.

Confidence building, I walk to the second target, again refusing to look as I set my arrow free. The crowd goes wild again, and I blink open to find another perfect shot. How is this happening? Magnets? Some invisible zip-line system? There's no way my actual skill is getting the job done, but I don't even care, the collective energy behind me putting an extra pep in my step. I practically float to the third target where the enormity of the moment comes decidedly clear.

This is it. The winning shot that solidifies Merida's hero status. Not only do I have to hit the bull's-eye, but I have to obliterate the arrow that's already there. Merida's confidence, her capability: This is where she defies the odds and takes her future into her own hands.

I have to do the same.

Seconds ago, I wouldn't have thought I could make it here. But now? It feels inevitable. Carefully, consciously, I set my aim, feeling the arrow's feathers brush against my cheek. To my left I hear Queen Elinor cry, "Merida, stop!" even as the crowd urges me on, but I tune it all out, taking a deep breath as I release the fateful arrow.

This time I keep my eyes open. I want to see this fairy-tale moment come true, to witness the exact moment a wish becomes a certainty. My arrow flies true, not only hitting the target but barreling through the awaiting shaft and splitting it in two.

I drop my bow, hands covering my open mouth. A wave of relief flows through me as the people of Scotland rush to my side, guests cheering and bagpipes sounding in victory. Crowds are usually my least favorite place to be, but today, with everyone chanting my name and smiling at me with glee, I don't immediately start hyperventilating. In fact, it's almost fun.

Even Dorothy, who should be pitching a fit as Queen Elinor, can't help but congratulate me, smothering me in a sweaty hug. "I'm so proud of you, sweetie!" she squeals, and I squeeze her back, releasing all that pent-up negative energy. Two of my failed suitors come up from behind and hoist me on their shoulders. Normally, I don't let strangers touch me, but from this high vantage point, I search for Madison, desperate to share this moment with my best friend. Where is she? I know she has to be here, I can almost feel her positive energy.

"Madison!" I yell, though my voice is lost in the roar. I keep looking for her blonde ponytail, but the guys whip me around before I can zero in.

So many faces, so much celebration, and yet finally, a familiar face comes into view: Charming, barreling his way through the swarm to get to me, his beautiful face beaming with pride. My heart races back into action and the closer he gets, the more I know I have to be with him right now.

He extends a hand as I slide down the strangers' shoulders; I let myself fall into his chest, and he easily catches me, securing his arms around my waist as I wrap my legs around his. For once in my life, I move without thought, letting my desire pull me in the right direction. And my heart must know what it wants because here, inches apart from this completely irresistible guy, I couldn't dream of anything more magical.

He smiles warmly, dimple deepening as he pushes back my orange curls so that there's nothing between us. "So," he breathes, dark eyes dancing all over my face. "I know you just proudly asserted your independence and all, but, um, I was wondering if I could take you to the ball? Or maybe . . . for coffee?"

I take a cue from my good friend Merida and kiss him, following my instincts to go after what I want. Why shouldn't I? No matter what tomorrow brings, today is a perfect moment. His lips press into mine, mirroring my want and need to feel him all over. My legs squeeze his torso tighter, and his right arm works up my back to my neck. People must be staring, but my curls block my vision, keeping Charming and me enveloped in our own private passion.

Eventually, I pull back, wanting to see his face. He looks up at me adoringly, and I take a mental snapshot to save forever. Slowly, he sets me back on the ground, but we don't move apart, neither one wanting to let go.

"So, was that a yes, or . . . ?" he jokes, and I playfully hit him in the chest.

"You better be careful," I tease. "I'm surprisingly good at archery."

"Oh, trust me, I kept a very close watch." He pulls me in even tighter. "It was very attractive."

I'm about to press him for details on this when I hear a voice call, "Lanie?" I turn to see a very confused, very upset Madison, wearing a green-and-brown tartan minidress with a DunBroch clan charm necklace. Mouth hanging open, eyes hard, she keeps her distance, trying to understand the scene before her.

My brain short-circuits, not knowing what to do with her looking at me like this. Like I'm the villain in her movie. Like I broke her heart. "Hey," I choke out, releasing Charming. "I was looking for you, but—"

"Who the hell is this?" Madison gestures wildly at Charming. His eyebrows shoot up to the sky but still he smiles, doing his best to defuse the situation.

"You must be the famous best friend I've heard so much about," he says, extending a hand. "I'm so glad I finally get to meet you, Cinderella. I'm Prince Charming."

Oh no. Madison's face goes stone-cold, her head turning so slowly she looks like one of those demonic dolls in horror movies that suddenly murders an entire family. "Excuse me?" she spits.

My insides freeze. Fairy tale, over.

MADISON

"PART OF YOUR WORLD"

I cannot freaking believe this.

I've been standing out in the hot island sun for hours in this itchy plaid dress to support Lanie, who I thought would be stress barfing all over the place. Turns out, not only is she fine, she's thriving! Lanie, the girl without a drop of Disney blood in her veins, just destroyed the Merida game without a hitch. Lanie, who hates the morning coffee rush but willingly threw herself into a crowd of adoring strangers. Lanie, standing lip to lip with an absolute hottie, who, I'm sorry, is Prince Charming?!? WHAT. EVEN. Do I even know her at all?

"Madison, don't be mad," Lanie says, pulling off her enormous curly wig.

I turn my back to her, barreling back through the crowd. It took me forever and a day to find her, but now I don't even want to look at her face. "Mad? Now why would I be mad?" I call over my shoulder, stomping out of Scotland.

She doesn't respond, but I can hear her on my heels, offering a stream of "excuse me, pardon me" apologies to her partying clan members. I know she must be panicking, mind racing with what to say, but at the moment I don't care. I rage walk all the way to Agrabah, wanting out of Merida's victory party. Kind of hard to be the one person pissed at the hero of the moment, although none of those guests should have been happy at all because I'm pretty sure that's not how it goes down in the movie. Amateurs.

Once we hit the sandy marketplace streets, I finally face my friend. Hair matted to her scalp from wearing that heavy wig, ripped sleeves hanging around her wrists, she twists her hands nervously as a trio of horns sounds down the street, followed by a steady drumbeat stirring up excitement from all the Agrabah-area guests.

"What's that?" Lanie asks, looking toward where the music is coming from.

"Uh-uh, no, we are not changing the subject," I say as she snaps her attention back to me. Though admittedly it's a little hard to concentrate when a chorus of male voices insists we get hyped for the arrival of Prince Ali. Seriously? The Prince Ali hero moment is happening right now? Great. OF COURSE. I pull Lanie into an alleyway, hoping the darkened corner will help block some of the over-the-top parade energy heading through the old bazaar.

"So, care to share what is going on with you?" I press, working overtime to ignore the dancing camel caravan stomping past. "All week long you've been in this faraway funk and then turn around to perfectly embody a princess?"

The Genie high-steps by, chest puffed out as he prances and twirls a fire-tipped baton. Lanie scrunches up her nose. "I wouldn't say *perfectly* . . ."

"Stop it, Lanie," I snap. She recoils at my forcefulness; we've never fought like this before. We've never fought, period. But I've also never felt this kind of betrayal coming from my best friend. "I saw the whole thing! You hit every beat flawlessly: ripping your dress, hitting the targets, speaking the lines? You crushed it like it was nothing."

Lanie plugs her ears as bells jingle and swords spin through the air. She yelps, "It wasn't nothing! That was hard for me! My whole body is probably covered in connect-the-dots hives right now."

I blow right past her rebuttal as a ginormous elephant proudly trots in my peripheral. On its back, Aladdin (or, I'm sorry, "Prince Ali") preens for the crowd, waving and flashing a pompous smile as his feathered turban flutters in the breeze. But even this iconic moment can't pull me out of my frustration. "You know, for a second back there I thought, *Wow! It happened! Lanie's letting herself have fun!* But why, then, couldn't you have that same fun with me? Almost every time

I've seen you you've been this tortured ball of weird energy, and I've tried—really hard—to reset your aura. To be your guide through all this. I wanted us to have a fun spring break together, but instead you've been sharing all your fun vibes with some guy. No, not some guy—a guy you said you didn't even know—Prince Charming!"

Lanie cringes as fifty-three purple peacocks glide by. Her eyebrows wrinkle as she says, "I wanted to tell you. . . ."

I groan. "So then why didn't you? Why did you hide this from me?" I ask, tears building. It feels ridiculous to be this emotional while an inflatable gorilla is blocking out the sun, but here we are. "You've clearly been spending a lot of time together, but why the secrecy? I gushed about Val and shared all my feelings. Why couldn't you do the same? Did you think I wouldn't be happy for you, that I'd be mad?"

"You are mad!" She throws her arms out.

"Because you hid this! You *lied to me*, Lanie. I specifically asked you if you'd met Prince Charming and you said no!"

She stares at the ground, kicking the sand. "I knew my meeting him first would set you off."

"Set me off?"

"Yeah." She doubles down despite the fresh flush of red on her cheeks. "Only you could meet him because that's the way it happens in the story and in your bubbly little head. I ruined it from day one without even trying."

Bubbly little . . . Is she for real? "Great. Now my best friend thinks I'm an idiot, too?"

"What? I didn't say that!"

"You just did! I'm just some immature joke for you to keep around and make you feel better about yourself. Anytime you mess up—which is never, by the way—you can look at me and say, 'Well at least I'm not as stupid as Madison!'" I tap the sides of my skull like my head is exploding with all my dumb, "bubbly" thoughts.

Lanie's mouth drops. She steps back like an arrow hit her heart. "That is not what I said. I meant *bubbly* as a *good* thing. Some of us don't have an effervescent thirst for life like you do."

"Right, because traveling to the Florida Keys is such tooooorture. Winning a once-in-a-lifetime vacation with your best friend is pure aaaaaagony." I drag out *torture* and *agony* while pulling down the sides of my mouth in dramatic ennui.

"It's not as easy for me to unwind, I—"

"Isn't it, though?" I interrupt. "All week you acted like you hated being here when really, you've been loving every second! That's not fair, Lanie. Coming here was supposed to be a dream come true." I wipe my eyes furiously, not letting a single drop roll down my cheeks as some beautiful belly dancers come skipping by, a rainbow of sheer ribbons trailing in their wake.

"And that's why I didn't say anything—I felt guilty, okay?" Lanie sniffs, face all splotchy and red. "Guilty that I was miraculously enjoying this trip while my Disney obsessed BFF was stuck scrubbing floors and missing all our activities. Which, thanks for that, by the way."

"Thanks for what?"

"Abandoning me left and right! You signed us up for

snorkeling and canoeing and then left me to do everything on my own!"

I cross my arms. "That wasn't my fault and you know it."

"Yeah, well, someone else was there in your absence. And I didn't go looking for him; I didn't even think our interactions were real." She scraps her fingernails through her short hair. "I didn't tell you because I was protecting myself. I couldn't let myself believe I liked him or that he liked me, and I knew if I told you, you'd spin the happily-ever-after fantasy out of control."

"No, I wouldn't have."

She rolls her eyes. "Please. You would've chosen our wedding invitation font the second I let the secret loose. And by the time I figured out there was something there, it was too late to come clean. God, Madison, do you think I would intentionally hurt you? I didn't mean for any of this to happen."

The more she talks, the worse I feel. Because of course Lanie falls in love without even trying. Everything in her life always works out; she may stress about it, but she still has the perfect career and life trajectory all lined up. It's not fair. She has no idea what it's like to never be good at anything, to be totally clueless when it comes to The Future. I try so hard at things that come naturally for her and she just takes them for granted. God, she even mastered Disney life in a few short days, and now she's pitying me? Feeling bad that once again poor, simple Madison is always a few steps behind? I've had about enough of that.

"No, of course you didn't," I say in a condescending tone. Drumbeats fuel my anger, marching right into my core. "You don't mean for anything to happen. You just float along in your perfect Lanie bubble, and you know what? I don't need you feeling sorry for me."

She grits her teeth, shielding her vision from the white Persian monkeys waving past. "What the hell does that mean?"

"Oh, you know what it means." I tsk my tongue. "Your stars have been aligned since birth, and yet you act like it's some big burden to have it all figured out."

She squints as sunlight bounces off piles and piles of gold coins raining from the sky. "Right, because it's soooo great to have every twist and turn of your life ironed out before you've even lived it."

"Better than floundering at every single step!" My arms flail out as the final verse of Prince Ali's big debut builds all around us, getting louder by the second. "Lanie, I would kill to have your life. To know without a doubt that I'm destined for something great, to lean on reality instead of stupid horoscopes to make decisions. You even have a parent guiding you through every step, whereas mine couldn't care less. I have . . . no one anymore." I swallow hard, fighting back tears. "All my life I've been waiting for a sign on where and how to start, while you already have it figured out."

"Well, maybe I don't want that!" she yells with a fire I didn't know she contained. I stumble back, knocking into a man balancing a cage filled with warbling birds. Despite the chaos, Lanie can't stop now. "Maybe having zero surprises ahead makes me feel like I've lived my whole stupid life before it's even begun! And I hate it!"

Trumpets blaring, drums pounding, the exultant praise for Aladdin's transformation pulses through my bones. I bury my face in my hands. Between Lanie screaming and the high-pitched chorus ringing through the desert, there is WAY too much happening right now.

The streets of Agrabah erupt in applause as the song comes to its end. Lanie and I stare at each other, her emotional reveal hanging in the sudden silence. Her chest rises and falls, but there's a calm across her face, like releasing all these secrets finally set her free.

"I hate it, Madison," she repeats, though much quieter this time. "You know, when I first met you, I was so jealous. I looked at you and wondered what it would be like to float through life instead of steamrolling, to appreciate the present and revel in what you love without always worrying about what you *should* do. You're like"—she chokes on her words, bottom lip trembling—"this magical ball of light letting yourself hope and dream at all times. I couldn't give myself that space . . . until I came here."

I've never heard Lanie talk about herself this way. She can be self-deprecating, sure, but I figured that was her way of downplaying her success in front of a screwup like me. The fact she could ever be jealous of me? I don't know what to think, let alone what to say. I hate seeing her cry, but I let her wring it all out.

"So, how long have you been having this school crisis?" I ask, bypassing her compliment for now.

She wipes her nose on her tattered sleeve. "I don't know . . . a couple of months?"

Months? *Months?* Somehow this hits harder than her Disney deception. "Why didn't you say something?"

"I didn't know what to say; I barely knew what to feel. Anytime these doubts popped up, I just pushed them back down, telling myself I had to go on no matter what."

To think that all this time we've been pouring coffee and hanging out she's been harboring this cyclone of confusion, all while playing the role of the perfect student and future doctor. It makes me feel like I've been spending time with a total stranger. "Lanie, I tell you everything. The second anything interesting happens to me I always think, *Ooh, gotta text Lanie.* And right now it feels like you tell me nothing. I don't get it. Am I not a good friend to you? Do you not trust me or something?"

"No!" she bursts. "I don't trust *me*. I don't know how to listen to my gut, and I didn't want to add my uncertainty to yours. You've had a hard enough time trying to pick a major and a plan, I didn't want to bother you."

I walk up and down the alleyway, processing this sudden info dump. Lanie admires me, but she doesn't open up to me. She thinks I'm magical, but not magical enough to help her with her problems. None of this sits right, and I don't know whether to cry or scream or sink into the sand.

"Well, I'm officially bothered." Because really, if Lanie's

not going to be honest with me, what are we doing with this friendship? The last thing I want is another person stringing me along because they don't think I have the emotional intelligence to get real. Part of me knows Lanie didn't do this on purpose, that her overachieving brain probably forced her to figure this all out on her own, but the bigger part of me is too disappointed to let that truth take hold.

We stand in silence, hollowed out from our first fight. There's no precedent for what to do next; I've fought with plenty of girlfriends, but this is on a different level. My instinct is to hug her and work this all out immediately, but I don't even know what that means right now. Lanie runs off in the direction we came, and I'm too tired to chase after her. Tears forming, I look up and blink rapidly to keep them at bay just as a magic carpet sails across the sky.

Yup, this is definitely a whole new world.

❋

Hours later, I'm still reeling from my fight with Lanie. The things we said, the way we yelled . . . it plays over and over like a nightmare-clip show. I want her to be honest with me, but how can she do that if she's not even honest with herself? How can I prove that I only want what's best for her? That's the worst part—I don't know how to fix it.

I sit at the top of the Lighthouse, legs dangling over the side as I rest my arms and head on the railing. As the bright beacon spins 'round and 'round, island landmarks wave hello for as far as I can see, from Rapunzel's tower and the emperor's palace, to the Cave of Wonders and Seven Dwarfs' mine. Tomorrow is our last full day here, and there are still so many parts of the island I've yet to explore. I wanted to take it all in, catalog every detail; I've spent my whole life going to Disney parks, but this place is on a different level. The amount of planning and storytelling happening here . . . it all went by so fast, but I feel like my story isn't close to being done here yet.

Because as amazing as Happily Ever Island is, I have so many ideas on how it could be even better. Things like videography packages, good versus evil elimination games, a princess pampering spa, animatronic sidekicks: I shared it all on my list to Val last night (which sadly ended up being strictly business since she had to help with the evil Queen/poisoned apple hero moment right after). But do these ideas have any weight? Do I have the skills and drive to try and make them real, or am I flitting off to fantasy once again? Lanie says she admires my spirit, but most of the time it still feels like I'm some aimless woman-child clinging to make-believe. Am I ever going to feel grown up?

Down below, a cast member plays "A Dream Is a Wish Your Heart Makes" on a violin, and the solo strings are so tender, so syrupy sweet that before I know it, fat tears are running down my face, my mind a mix of everything I'd hoped this week would be and the truth of what transpired. Running through the utilidor toward the floating lights, watching ice

259

castles come to life: The behind the scenes moments captivated me most of all. I don't want to say good-bye to these magical new perspectives yet.

"Hey," a voice calls quietly from behind. I wipe my cheeks and turn to see Val, her arms clutching multiple take-out boxes. My heart bursts at the sight of her; is there anything more attractive than a hot girl bringing you food? "I didn't see you at the dinner at Tiana's Palace. Thought you might like some gumbo."

"Thanks," I sniffle, giving her the biggest smile I can muster. "But I'm more of a jambalaya girl."

"You will eat it and you will like it." She sits down next to me, passing me a spork before noticing how puffy my face must look. "What's wrong?"

"Oh, I'm just rehearsing for tomorrow," I lie, pulling on my ponytail. "Making sure I can turn on the waterworks to make my fairy godmother appear."

She rolls her eyes. "Bull. What happened?"

"Are you calling me a liar?"

"Yes. I saw you arguing with Lanie. . . ."

"Fine. We got in a huge fight. It was awful." I give her a quick recap, including all the ridiculous details of the Prince Ali backdrop. "And now I can't get over something she said."

Val stares at me expectantly. "Which was . . . ?"

I hesitate, almost embarrassed to reveal what I'm confused about most. But Val hasn't given me any reason not to trust her. "Well, Lanie told me that sometimes she's jealous of me, which is really confusing since she's the one who's always had it all figured out, while I'm like a real-life Peter Pan too scared to grow up."

A warm breeze ruffles her hair as she says, "Hmm. Sounds like you could use a beignet."

My eyes tear up again. "I really, really could."

Val gets to work opening up all the take-out boxes, revealing a straight-up feast of shrimp, red beans and rice, and, of course, Tiana's signature puffed pastries. I haven't eaten all day, and even though my stomach grumbles wildly, I can't take my eyes off her, going to all this trouble to take care of me. Is this what having a real girlfriend is like? Someone who listens to you and makes sure you're fed? Because if so, I'm in.

Her eyes twinkle every time the spotlight spins our way, making it really hard to stay so sad with her looking so cute. Once she has everything laid out, we both swing our legs back up from over the side, sitting cross-legged facing each other. We each take a box and with utensils at the ready, she says, "So, continue. You're having an existential crisis."

I nearly choke on my gumbo. "That is *not* what I said!"

"Well, good, because I have some news."

"Oh, so we're done talking about me, then?"

"Shh, this pertains to you."

"Uh-huh, sure." I go for another bite, pretending to be mad.

"So as promised, I took your ideas to our cast member morning meeting today," she starts after finishing her bite of rice. "First of all, you should've seen Jared's face. Dude pouted so hard, I thought his face was going to implode."

"Exactly what we were going for!" I cheer.

"Right. So, besides that, which was a victory in itself, my boss was very impressed with my initiative." She holds her head high, cheeks filled with pride. "Everyone else was complaining about problems, but I came to the table with solutions. She said, and I quote, my 'determination to problem solve using real-world feedback is what defines Disney leaders.'"

My jaw drops open in a wide smile, my next bite left dangling. "That's . . . holy crap, Val. That's amazing!"

"I know!" She beams. "It feels so good to be recognized. I've been running around this island all week, picking up thingamabobs, sweeping up snowflakes, and you don't even want to know how many corsets I've tightened, and that's just for Gaston! But I managed to set myself apart from the others, and I feel really, really good about my chances at landing a full-time role here."

A small pang of jealousy rips through me. Val gets to stay here, to spend every single day as a happily-ever-after. I eye the cast member name tag pinned on the left side of her snug navy vest: a white oval with tiny gold stars dancing along the border, her name in bold blue with a Lighthouse illustration emblazoned above. God, to see my name on one of those iconic tags! I'm happy for her but selfishly sad for me; another girl in my life off to do incredible things while I'm left behind with nothing but dreams to cling to.

"You are living the ultimate Disney nerd fantasy," I tell her, doing my best to keep my voice steady. "I kind of hate you right now."

"I know." She smirks. She sets down her food and tucks her hair behind her ears. "But wait, there's more!"

"More?" I gasp. I'm not sure if my heart can take it. If they are suddenly creating a Disney princess in her image, I will just melt down the side of this lighthouse. They totally should and I would buy the hell out of that merch, but still. "Stop torturing me!"

Ignoring my comment, she continues. "After my boss finished lavishing me with praise in front of the whole team, I took her aside to explain how I gathered all these ideas based on guest input, specifically yours. I told her all about how you're this smart, passionate, if not slightly arrogant Disney talent that we should hire. I hyped you up so hard she wants to meet you before you go home."

This time I actually do choke. I'm sorry, what did she just say? Through a bite of chewed-up shrimp, I gag out, "Huh?"

"To be honest, working with you would probably be impossible." She sighs, casually looking up at the stars. "Being around Jared is hard enough." Val's lips bend to the right in a playful smile. "I mean . . . as long as that's what you'd want?"

I force myself to focus on her words and not her very kissable face. "You really think I could?"

"I do," she says matter-of-factly. "You're a hospitality natural. You care deeply about the brand, obviously, but you're equally invested in the happiness of others. I mean, look at you." She flicks her wrist up and down. "You're wearing a flannel tartan dress in the Florida heat just to match your friend's hero moment."

I look down at my very uncomfortable outfit as fireworks burst in my chest. Hospitality? I never would have thought of it. I do like making people smile, and the only compliment Barry's ever paid me has been about how despite the fact that I'm always late and sometimes make espresso wrong, I do give excellent customer service. Every time the idea of working for Disney has waltzed through my brain, I've shot it dead, reminding myself how I'm not smart enough. But could this be my angle? Is there really a chance?

The familiar flicker of doubt makes itself known. What could I contribute here, really? Photo packages, spa days? I'm sure any fan would have similar suggestions. As my head spins, I become very aware of how far up off the ground we are; I scoot my back against the Lighthouse's center for extra stability. "I always figured I'd have to be some kind of super genius to work for Disney," I admit.

"Yeah, well, we can't all be brilliant," she teases, pressing a finger into my shoulder. "You'll have to make up for it in heart."

I stare at her, watching both the spinning light above and the night sky fight over who gets to make her look more beautiful. Whether bathed in moonlight or drenched from the beacon, she glows, her soft skin and mischievous eyes pulling on my heartstrings. But what's more than that, she believes in me. She's seen something no one else has ever recognized, not even myself. And there's still so much I don't know about her, so much I want to be part of. The way she's putting herself out there makes me hope she feels the same. "Why are you doing this for me?" I whisper.

She looks away, suddenly shy. "Because," she says, tone softening, "I like being around you. You make feel like it's okay to be vulnerable sometimes, like it doesn't always have to be me against the world." She gives a small smile, cheeks turning pink. "You're special, Madison. More than you know. You deserve a shot at your dream."

First Lanie revealing her admiration for me, now Val? It's a lot, almost too much, amplified by the fact that my body is screaming to kiss her, our starlit setting too romantic to ignore. But as much as I want her, I pause, deciding to start very small; to dip my toe instead of diving straight into the deep end as usual. Val is too important for me to mess things up. I clear away the food to sit right next to her, our arms and thighs touching, and I reach out, hovering my hand over hers to give her a chance to move if she'd like, before touching down. We've held hands before but only while running, clutching each other for stability. But this is slower, closer; her skin humming against mine. It feels so good just to be near her, like I can do anything with her by my side. She doesn't pull away.

"I think you're special, too," I whisper, breathing in her sweet scent. "I've never met anyone like you."

"And you never will," she teases. Except that she's right.

Together we listen to the violinist below play through

several more Disney ballads, and eventually Val rests her head on my shoulder.

Everything else fades away, and I sink into the happiness of being right here, right now, the two of us snuggling together under the stars. And even if one came shooting across the sky, I wouldn't wish for anything else.

LANIE

"THE NEXT RIGHT THING"

fter my horrible fight with Madison, I decide I have to end things with Prince Charming. But how?

No one ever really gets dumped in fairy tales. *Happily ever after* is a status quo that's never challenged, the camera consciously moving away before revealing the future breakup or divorce. My mom has never once talked positively about my dad, a guy who left so early I don't even remember him. But at one point they must've been in love, right? Skipping into the sunset together? My family is living proof there's no way everything just magically falls into place after every sweeping kiss. There have to be fights, friction: Two people do not figure each other out the second their lips touch.

And as much as I'd like to take that journey, I don't think Charming and I have time for all that. I'm about to go home and then what, we start a long distance relationship where I'm always in class and he's doing . . . whatever it is he does? I haven't dated much, but I know myself enough to foresee my anxiety twisting in unhealthy ways. Better to leave things off as they are now.

I wish I could communicate all this without having to say the words. Where is that Genie when you need him?

By the time I get back to Scotland after the parade in Agrabah, everyone is still whooping it up, beer steins overflowing and bagpipes blaring. Now that my entire clan witnessed my archery triumph, it's impossible to slip by unnoticed, with guests and cast members alike shouting congratulations and compliments my way.

"Merida! Where did you learn to shoot like that?"

"You can shoot to win my hand any day!"

I smile meekly, uncomfortable with so much praise and attention. All I want to do is change out of this heavy, ripped-apart dress into something normal before I break the news to Charming.

In an effort to sneak through the courtyard unnoticed, I accidentally bump into Sal, who's clearly achieved his ideal state of being as the king of DunBroch. Still wearing his tartan-swathed armor and crown, he cheers upon seeing me, his face red with joy. "Well, there ya are, lassie!" he exclaims in a brand-new, very thick Scottish accent. Apparently, alcohol

brings out the inner Scotsman in him. "We've a been celebra-
tin' ya! Where've ya been?"

"Just needed some air, I guess."

"But this is yer moment! I'm so verra proud o' ya!"

I laugh, enjoying watching my fake father in his element.
"Aren't you supposed to be mad at Merida, though?"

He frowns dramatically, sloshing his stout. "Eh, I dinna
care 'bout that. We're on vacation! Have some fun!" Suddenly,
he remembers something. "Oh, there's a young lad waitin' fer
ya back inside."

"Wait, what?" I panic.

"Aye! That Charmin' fella, he's up in yer room."

"I gotta go!" I sprint toward the castle. With every step my
nerves click higher up the scale, adrenaline coursing through
me. *How am I going to share this decision with Charming? Will he hate
me? Will I hate myself? What if I'm making a huge mistake? What if
denying the inevitable is the mistake? What if, what if, what if—*

I hit the brakes just outside my door, pressing myself into
the cool castle stone. I can't let my anxiety take over right now;
for once I need to speak from the heart and not my spinning
head. Focusing on my breath, I work on regaining control,
closing my eyes as air cycles in and out. Through concentrated
effort I stop the *what if*s and replace them with *you can do this*,
forcing my body to accept that I'm not in mortal danger even
though what I'm about to do makes it feel that way.

My resolve cracks the moment I open the door and see
Charming sitting on the edge of my bed. Elbows on his knees,

clasped hands propping up his forehead: it's the posture of worry, a pose I often find myself in moments before a test. Yet upon my arrival he leaps to my side, concern washing away into relief.

"You're here," he breathes, wrapping his arms around me. Against my better judgment I melt into his chest, letting myself linger in this last bit of closeness. "Is everything okay with you? With Madison? I wanted to chime in back there but didn't feel like it was my place." He takes my hands, intertwining his fingers in mine. For a second, I stay there, committing this sensation to memory; I never want to forget what it's like to have someone willingly offer their hands in support. Every part of me wants to pull him in closer, but if I do, I'll never be able to let go.

"I need to talk to you," I say softly, avoiding his eyes in favor of the floor. "About the ball."

He snorts. "Sorry, I just have to point out the hilarity of that sentence." I try to smile, but the muscles refuse. He picks up on my emotion and adds, "Wait, you're serious."

I nod, and he guides me toward the edge of the bed, hands still locked. Okay, I definitely have his attention: It's now or never.

"I can't hang out with you at the ball," I spit out so fast I almost trip over my own words.

"Because . . . ?"

"Because it's supposed to be Madison's big moment. She's Cinderella; you're Prince Charming." As soon as I say the words, I know they're a flimsy excuse.

He stares blankly. "And?"

"And Merida doesn't really factor into that equation?" I try meekly.

His mouth twists. "Okay, I mean, obviously I came here to play this character, but that's all that is: playing. Our feelings for each other shouldn't affect Madison or the amount of fun any of us can have. I don't see why me pretending to be a fictional prince should keep us from hanging out."

I wish it were that easy. I wish I didn't keep all my secrets so she wouldn't hate me. Because right now I would do anything just for us to be on better terms again. Obviously, I haven't been acting myself this week. I need to rid myself of all distractions to figure out a way to get my one meaningful friendship back on track.

"One dance?" He smiles, using that dimple magic against me. "One little dance? I'm sure the prince dances with other eligible ladies before Cinderella shows up, right?"

I don't actually know. Madison would, but I can't ask her now.

"Lanie," he says softly, drawing my attention up from off the floor. I've never heard him say my name before, but I like it. A lot. Never before has my name sounded sexy: like a sultry secret miles away from brainy Lanie. My eyes betray me, looking at his mouth and begging him to say it again. "It is Lanie, right?"

I nod, the back of my neck starting to burn.

"I can tell you're conflicted," he continues. "I really love how much you care about your friend. And I don't mean to make things harder for you, but . . . I care about you, too. I've had a lot of fun exploring this place with you, and there's no one else I'd rather end this experience with. Can't we make it work? Figure out a way for Madison to get her happy ending while making some space for us, too?"

Us. Such a simple word, and yet it says so much. I've never been part of an us, not a romantic us, anyway. I don't know the first thing about balancing the needs of us; I can barely navigate the needs of me.

"It's just that . . . I'm not very experienced with *this.*" I gesture to the space between us. "When I came on this trip, I figured I'd just hide on the beach with a book. I didn't plan for anything like this to happen."

"Well, to be honest, you weren't exactly in my plan either." Charming shakes his head. "Or, I don't know, maybe this was supposed to be the plan all along. If the past couple of years have taught me anything, it's that life makes zero sense and plans can easily fall apart."

I try to imagine my life plan falling apart. If med school, graduation, and joining Mom's practice suddenly all fell by the wayside, how would I feel? Would I be sad? Would I feel free? If all that certainty disappeared, would it be a relief or would I miss reaching those goals, knowing what should have been? "I don't know what that's like," I admit.

He omits a hushed *hmm* sound before saying, "Consider yourself lucky. Having your life turn upside down without warning is a scary place to be." His eyes darken, caught on some troubling memory. I want to ask him what he means, to find out what caused the pain casting a shadow on him now and how he found himself on an island devoted to happy endings. But if I open that door, a whole world of information will come spilling out, and the more I know about him, the harder it will be to walk away.

Still, his whole demeanor has changed, strong shoulders hunched. I scoot closer to offer comfort, and he instantly accepts, releasing one of my hands in favor of my knee. "Look, I'm not trying to pressure you. If you don't want to go to the ball with me, I will understand. I won't like it, but I'll understand. All I'm trying to say is don't let whatever's doubting you hold you back. You may not get a second chance, you know?"

"This just isn't me," I say, gesturing to our castle setting. "I'm not a princess. I don't even know if I believe in fairy tales or happy endings." He starts to say something, but I push on. "After tomorrow we'll be on our separate ways. I have so much to figure out about my life, my future . . . I don't know if I'll be able to do that if my head is in the clouds."

Sad brown eyes blink back at me with disappointment. "Lanie, we haven't known each other long, and I can't tell you what to do. But I do know that life isn't all or nothing. It's not all rain or rainbows, work or play. You can have a little of both. I went through some rough times recently, but I'm here to tell you that if you don't mix it up, you'll drown."

I want to hear him. I do. But I have no idea how to let those two spaces coexist. My head and my heart have never worked together, my brain so insistent on driving that everything else has taken a permanent back seat. As much as I want to dance with Charming, I just don't see the point. "I'm sorry" is all I can say.

He lets out a long exhale through his nose, running frustrated fingers through his dark curls. "Okay," he whispers, standing up. Charming kisses the top of my head before stopping at the door. "By the way, my name is actually—"

"Wait!" I call out before he can reveal. "Don't tell me. It will just make everything harder."

He sighs, softly closing the door behind him. I stare at it for far too long, selfishly hoping he'll come running back. That everything is fine and that I did not just say good-bye to Prince Charming.

Instead, I end up sobbing into my pillow for what feels like an eternity. If I made the right choice, why does it feel so bad?

MADISON

"BIBBIDI-BOBBIDI-BOO"

I have been waiting for this day. Not just since the beginning of this week, but since the moment I first saw *Cinderella* on the screen. I remember it vividly: me, sitting on Grandma Jean's couch, a giant bowl of popcorn mixed with M&M'S in my lap. After falling off my tricycle and scraping my knee, I was a mess, but Grandma Jean scooped me up, saying she knew the perfect fix.

From the moment those golden title cards sparkled on screen, I was glued to my seat, transfixed by Cinderella's story. I loved her funny mouse friends and ridiculous stepsisters, and her magical makeover? Forget it! I was gone. Grandma

Jean had to sew sequins on to every article of clothing I owned including my underwear so I could sparkle like Cinderella.

My little toddler self looked up to her. How she was so kind despite her life being so rotten. How she made a terrible living situation tolerable. Being raised by my grandma instead of my parents sometimes made me feel like my home life was weird, but anytime I didn't feel normal, I reminded myself how Cinderella had an unconventional family, too, and her life turned out okay.

Today, I get my chance to walk in her shoes.

Or slippers, I should say.

I throw myself into my morning chores, hoping busy hands will quiet my busy mind. I should be skipping about to an endless refrain of "Bibbidi Bobbidi Boo"—four-year-old me demands it!—and yet I can't stop thinking about my fight with Lanie and my snuggle sesh with Val. Both of these smart, awesome women in my life see something equally special in me; they're rooting for me to find my way. But what is that way, exactly? Do I really have what it takes to make magic for a living? Now in the harsh light of day, I'm not so sure.

At least today is all about the fantasy.

The doorbell rings as I'm sweeping the foyer. When I answer the door, a royal courier bows and hands me a wax-sealed envelope.

"An urgent message from His Imperial Majesty," he says with a flourish.

I curtsy. "Thank you." Running my fingers over the creamy parchment, they itch to break open the seal. But, being the obedient Cinderella that I am, I run up the stairs and burst into Lady Tremaine's room, where she's leading my stepsisters in yet another failed music lesson.

Stepmother slams her fists into her piano's keys, a dissonant tone filling the room. "Cinderella, I warned you never to interrupt our—"

I skip over and present her with the envelope. "But this just arrived from the palace!" I cheer.

"From the palace?!" My stepsisters cry in unison, running to my side. We're all deep in character now, following the beats leading up to the ball. This is our last hurrah as a dysfunctional family, after all, so everyone's committed to doing it perfectly.

Drizella rips the letter from my hands. "Give it here!" she demands.

Anastasia fights backs. "Let me have it!" she snaps, grabbing it from her sister. They squabble for a second, all arms and high-pitched squeals before Lady Tremaine snatches the envelope with her bony fingers.

"I'll read it!" she announces to end the bickering. She takes her time, making a big show as if she is literally discovering this event for the first time. "Well . . . there's to be a ball!"

My sisters gasp. "A ball?!"

Quelle surprise!

"In honor of His Highness, the Prince!"

"Ooh, the Prince!"

You don't say!

"And, by royal command, every eligible maiden is to attend!" Stepmother proclaims. Everyone rejoices in this oh-so-unexpected news, their bustles bouncing up and down until I try to join in.

"Why, that means I can go, too!" I exclaim sweetly, pressing my palm to my heart.

Drizella bursts out laughing. "Her? Dancing with the Prince?"

Anastasia mocks me with a deep curtsy, saying in a nasally voice, "I'd be honored, Your Highness, would you mind holding my broom?" They link arms and dance around the room. Man, these two are on point. As Cinderella I should be offended by their judgment, but as Madison, I'm in awe of their live-action role-play skills.

But I stand my ground. "Well, why not? After all, I'm still a member of the family. And it says by royal command, EVERY eligible maiden is to attend."

With a raised brow, Lady Tremaine scans the letter again before reluctantly replying, "Yes . . . so it does." She pauses, evil schemes rolling through her head. "Well, I see no reason why you can't go. *If* you get all your work done."

"Oh, I will, I promise!" And with that, we go through the whole song and dance of everyone piling an obscene amount of work on me, even though we all know I don't have to lift a damn finger and I'll still be at that ball. I busy myself anyway, knowing I need to stay out of my room long enough to let a fellowship of mice and birds design a dress out of scraps.

After a few hours of hard labor (and some ignored chores; seriously, Stepmother added *clean the boiler* to my list, and I'm not even totally sure what a boiler is?), I wearily climb up my tower to find my "mother's" dress waiting for me, updated with Drizella's beaded necklace and Anastasia's sash. It's lovely, all pink and white and covered in ruffles. Light projections of mice and birds flutter around the room as they chant, "Surprise! Surprise! Surprise!"

"Oh, I never dreamed it! Thank you so much!" I say to my imaginary friends. I grab the dress and twirl around, giving the garment time to shine. It's too bad that the second I don this and go downstairs, it will get ripped to shreds, because it really is a screen-level worthy piece of costuming. If Imagineering can make this simple dress look so exquisite, I can't WAIT to see my actual gown. *Eeeeee!*

After a quick shower, I dress and run down the stairs, where my pretend family is getting ready to leave. They're all bustled up and heading out the door as I call out, "Wait! Please wait for me!"

Anastasia and Drizella turn, bright poufy feathers tucked into wigs spilling with ringlets. They both looking amazingly over the top, rocking their characters' confounding color palettes—Drizella in olive and robin-egg blue; Anastasia in a clash of pink and maroon. They could easily march in a Disneyland parade and completely steal the show. Even though they'll be clawing me apart in a second, the three of us share a knowing smile before slipping back into our antagonistic states.

"Mother, she can't!" Anastasia cries as she stomps her foot.

"It wouldn't be right!" Drizella chimes in.

"Girls, please!" Lady Tremaine sighs, quieting her fake offspring. "After all, we did make a bargain."

She steps closer, casting a shadow over me. My fashion success has put a wrench in her self-serving schemes, and there's no way she's letting that fly. A shiver runs down my spine as her green eyes bore into mine, her absolute distaste for my very existence conveyed in just a subtle twitch of her upper lip. I inch away, trapped between her and the staircase. There's no turning back now.

"How very clever," she sneers as she gently takes the end of my necklace in her hand. "These beads . . . they give it just the right touch. Don't you think so, Drizella?"

Drizella crosses her arms, sticking her nose up in the air. "No, I don't I think she—" Realization flashes in her eyes. "What? You little thief! They're MY beads! Give them here!" She charges toward me and rips the blue-green pearls right off my neck, glass beads scattering all over the floor.

"No!" I cry out, not even in pretend as the remnants of my necklace roll away. Drizella's eyes widen in shock; it's one thing to passively observe this on-screen but quite another to be the instigator. She cringes in apology, and I blink back to let her know it's okay. It's all part of the show.

We wait for Anastasia to join in the dress destruction, but after seeing the initial pass, she's frozen in place. Stepmother has to physically nudge her to shake loose an "Oh, and look! That's my sash!" Her voice catches as she tentatively approaches, jaw clenched. "She CAN'T!" Hands hover over my waist, unsure of how to rip the light pink sash away without being hurtful. One simple rip and the whole dress is already coming undone, designed to fall apart. Even with it being an act, it's still humiliating, leaving me exposed and vulnerable. I knew this was coming yet had no idea how it would really feel, my brain always skipping over to the good parts and ignoring this heartbreaking moment.

But rather than continue the free-for-all, my sisters break character, spinning on their heels to face our visibly disturbed matriarch.

"I'm sorry, I don't like this," Anastasia announces, dropping the sash.

"Me neither." Drizella puts her hands on her hips. "Can't we all just get to the ball already? It's been a week, and I want to dance." My heart leaps as my stepsisters take my sides in solidarity, shoulder to shoulder in Tremaine girl power.

Stepmother is not having it. Eyes on fire, nostrils flared, she came here to wreak havoc and will not rest until she sees it through. "Worthless, all of you!" she bellows, hitting her cane against the tiled foyer. "After all that I do! After all that I've done! And this is how you end things?" Her arms fling wide, her gauzy shawl slipping down her purple gown as she stares as us with such ferocity, I feel her tunneling into my soul. Fueled by anger she seemingly grows another foot taller; Lady Tremaine isn't a witch (that we know of), but I wouldn't be surprised if she somehow engulfed the château in flames just to spite us.

"Oh my god, just give it up already!" Drizella sighs over the dramatics. "We get it—you're evil. You win Queen Villain or whatever you're going for here. But I'm done and am ready to party."

"Same," Anastasia chimes in. "Being mean is too exhausting, and I need some snacks. Cinderella, find us at the ball later?"

I nod, clutching my tattered bodice. They pick up the ends of their gowns and glide away to their awaiting carriage. But Lady Tremaine hangs back, hovering above me but still decked in shadows. This woman is the master of *not* finding one's light, somehow always bathing her sneers in a blanket of darkness. Knowing that she's not a cast member who wasn't specifically trained to strike fear in the hearts of guests makes her menacing even more concerning.

Tilting her pointy chin to the top of the stairs, she glares at me from the corner of her yellow-green eyes. "Putting on a fancy gown doesn't change who you are, Cinderella," she taunts in an octave below her usual cadence. We're outside the realm of make-believe now, her words completely her own. Goose bumps spread across my exposed skin. "Take it from someone who knows: Dreams are for fools, and you'll never live up to the fantasies in your head. And of course, what do *you* have to contribute anyway? Probably nothing worthwhile."

A sinister smile curls across her lips as she finally exits, leaving me to take in the wreckage of torn-up fabric and broken jewelry scattered all around me. I stand there, shaking, telling myself it was all for show but unable to let that truth sink in. The way Lady Tremaine looked down at me—like I was nothing, like I would never make it anywhere—hit deep down, stirring up all those old feelings I've held on to for far too long. She knew, I don't know how, but she knew how to break me, hitting a nerve too raw to contain. I thought I would have to force myself to cry, but the tears come easily as I run out into the night, barreling through the darkness. I race through the garden, flinging myself onto a stone bench.

I bawl uncontrollably, and for a second, I wish we could stop this reenactment so I could compose myself. It's one thing to be in character, but it's completely another to be inconsolable. At this point I'm going to be so red and splotchy, it will take some serious magic to turn things around! I need my friend; I need Lanie and her sensible ways to tell me everything will be okay, that I'm not some hopeless screwup going nowhere. I lay my head on the garden bench, cool against my flushed skin. The night is so quiet all I hear are my stuttering sobs until a gentle voice says, "There, there."

I jerk back, one last sob caught in my throat. *Lanie?* But no, out of literal nowhere an elderly white woman has appeared next to me, wrapped in a blue cloak tied up with a pink bow. My fairy godmother! How in the . . . ? Where did she come from?

"Wha— I don't believe it!" I gasp. I look around, trying to find the trapdoor or other hidden sorcery that make this person materialize out of thin air.

She chuckles, cheeks full and rosy. "Nonsense. If you didn't believe, I couldn't be here. And here I am!"

Little iridescent sparkles hover in a halo all around her. Are there light projectors hidden in the trees, or . . . "Okay, but seriously, how did you get here?" I ask even though Cinderella never pressed for details.

"Oh, come, now, dry those tears," she says, sticking to the

script. "You can't go to the ball looking like that!" Fine, if she's not going to reveal her magic, then she's right, it's time to move along to the good stuff. I wipe my face clean, climbing up out of the dirt ready to be transformed. Let's do this!

She rolls up her sleeves, winking at me as she pulls out a twinkling magic wand. "Now then, the magic words . . ." My heart starts to race as playful orchestral music pipes in throughout the garden, the hopeful bounce of "Bibbidi-Bobbidi-Boo" flooding the night.

The Fairy Godmother lip-syncs the sweet, nonsensical lyrics while she skips over to a massive pumpkin, twirling her wand over its bright orange rind. It pulses up and down, wiggling in the dirt before leaping into the air, its leafy vines coiling and extending into four sweeping circles.

"Oh my god!" I call out, quickly covering my mouth. Unlike Cinderella, who observes all this wizardry with a quiet grace, I'm unable to contain my excitement. My eyes flit around looking for secrets, trying to find the hidden cast members turning dials and flicking switches to make all this come to life.

The gourd grows and grows right before my eyes, a swirl of sparkles wiping away its saturated color and leaving behind a glittering silver exterior. The Fairy Godmother waves her arms wildly as a cyclone of stars shoots from her wand; their light bursts through the darkness until the spell reaches its most frantic point, the music swelling with a background chorus of *aaahs* that sound just as amazed as I feel.

And there, rising out of the pumpkin patch, sits an elegant, shimmering coach, golden accents gleaming against its jack-o'-lantern frame. It's . . . it's . . . it's perfect, even more whimsical than the Cinderella carriage they use for weddings at Disneyland. While I'd gladly take a ride in either, this remarkable transport before me looks exactly like I'd dreamed, pulled from my heartstrings and made real.

"It's beautiful!" I cry, running toward it the second the music fades. I can't help but touch every detail—the wire-thin wheels, the pink velvet curtains in the window, the golden *C* inlay on the door—marveling at the accuracy. If only Grandma Jean could be here, her heart would be a puddle of pudding just like mine.

"Yes, yes, isn't it?" The Fairy Godmother smiles with self-satisfaction. But of course, the magic doesn't stop there. She proceeds to whip up the rest of my carriage team, pulling four white horses, a coachman, and a footman out of the darkness, each smiling and preening and ready to whisk me away. But with each transformative refrain of "Bibbidi-Bobbidi-Boo," I find myself getting more and more distracted, doing mental gymnastics to figure out how this is being accomplished. Where are they coming from? These are real horses. . . . Were they just waiting backstage? How were they able to stay so quiet until their big reveal? I picture Val tucked away somewhere, pockets full of sugar cubes while she calls cues into her headset. Is she watching me now, laughing over how geeked out I am? I want to get lost in the moment—I really, really do—but even more I want to know how the impossible is coming true. For the first time in my life

I'm actually less excited by the fantasy and more interested in the reality of what it takes to make dreams come true.

Talk about a magic spell.

Finally, it's time. With a transport and team designed for a princess, the Fairy Godmother beckons for me to get going. "Well, well, hop in, my dear! We can't waste time!"

I pick up the ends of my tattered dress. "But, uh . . ."

"Now, now, now, don't try to thank me," she interrupts, turning away with a bashful smile.

I have to wonder if this woman is a cast member with how effortlessly she's commanding this whole scene. But still, I gotta get that dress! "I do but, don't you think my dress . . . ?"

Without looking, she answers, "Yes, yes, it's lovely dear, love —" She gargles her words once she truly sees the remaining scrap of fabric hanging from my body. "Good heavens, child! You can't go in that!"

She scurries up to me, pretending to take measurements and choose a fabric based on my eye color. With all her hustle and bustle, she takes a quick second to squeeze my hand and give me a knowing nod, her kind face beaming with thrill. "Just leave it to me, what a gown this will be!" she says in an excited whisper.

She steps back, arms raising slowly as sparkles spill from the tip of her wand over to my feet, building into a whirlpool of light around my body. A flurry of strings accented by *oohs* and *aahs* plays; oh god, it's all happening so fast! A tingle runs through me as the Fairy Godmother sings her iconic chorus.

And somehow, pulled from the screen and draped over my

286

body is the most incredible garment created by Disneykind. To say it sparkles is an understatement: It radiates, casting a glowing aura on the ground. I thought it would be heavy, but the fabric feels like starlight, gauzy and rich at the same time. I give it a twirl and watch in awe as the silvery sheen floats all around me, and there, poking out from under the fluffy petticoat, are the iconic glass slippers.

Oh. My. God. THE GLASS SLIPPERS! And they're . . . surprisingly comfortable? They smile up at me, the toes shimmering against my dress's hem. I love them and don't ever want to take them off. Lose a shoe? Forget that! I'm stuffing these in my suitcase and wearing them for the rest of my life.

"Did you ever see such a beautiful dress?" I ask no one in particular. Because of course they haven't: This is unreal. I can't stop spinning; I can't stop smiling! I float over to the garden fountain, admiring my reflection in the inky water. Yes, yes, it's all there: the gloves, the earrings, the headband with the sweeping updo. I am the most Cinderella-ed Cinderella of all time. "It's like a dream! A wonderful dream come true!"

"Yes, my child, but like all dreams, I'm afraid this can't last forever," the Fairy Godmother says with a frown. "On the stroke of twelve, the spell will be broken and everything will be as it was before."

"I understand. It's more than I ever hoped for." Because it really is. Yes, I look freaking amazing and this entire day has hit every note, regardless of how sour or sweet. But it's even more than that. As much as I love being in this moment, I have a sudden realization.

I want to *make* moments like these, to help create this mind-bending level of fantasy for others. I want to grab the stars and polish them up to an unbelievable shine, scattering them at the feet of those who need them most. I want to put my lifelong study of happily-ever-afters to good use and make my own dreams come true in the process.

This is it! This is my path.

And finally, I know exactly how to start.

LANIE

"SOMEDAY MY PRINCE WILL COME"

I hear it before I see it.

A frantic clattering of hooves and wheels pounding down the dirt paths to DunBroch. Most of my clansmen left Scotland at sunset to attend Prince Charming's ball, everyone eager to attend the biggest party of the week. Staying behind while the rest of the world rages is what I'm best at: brainy Lanie alone in the dorm with her books. But Merida's room is sadly lacking in reading materials, so instead I wander around the castle, daydreaming about frilly dresses and royal engagements, things that rarely, if ever, cross my mind.

They're not unwelcome, though. In fact, I kind of like thinking about something that's just pure fun. Fanciful, joyful thoughts that have no bearing on my future or career, existing only to make me smile.

It's nice. I wouldn't mind them stopping by more often.

But in fact, something else entirely makes an appearance, breaking through my solitude. Confused by all the commotion I look out the window to see a glowing pumpkin led by four white horses come barreling into the courtyard, dust flying everywhere as it comes to halt. What in the world? Did someone steal Cinderella's carriage for a joyride around the island?

I run outside to get a better look and am instantly transfixed by the glittering coach, its silver sparkles completely out of place in Merida's rustic setting. Curious to see who would carjack such a magical transport—a villain, maybe?—I tiptoe toward it, trying to sneak a peek through the carriage window, but then Madison, looking like she just waltzed off the movie screen, spills out of the pumpkin, glass slippers gliding on the dirt.

"Oh my god!" I gasp as she floats toward me. She is an absolute vision, a real-life incarnation of Cinderella from her silver-gloved hands to her impossibly glittering gown. She looks so perfect, so exactly right, she has to be high on cosplay realness, and yet if that's true, why is she here? Shouldn't she be making her grand entrance at the ball? "You look amazing!"

"I know, right?" Madison beams, giving a dramatic twirl for effect. "I mean, this is next level. The shoes are actual glass!"

I cringe. "Yikes! How does that feel?"

"Honestly? I've worn worse. I do have a little foot sweat

going, but that's to be expected. Glass isn't exactly breathable. But it's fine, I won't be wearing them long anyway," she says with a wink.

"Oh of course, because you'll lose one running down the castle stairs?"

She wiggles her eyebrows. "No, because I'm giving them to you."

I stare at her, unsure of how to respond. I've spent the last twenty-four hours haunted by our fight, feeling so far away from my best friend that I didn't know how we'd ever come back together. Planning big, thoughtful gestures has never been my thing, and after how I deceived her, I didn't expect Madison to be the one to make the first move. But now she's here, fully ascended into her truest form, offering me a shoe? I don't understand at all.

"Madison, I—"

"Don't try to fight me again; I won't take no for an answer." She puts her hands on her sparkly hips.

"About that . . ." I say. A geyser of nerves shoots up into my chest, but I press on. "I just want to tell you that I'm so, so sorry. About everything. You are my best friend, and I will do whatever I can to regain your trust. Your friendship means the world to me, and I can't believe I screwed things up so badly."

She wafts over to me, her movements like a cloud. "I'm sorry, too. I shouldn't have lashed out about how easy your life seems. I know you work hard, and I'm here to help you find a new path if that's what you want."

"And I didn't mean to imply that you're immature or

flighty!" I cringe at the thought. "I get jealous sometimes of how you're so carefree, and it all came out wrong."

Madison continues. "I pushed you into this world and then left you all on your own. I think we both got swept up in unexpected story lines, but the most important one is right here." She reaches for me, clasping her gloved hands around mine. "How about this: Let's promise each other to be honest and open from here on out."

"Deal," I agree, squeezing her palms. She beams back at me. "And I'll start: I honestly don't know what you're doing here and not at the ball."

She releases me and spins out in a dramatic twirl, ending on a perfect princess pose. "So! Okay, as it turns out, my life has been building up to this moment in ways I never could have imagined. In fact, I want tonight to be the maiden voyage of Madison Makes the World a More Magical Place, with you as the star!"

"Okay . . . I still don't understand."

"I know. I'll explain it all on the way there. But the too-long-didn't-read version is that you're playing Cinderella tonight."

Okay, now I'm *really* lost. "What?"

She gestures to the pumpkin coach like she's a game show host. "I know it's not a dark chocolate pumpkin marshmallow chai, but I brought you *this* pumpkin as a peace offering!"

Madison passing on playing a princess? None of this makes any sense! "You seem really psyched about this, but no matter what you're scheming, there's no way I could take this from you."

She bites her lip, sighing impatiently. "You're not taking, I'm giving. It's a win-win, I promise. But please, as always I am reaaaaaaally running late, so get in the carriage and I will spill the whole plan, okay?"

"But, the thing is—" I break off, saddened by the truth of what I'm about to admit. "I ended things with Charming."

She shakes her head. "Wait, what? Why?"

I shrug. "Because . . . a lot of reasons. We're going home tomorrow. I don't even know what will be waiting for me there. And, I already had my hero moment. Now it's time for yours."

She wrinkles her nose. "Okay, I appreciate this and every-thing, but, Lanie, you like him. And clearly he likes you. Girl, he is CUTE! You don't have to break up! That makes no sense!"

"But, we'll probably break up anyway, don't you think? What kind of future could we have? I don't even know where he lives and I have so much more school ahead of me and—"

"Hold up," she interrupts. "Let me stop you right there. First rule of Madison's Daydreaming Academy is that love defies logic. You do not have to have this figured out now."

"Yeah, but—"

She presses a gloved finger to my lips. "No buts. Follow your heart, not your head."

"But—"

"I SAID NO BUTS!" She narrows her eyes. "Now tell me the truth: Do you *want* to dance with Charming? Would that make you happy? Or more stressed out? Because we can figure out something else magical for you if so."

I take her hand in mine. "No, no it all sounds . . . amazing, actually. It's just important to me that *you* get your special moment."

"I am getting it," she reassures me. "It's just looking different than I thought."

I don't know what to say; I don't know what to think! Madison wants me to play Cinderella? At the one social event she's been waiting for her entire life? What is going on? I can't imagine what would make her flip the script like this, but if she's so insistent on giving up her crown, there must be a good reason. There's a spark in her blue eyes I've never seen before, and she's so happy, so fired up, I guess I need to let her see this through. "If I say okay, can we please promise to never fight again?"

She melts into me. "OMG, yes. That was awful! No more fighting ever." We seal our wish with a hug, relief coursing through me.

Then Madison all but pushes me into the pumpkin, which is surprisingly plush inside; soft pink fabric covers every surface stitched with silver thread along the seams. Despite the fact that I'm sitting in a gourd, it actually feels quite spacious. . . . That is until Madison climbs in, her massive dress filling up every available nook and cranny. Her gloved hand taps on the window behind her as she calls, "Monsieur, to the ball!" and the carriage takes off, escaping into the night.

She immediately starts undressing, which is easier said than done. Changing out of a fairy-tale ball gown while traveling in a high-speed pumpkin is no simple task, but Madison is on a mission, quickly squirming out of her corset while instructing me to strip as well.

"So, give me the one-minute rundown on Charming," she says once she's successfully removed her legs from her skirt. "Like I know he's super cute, but what else?"

I blush, and not just because I'm sitting in my underwear. No more secrets, I owe her that. "Well, he's funny and considerate. When we're together, I feel less like an anxious stress ball."

"Aww!" Madison gushes. "That's so rare for you!"

"I know!" We hit a bump in the road, gossamer fabric flying everywhere. "What about you? What is this all about?"

We trade outfits, Madison shimmying into my casual Merida attire before helping me tackle Cinderella's gown. "Okay. So you know how I've pretty much never found My Thing? Well, I think I finally did . . . working as a real Disney cast member! Val thinks I have what it takes to help make people's dreams come true, and I honestly never thought it was possible. But then I realized, I just might have something to contribute—passion and Disney knowledge and a hunger to keep learning. In any case, I can figure it out, work my way up to a career here. And there's nothing I want more."

I pause mid-bustle, breathless with pride. I've never heard Madison talk like this before: excited about the future, excited about herself. "Really?"

She nods, glowing with happiness. "Really! And what better way to start my marathon of dream making than with my best friend?" She claps her hands, bouncing in her seat as an unstoppable smile spreads across her face.

A lump of joy catches in my throat as I watch her bop back and forth in goofy glee. My dear sweet aimless best friend has finally found something to be excited about, something to pour her whole generous heart into and be proud of. I know how long she's wanted this and how desperately she's searched; to see her at the exact beginning of what's to come is so over-whelming wonderful, I can't help but cry.

"Gah! What are you doing?" Madison recoils as my tears threaten to drip on the dress.

"It's just . . . that . . ." I struggle to speak, my words bump-ing around in tandem with the carriage. "You've searched for your calling for so long, and . . . this place *really is* Happily Ever Island!"

She smiles, shaking her head at me. "Oh, Lanie, did my little Aquarius just suddenly become a dreamer?"

I laugh and wipe my face. "Says the Gemini who finally made a decision!"

"Ooh, astrology burn!" She gives me a playful shove. "I love it. But you're right, it's like I've grown or something," she says with a shoulder bounce. "And see? It's never too late to shift your path." She eyes me knowingly. "Look at us: Two very amazing people with very bright futures."

"Agreed," I say with a sniffle. If Madison can figure out what's next, so can I.

The road beneath shifts from dirt to cobblestone, signal-ing our imminent arrival at Charming's castle. Madison kicks it into high gear, fast fingers working up the buttons on my bodice and through my messy hair. Even without a brush, she manages to give my short strands some volume, using her glittering headband to pouf out the front.

"Ugh, this is much easier when a fairy godmother dresses you!" she says as we struggle to pull up the elbow-length gloves. "Still, you look pretty damn princessey, my friend."

There's no mirror in the pumpkin, so I'll have to take her word for it. I'm doing my best not to let the weight of all this fabric drag me into an unwelcome pit of stress; every time I start to feel my nerves twitch I just look at Madison, blissfully working away to make me a star. The final touch is the shoes, which she hands over to me with the caution and care of a surgeon handling a heart, which I guess in her eyes, they are.

"You were right!" I exclaim once the glassy gems are on my feet. "They are surprisingly comfortable!"

Madison wiggles her fingers as she whispers, "Magic! Oh! Speaking of which . . ."

Our pumpkin coach pulls up to the castle, and even though I've seen multiple royal estates in the past week, this one blows them all away. Both our jaws drop as we take it all in: white stone lit up in an ombré of blues, blurring the lines of structure and sky. Turrets so tall they seem to scrape the stars. Warm light spilling from every window and door, a mixture of laughter and symphony inviting all to join in the merriment. Less imposing than the Beast's castle, more stately than Merida's, Charming's home is a picture-book manor of majesty, befitting such a handsome prince.

I wonder what he'll think when he sees me tonight. Will he be excited? Upset? Frustrated after I made such a big deal about not coming? I'm hopeful he'll forgive me and let the magic of the evening carry him away. But . . . but . . .

As the footman swings open the carriage door, I'm suddenly scared, my stomach churning with its usual undercurrent of nausea. Madison, easily detecting my emotional state, snaps her fingers in my face and forces me to focus on something else.

"Hey, hey—no stress barfs," she demands. "Tonight is going to be amazing and vomit-free." She takes my gloved hands and I squeeze tight, wishing we could enter the ball together.

"Madison," I say with a shaky tremor. "You're sure about this?"

She beams, clutching me tight. "A thousand percent. Go get that prince—I've got my own princess to hunt down."

"I love you," I tell her.

"Love you, too, babe." She winks. "Now go! You only have until midnight!"

Once outside the carriage, my feet wobble in the glass slippers; I'm still not entirely comfortable wearing a dress, especially such an iconic gown that's practically dripping with romance. It's foreign, sure, but not in a bad way. Even with so much fabric on my body I feel light and airy, like if I jumped, the warm night breeze could simply carry me up the entry stairs. Madison's always forcing me to twirl, so I give it a go, spinning 'round and 'round to watch the silver sheen magnify by the castle's glow. I can almost feel the sparkles melting into my veins and filling me with a bubbling excitement.

Tonight is going to be good. I am going to *make* it good.

Picking up the ends of my dress, I hurry up the many, many stairs until I'm breathless in the grand foyer, a soaring hallway painted in a soft blush and lined with red carpet. Two rows of guards nod at me as I tiptoe past; I honestly have no idea where I'm supposed to go and consider asking one of them for directions. But instead I follow the music, a flurry of strings and horns signifying the pageantry ahead. With every step, my anticipation grows and my heart flips over what's to come. Soon, I will be dancing with Charming, his arms around me, our faces close. The thought alone makes me pick up the pace until I've found the ballroom and the party already in full swing.

From the balcony I take a beat to enjoy the scene below. Every island guest is here tonight, dressed to impress, swaying in a sea of metallics and jewels, tiaras and tunics. Cast members weave throughout the crowd carrying silver trays loaded with appetizers and champagne flutes; a modest orchestra plays a waltz under a crystal chandelier. I spot Dorothy and Sal gliding across the floor in each other's arms, as well as many others who've popped up throughout the week. But they all fade away when I see him.

Charming, standing before his throne and bowing for every guest who saunters past. Dressed in a long-sleeved tunic with gold-and-red adornments, crisp white against his dark skin, he looks so devastatingly handsome I have to hold on to the handrail for fear of literally falling for him. I want to go to him, to leap into his arms, but I'm overcome by the beauty of it all, my glass feet frozen. I will him to see me standing here alone atop the stairs, and after one more polite bow he does, brown eyes meeting mine from across the room. He squints, laughing to himself as he tries to decide if it's really me, but ultimately his heart takes over, propelling him through the crowd and up the stairs until we're together again. He hugs me and spins me around, my skirt flying as our bodies collide in joy.

He presses his face into my neck, squeezing my waist. "How?" he asks breathlessly. "I thought . . ."

I take his sweet face in my gloved hands, rubbing my thumb over his dimple. "I guess we have our own fairy godmother."

Amid whispers and extra confused stares, he leads me to the center of the ballroom, music swelling right on cue as the lighting dims for optimal romance. Guests form an adoring circle all around us, but I keep my gaze on him, the only magic I'm interested in tonight. As he guides my right arm out in the proper waltz stance, I realize I've never once in my life danced like this, and certainly not in glass heels.

"Do you know how to waltz?" I whisper as my left hand awkwardly grabs a fistful of dress.

"Not at all." He laughs. "I skipped my waltzing lesson to hang with you. But follow my lead, I guess?" And I do, instantly losing myself in a swirl of scenery. The costumes, the music . . . him. This amazing guy is holding me close: me! Even after pushing him away he's here, guiding me through this daydream. He's too good, too wonderful: I can't believe I was going to let this moment pass me by.

But before I can truly float away, Cinderella's voice comes chiming in over the orchestra, her dreamy vibrato breaking my trance as she sings "So This Is Love."

I pinch Charming's hand. "Oh shoot, are we supposed to be singing?" I panic.

He frowns, looking around the room as if there are cue cards hidden in the corner. "Uh, I do not know the words if we are. My Prince Charming itinerary literally featured no dialogue for tonight except for 'Wait, don't go!'"

"A man of few words."

"Yes, but they are good ones. Because I don't want you to go."

Charming leads me into a spin, and for the briefest of moments, I spot Madison on the edge of the crowd, snuggled up next to a very fancy Val. My heart skips a beat at seeing the two of them together; I'm glad they found each other. I send my friend a subtle thumbs-up behind Charming's back, which she returns, but even those few seconds looking away from him are too much. I realize I need more, not just of his handsome face but of who he is deep down. I've crossed the point of no return, and I want to see what's on the other side.

"I'm ready now," I tell him once we're pressed up against each other again. "Tell me about you. The real you."

His mouth pinches in doubt, but his eyes shine in triumph. "You sure? It won't ruin things?"

"It's a risk I'm willing to take."

"Fair enough." He grins, letting go of my waist to bend into a deep bow. "Fairest Lanie, my name is Ethan Young. It's nice to officially make your acquaintance."

"Ethan." I blush, dipping into a curtsy. "Hello."

Our waltz resumes as he continues. "So I'm a junior at UW-Madison, Communications major. I like books and movies, comedies mostly. I dabble in cooking, though I'm much better at eating."

"And Disney?"

He shrugs. "More of an accidental fan. See, I came here with my mom: She's been battling cancer for the past two years, and when she finally kicked it this winter, she decided we needed an emotional reset. She won the tickets here, and I couldn't say no as her plus-one, and besides, we watched *a lot* of Disney movies while she was recovering. It was actually kind of fun. She's been busy playing Maleficent this whole time, which is very against type, but she's feeling pretty badass after defeating cancer."

"Your mom . . . is Maleficent?" I think back to that day, how Ethan was so excited to be part of that scene. "So that's why you wanted to join that hero moment."

"That, and dragons are awesome. She's here tonight, somewhere. . . . We'll have to go say hi."

"Okay." I don't know what else to say. We've barely scratched the surface, but I can already feel myself falling harder, the details of his world pulling me in. I want to know more, more, everything at once; who are his best friends and what does he do when he's all alone? What is his favorite food, favorite book? The ball would end long before I could find this all out, but I'm hoping tonight won't be the last page in our story.

I look at him in awe, mind racing with questions, but when I don't say a thing, he asks, "So . . . what do you think?"

"Hmm, let me see." I tap my chin. "Cute guy who loves his mom and knows how to cook? Ugh, pass."

He feigns shock.

"I'm kidding, obviously!" I cry. "You really are Prince Charming."

Ethan pulls me in until our lips are close enough to touch. It's hard to breathe, let alone think of an answer when he asks, "And what about you, Dr. Lanie?"

"What about me?" I sigh, eyes trained on his mouth.

"Do you think you'll live happily ever after?"

For once in my life, I'm not worrying about the future. Here—right now—is exactly where I need to be. Tomorrow we'll be packing our suitcases and flying home to Chicago, where a stack of books and an irate Mom will be waiting. I don't know what will happen with my career, my life, or this beautiful man holding me tight, but if pretending to be a princess has taught me anything, it's that I don't have to be just one thing. I can be smart and silly. Focused and frivolous. My heart and my head can each play a part on where I'm going next without having the path drawn in permanent ink. Is that scary? Yes. But is it okay? I don't know! And I don't need to have it all figured out just yet. Tonight is about starlight and slippers, pumpkins and princes, and there's nothing wrong with that.

"You know, I'm not sure," I say honestly. "But I'm excited to find out."

❀

We dance for hours, cycling through every craze from the waltz to the floss, and seeing Sal dab it up on the dance floor made me laugh so hard I almost cried. I'm not even sure how my feet are not screaming in these slippers, but I'll take it; any magic that keeps me in Ethan's arms is okay by me. Throughout the night I tried to find Madison again, but she's completely disappeared. Maybe she's snuck her way behind the scenes or is making out with Val in a royal bedchamber, but either way, at a quarter to midnight, I suddenly have an idea on how to return the gift she gave to me.

"Hey, come with me," I say to Ethan, dragging him away from the ball after a lively samba.

"Where are we going?" he asks. "Are you luring me into your pumpkin?"

I snort. "Oh wow, that sounded surprisingly dirty."

He stops in his tracks. "That's not what I— Actually no, I stand by it."

I press my palms into his chest as he kisses the top of my head. "C'mon, we don't have much time, and I want to do something for Madison."

We race out of the castle into the cool night air; it feels good against our flushed cheeks. It's so calm out here compared to the packed party inside, but with the minutes ticking away, there's no time to enjoy the serenity. Halfway down the massive flight of stairs, I stop and remove my right shoe, leaving it alone in the moonlight.

"How do you know she'll find it?" Ethan asks.

"Trust me, when the clock strikes twelve, she'll be out here," I confirm. "Madison's a stickler for Disney details."

"Won't you be walking all lopsided now?"

"Not if you carry me." I hop into his arms, something I never would have done a week ago. But it's a whole new world now, and I'm letting my heart lead the way.

"As you wish, Princess." He kisses me lightly before adding, "You know what? I get it now."

"Get what?"

"Prince Charming! His deal! Maybe he's less swashbuckling than the other dudes, but in the end he falls in love, and there's nothing boring about that."

I smile. "I'd have to agree."

"What should we do now? Hide behind this fountain and watch her find the slipper?"

I swallow down a laugh. "I have to say: For someone so good looking, you are really quite dorky."

He beams. "You love it."

From the comfort of his arms, I reply, "You know, I think I do."

MADISON

"A DREAM IS A WISH YOUR HEART MAKES"

It's weird to watch your best friend chase after your former dream. Seeing Lanie slip on my Cinderella persona and float up the castle stairs is like a strange out-of-body experience, the glittering gown waving good-bye as I pivot toward something even better. Look at me, growing up! But not all the way, because gross. After all, I'm still sitting here in this pumpkin coach committing every single detail to memory but whatever. How often do I get to admire fairy-tale settings like this? Besides my yearly pilgrimage to Disneyland, of course. No wonder they chose Cinderella's royal abode as Disney World's signature icon: This castle is EVERYTHING. I could sit here all night admiring the towers and shimmering arches, but like I told Lanie, we only have until midnight, so I better get a move on.

Once inside, it hits me how incredibly out of place I am in Merida's casual dress. I got so caught up in the moment I didn't think to bring a backup ensemble, but I hate not matching the theme. Everyone around me is sporting massive bustles, feathered hairpieces, and elbow-length gloves; meanwhile my long-sleeved blue gown is like three centuries out of style. Next time I stage a spur-of-the-moment surprise gesture like this, I need to be better prepared.

The ballroom is seriously to die for, with enough music and food to last well into tomorrow. Even though Disney kind of lets you inside the castles at the parks, it's never like this, all free range to sneak away to wherever you heart desires. Part of me wants to run wild through every corridor and ransack the closets to change into a more appropriate outfit, but all I really want to find is Val and tell her how I feel—finally put it all out there and have a real conversation about us—which may prove difficult since the castle is packed with literally every person on the island tonight.

I weave through the room to the sound of harpsichord and strings, grabbing some passed cheese ball hors d'oeuvres as I go. *Mmm, cheese.* Suddenly, the lights dim as a circle forms in the middle of the room; I can't see but the couple of the hour must have encountered each other for the first time. Brie in hand, I fight my way to catch a glimpse of Lanie and Charming, but there's too much tulle and too many tiaras in my way to get a good look.

The guests in front of me twitter in confusion.

"Is that Cinderella?"

"I thought that woman was playing Merida, though?"

Ha-ha! Yes! I didn't even realize how pulling a freaky Friday with my bestie would leave guests confused about Cinderella's identity, just like in the movie. I AM A GENIUS! I smile to myself, wondering if Val will now be searching for me, too. She has to have noticed it's not me out there and is probably furiously flipping through her clipboard for answers. I will have to gloat about this moment to her later.

Finally, I spot her, standing by the orchestra like a 1940's vixen ready to take the mic and melt hearts. She looks . . . Goddamn. One side of her hair is pinned up in an elaborate twist, with sparkly bobby pins so small they look like starlight woven through her dark locks. She wears an off-the-shoulder form-fitting sapphire-blue gown that's completely wrong for the time period but hugs her curves so perfectly who even cares. But what I really can't take my eyes off of is the simple swipe of pink gloss across her lips, tugging at my insides in a way that is deeply unfair. She has no right to be this beautiful.

Would it be wrong to steal Cinderella's thunder and kiss Val in the center of the ballroom? Maybe. Can I control myself not to? No guarantees.

She catches me mid-ogle, shaking her head at me from across the room. After whispering something to the cello player, she saunters my way, silk-covered hips putting me in a state.

"So, what, you ditched your own fantasy?" Val laughs in disbelief.

I shrug like it's nothing. "Who said I did?"

"Um, Lanie wearing your dress out there says you did. I was just about to send out a search party for you since I thought you'd be dead before giving this up."

I smile, happy she already knows me this well. "Yeah, well, dressing up was fun, but as it turns out, I found a fantasy that's even more satisfying. See that out there?" I point to the dance floor. "An amazing person helped me realize that I can make dreams come true. I worked real magic to help two people realize they are in looooooove."

Val raises an eyebrow, but I can tell she's impressed. "I see."

"By the way," I say. "You look like an actual fairy-tale goddess right now."

"You think?" She turns around real slow, pausing with her backside to me to give a flirtatious glance over her shoulder.

That's it, she's too cute. I can't think of a more perfect place to officially start our love story. This is happening now. "Val, I want you to know—"

I move in closer, but she stops me with a "Be right back; I have to cue the music."

The string quartet kicks off "So This Is Love," a ballad so on the nose I feel like Val is reading my mind.

She returns, grabbing my hand. "C'mon, let's watch your friend."

"Oh, there's no way Lanie knows the words to this, or that this song even exists."

"Even better!" She laughs. Val pushes through the crowd of onlookers, most of whom recognize her and let us through for a front-row seat of the royal waltz.

Lanie, my beautifully awkward friend, floats in the arms of her handsome prince, having the time of her life. I've never seen her so light, so uninhibited, and I know I made the right choice, especially as Val's hand slowly meanders to my lower back, making all my arm hair stand at attention.

As she spins across the room Lanie's eyes briefly meet mine, an even dopier grin spreading across her face. Upon seeing Val and me together, my best friend shoots me a quick thumbs-up behind Charming's back, which I instantly return. What a dork, I love her.

"I still can't believe you gave up this big moment," Val says, watching them. "All the cast members are seriously confused as to why Merida showed up in Cinderella's slippers."

I turn toward her, our hips touching. "I just thought . . . What's the point of dancing with a prince if he's not what I'm after?"

"Oh yeah?" She angles herself my way, the light catching her glossy, grinning lips. "And what's that?"

Okay, this is it! I have totally fallen, swept away by a pretty girl's smile, unable to resist. But it feels different this time. I'm not just swept by the magic of the perfect musical cue, the dreamy setting, the opulent costumes. I'm swept by this smart, witty, beautiful woman who geeks out about the same things I do, whom I can't wait to do it all with—the magical moments as well as the real and messy ones. I curl my arm around her waist and move our torsos to touch; we're so close I can almost taste that lip gloss. "Val, I know I said I wasn't looking to be tied down, but that was before and I need you to know . . ." I close my eyes and lean in for the kiss but instead of her mouth I'm met with her fingertips, lightly keeping me just beyond reach.

"Can you hold that thought?" she whispers. "I'm still technically on the clock." My heart sinks. Did I do it again, misread the whole situation? Then she continues, uttering the six most magical words I've ever heard. "But I get off at midnight . . ."

I swallow hard. "Twelve-oh-one, then?"

"It's a date."

Val leaves me to do a quick round of check-ins, so I head over to the bar, helping myself to a glass of something pink and bubbly. Mid-sip I spot my stepmother alone in literally the only dark corner of the castle. Good god, this woman. Even when everyone else is letting go and letting loose, she still looks ready to crush the dreams of anyone who dares cross her path.

"Hey, Ma!" I cheer, raising my glass as I walk over to her fortress of solitude. "Great party, huh?"

"Cinderella?" she gasps, examining my outfit in confusion. "What are you doing here? Shouldn't you be—"

"Dancing with the prince? Yeah, no. I'm good." I grin. "But I did want to tell you how completely awful you are, and I mean that in the best possible way." Green eyes glare at me. "No, seriously! Your commitment to being a nonstop nightmare was really something, so thanks for the ridiculously accurate Cinderella experience. Brava!" I give a chef's kiss and sashay away, ready to be reunited with my girl.

The music's tempo picks up the pace, and the room erupts into applause, everyone eager to dance now that Cinderella and Charming's moment has passed. I search for Val among the sea of bouncing heads, but she finds me first, wrapping her arms around my waist from behind and dragging me backward through a door.

"Hey!" I call out in fake protest. "Don't you want to dance?"

"I'd love to but, I need to check in with the kitchen," she admits once she's let me go. "Want to join me?"

"Do you mean, do I want to see even more backstage setup?" I reply. "Because you know the answer is always yes."

She leads me through the castle hallways, which are way less themed but somehow even more enchanting. I'm not sure I will ever tire of seeing how Disney really works. The kitchen is typical of any restaurant setup, chefs working overtime to send out mini masterpieces for the guests to enjoy. After she ensures everything is in order, Val and I tuck ourselves into a corner piled with plates of macarons, éclairs, and other French pastries, and start sharing stories as we snack. She tells me all about cast member life and some of the absurd fires she's had to extinguish over the past week; I laugh to the point of tears as she recalls the drama of Snow White getting poisoned apple stuck in her hair, the sticky potion coating adhered to the ends of her perfectly manicured bob. I tell her all about my new mission to become a Disney employee, and she gives me all her tips about getting into the Disney College Program, what kind of classes to focus on, and résumé suggestions. I've never—ever—been psyched to discuss this stuff, but talking to Val makes it feel less like work and more like an adventure I can't wait to take, especially since there's hope she may pop up along the way. Turns out she's a hospitality and tourism major at Western Illinois, which is only a couple of hours away from Chicago.

"I wish my Grandma Jean could see all this," I tell Val as I lick frosting off my fingers.

"Was she a big Disney fan?"

"The biggest. She took me on my first Disney trip and sat next to me for every movie."

"Ah, so she's the one to blame for all this." Val waves her hand in my general direction. I reach to smack her away, but instead our fingers entwine, sending a jolt from head to toe. The pastries are instantly dethroned as the most delicious thing in the room.

"My grandma always loved the fireworks." Val grins, eyes glimmering with a faraway memory. "Said they were just like me, that someday I would burst open and show the world all my sparkle."

"Well, she was right," I say. "Everyone on the island has been touched by your light. This place couldn't run without you."

"You really think that?"

"Hello? Obviously. Who else would rescue fair maidens from an evil stepparent or help ice queens complete their solos? You've been turning fantasy into reality at every step, especially for me."

She blushes, setting down her plate of treats. "You know what I think?"

"Tell me."

"I think your grandma Jean would be proud of you tonight," she says. I almost choke on my croissant. "I know I didn't know her, but I bet seeing her granddaughter follow Cinderella's kind, selfless footsteps would've really made her happy."

Her words pull at the last seam I've been trying to hold together. All this time, I've wanted to be like my grandma, to grow old without really growing up. I thought that's what she wanted for me, but maybe I was wrong. Maybe there is a certain kind of magic in finding your place, in learning about who you are and where you belong. It doesn't mean you have to give up the things you love or abandon parts of your heart; actually, it's about leaning into your instincts even more. I can go after what I want without apology and live my best life in my own way. And that's exactly what I intend to do.

A fat tear rolls down my face. "Thank you," I gasp.

Val bites her lip. "Oh shoot, I didn't mean to make you cry." She scoots closer to me, gently running her thumb across my cheek. Even after the tear is wiped away she holds steady, fingers lightly stroking my jawline, my earlobe. I lean into her palm and smell the vanilla frosting on her skin. All the commotion of the kitchen disappears as I hyper focus on this incredible woman looking at me.

"No, it's okay. I loved what you said. You have no idea how much that means to me . . . how much you mean to me."

She smiles in relief, moving even closer. Her hand slides back up into my hair, and with only inches between us, I almost lose myself completely just before spotting a clock on the wall behind her.

It's 11:58.

"Oh my gosh!" I jump back in alarm.

"What? What's wrong?" Val startles. I point to the clock. "Yeah, I know, my shift's almost over."

I take her hands in mine and say, "No, it's almost midnight! Glass slippers! I want to see Cinderella lose her glass slipper before the spell is broken!"

Val pinches her lips together trying to hold back a smile. "I'd make fun of you, but honestly I want to see that, too. C'mon." Palm in palm, we burst back into the ballroom to find a way more banging party than we left. The string quartet retired their bows in favor of a DJ who's playing hip-hop remixes of Disney jams: a killer version of "I Just Can't Wait to Be King" has everyone on the floor. Observing a crowd constrained by corsets try to dance it out would be amazing people-watching if I had the time, but among all the bustles getting down, Lanie and Charming are nowhere to be seen.

"We couldn't have missed them, right?" I shout against the thumping bass. "We still have a few seconds before—"

BONG!

The clock strikes twelve, ricocheting its warning throughout the room.

BONG!

Everyone stops dancing, necks craning to find the source.

BONG!

I can practically feel the floor vibrating, prompting my feet to move faster toward the exit.

"Go, go, go!" Val encourages me from behind, pushing

me through all the gyrating ball gowns. This is my last chance to witness a hero moment on the island, and I don't want to miss it.

BONG!

Breathless, we escape out of the castle to the top of the stairs, only there's no panicked princess in sight. No flurry of fabrics, no royal guard in hot pursuit: Val and I are the only ones fleeing into the night, which makes no sense at all.

BONG!

"Oh, that clock! Old killjoy!" I yelp up at the bell tower.

"Nice." Val nods in acknowledging my thematic reference.

BONG!

"But seriously, where's Lanie?" I ask. "The pumpkin coach is still here, so she didn't leave. . . ." Did she forget? Lanie doesn't have Disney filmography tattooed on her heart like me, but I'm pretty sure Cinderella losing her slipper at the ball has transcended general pop culture knowledge. Plus, we talked about it earlier, so where even is she?

"I can radio the team to see if anyone's seen them," Val suggests.

But that's when I see it. A small shimmer calling to me from halfway down the staircase; a tiny treasure waiting to be discovered. One glass slipper left behind, but there's no way this was an accident. Lanie knew I'd never miss this moment; she had to have left this here for me. I look around the courtyard wondering if she's hiding nearby, but when I don't see her, I move to collect my prize, pressing it against my heart and willing myself not to cry.

This is my hero moment. And I know exactly what to do with it.

"Fair maiden!" I call to Val, her sapphire dress shimmering in the moonlight. "Please, take a seat." I gesture to the step before me, and while she initially frowns, seeing the slipper turns her confusion into anticipation, lips curving to the right in that irresistible lopsided smile of hers. She sits, smoothing down her gown as I kneel before her.

"What are you doing?" She laughs, even though we both know.

"You once returned my ballet slipper, and I'm here to repay that favor."

Her hands fly up to her face. "I forgot about that!"

"It was meant to be, right from the start. May I?" I ask, motioning to her strappy silver heels. She takes a deep breath and nods, holding it in as I remove her right shoe. It's so quiet I can hear both our hearts beating furiously in the night, nervous but excited for what's to come.

I run my thumb against the smooth glass of the slipper and admire its elegant shape. Holding this iconic shoe, this sparkling symbol of magic and dreams coming true, makes me feel like I'm exactly where I need to be. This is my present but future as well; I feel it, I know it. My heart made a wish and now it's coming true.

Val props up her foot and points her toes, still holding her breath. Just before I slip it on, she gulps. "What if it doesn't fit?"

"Believe," I say softly. And with that, I easily slide the slipper on her waiting foot, a perfect fit from heel to toe. It fits, it fits! Not that I had any doubts, but as she wiggles the shoe against the starlight it feels like an extra glittering stamp of approval.

I stand tall and extend my hand; in her sparkling new footwear, Val rises up to meet me, grinning from ear to ear. Fingers entwined, I give her a spin, and she twirls like a goddess of the night, dreamy in silver and sapphire. I wrap my arm around her waist, dipping her into a gentle backbend. She reaches up for me, and we kiss, long and slow under the approving canopy of the castle. Our bodies melt together, and my heart sings over how good, how right, it feels to finally embrace this perfect princess. She sets me aglow in every possible way, and I will do whatever it takes to keep this fairy tale thriving.

I pull back, hovering an inch from her nose to get a better view. "So that was . . ."

"Pretty damn epic," she says breathlessly, skin rosy. "Do you think we should add that as an itinerary activity?"

I roll my eyes. "Oh, you want to be funny?" I tickle her torso, and she erupts in giggles. Then, as if this moment couldn't be any more enchanting, a rainbow of fireworks fills up the sky, their twinkling sparkles raining down all around us. It's so romantic I want to cry, but instead I kiss her again because I can.

"Fireworks!" she squeals afterward, pressing her hands to her heart. Her brown eyes glass over with tears, and I pull her in tight, both of us caught up in the emotion of the moment. As we hold each other close, the courtyard erupts in applause; startled, we both pop back, unaware anyone was watching our private embrace. But sometime during our kiss, all the castle guests flooded the steps, gloved hands commending our union.

"Are they clapping for the fireworks, or . . . ?" Val asks, fanning herself over the sudden attention.

I scan the crowd; with no eyes on the skies, it's clear we're the main attraction even as fireworks pop and sparkle. "No, they're cheering for us." I spy Lanie and Charming's goofy grins sneaking out of the topiaries, the two of them celebrating my and Val's kiss like some kind of magical touchdown, although to be fair it totally was.

"Well then," my princess declares, "I guess we better give them a true finale." In one fell swoop, she cradles my back and delivers the ultimate good-night kiss. Happily Ever Island responds in a thunderous standing ovation, a soundtrack of *oohs* and *awws* so pitch perfect you'd think they were from a movie. But no, this is real life. My life. The dreams in my head made real.

Lanie comes flouncing over, and we collide in a giant hug, laughing like dorks under the colorful show above. While fireworks are always the sign that my time at Disney has come to an end, this time it's different. This time wasn't just about making memories but starting something new. This time I'm leaving with more than I came with, with more hope than I thought was possible. This time I learned I can lean into being a grown-up while still keeping the magic alive in my heart.

And that is truly my happily-ever-after.

ONE YEAR, 3 MONTHS LATER

LANIE

"YOU'LL BE IN MY HEART"

Oh my god, Madison. What have you gotten us into now?"

The line at Java Jam! is at an all-time high, circling out the door and around the building. Ever since we got back from Happily Ever Island, Madison has been concocting a secret "magic" menu of drinks for in-the-know students, dropping new Disney-inspired flavors every Friday. There was the Simba's Pride (cinnamon and honey mocha), the Pixie Dust (peppermint and dark chocolate espresso), and, of course, the Never Grow Up, a seemingly disgusting but somehow delightful recipe combining every fruit syrup in the shop. It tasted like Fruity Pebbles.

But now, for her final drop before leaving for the Disney

College Program, Madison has debuted the Glass Slipper, a vanilla latte with two pumps of blueberry syrup, topped with whipped cream, shaved white chocolate, and sparkly vanilla pearls. We've been brewing her masterpiece since 6:00 a.m. with no end to the line in sight; it's almost lunch, and at this point, we may be here all day long. Normally, I can't wait to hang up my apron, but today I don't mind, since this is my last chance to hang with my best friend for three long months.

"Maybe next year we should set up some kind of drink reservation system," Madison says, furiously frothing her hundredth batch of whipped cream. "Ooh, like a FastPass!"

I can't pretend not to know her Disney references anymore. Last winter break, she took me on my inaugural trip to Disneyland, along with Ethan and Val. It snowed on Main Street; I openly wept.

I am forever changed.

"That could work. Do you think Barry will mind?"

"Please." She rolls her eyes. "He basically works for us now." She's not wrong. Even as professors fumed about late students and administrators threatened eviction over our long lines blocking fire exits, Barry's profits soared. He gave us multiple raises throughout sophomore year and rarely stops by unless it's to count his piles of money. It's the best-case scenario on all fronts. "What time does Ethan get in?"

"Later tonight. Eight, maybe?" I say, unable to hold back a smile. It's been a super-busy end to the school year, what with him graduating and me taking extra classes to catch up from my self-imposed sabbatical. I took a brief break from school after our trip to see how it would make me feel and found myself missing the rigors of academia. But when I still couldn't shake the feeling that becoming a doctor wasn't right for me, it was time for a serious heart-to-heart with my mom.

It was hard—really hard—telling her I wouldn't be joining her practice. She was upset at first, but once I explained what was in my heart, we eventually came to an understanding. In fact, it was her idea that I go into medical research instead, allowing me to delve into my studying superpower without having to work with patients one-on-one. Now we can still talk about developments in medicine without feeling like there's this giant pressure to perform. Our relationship isn't perfect, but it's so much better than where we were a year ago.

At least things are about to get a little easier in my romantic relationship: Ethan got a marketing job downtown and an apartment not too far from DePaul, so now I'll be able to see my prince all the time and not just every couple of weeks.

"I can't wait to see him," I add as I ring up another Glass Slipper.

"That boy is *very* nice to look at," she says with a wink. "But I won't be able to hang for too long; my flight for Florida leaves stupid early tomorrow morning."

"I know." I pinch my lips shut before I say more. Selfishly, I'm so sad she's leaving even as I'm simultaneously psyched for her. After her big Cinderella swap, Madison had a great meeting with Val's boss, who was impressed by her ambition. They stayed in touch, which helped her secure an internship at Happily Ever Island this summer. She can't wait to work side by side with Val, combining their love of Disney and love for each other in one big fantasy supernova. Since we left the island, the two of them have been writing letters—real paper letters—accompanied by little trinkets and decorations, too. It's so romantic, and so *them*.

Madison once sent Val a box full of sparklers; Val returned the favor with a pair of "floor model" glass slippers that were about to go into retirement. They've worked really hard to keep the spark alive despite the distance, and they complement each other in really amazing ways. Val celebrates Madison's glittery spirit while also highlighting her hidden talents, whereas Madison's always there to offer Val support, even without being asked. My best friend is no longer throwing her heart out into the abyss; she's found someone ready and willing to reel her in.

Madison pulls me away from the register, her eyebrows doing that weird waggly thing when she's having mischievous thoughts. "I have to show you the outfit I bought for the plane. It's a low-key Jessica Rabbit cosplay that is gonna blow Val's mind. I'm talking Roger Rabbit eyes popping out of her skull." She sticks out one leg and kicks it playfully, pursing her lips like the cartoon vixen.

"Subtle Jessica Rabbit?" I laugh. "Is that even possible?"

"Okay, fine, it's full-on Jessica, but whatever! I haven't seen Val outside of a screen in wayyyyy too long, and I want our reunion to be . . . memorable."

"More memorable than making out on the castle stairs?"

She smiles, cheeks glowing with the memory. "Probably not but YOU NEVER KNOW."

"You know, that's going to be a super-uncomfortable plane ride in all those sequins," I say as I check to see how much blueberry syrup is left.

"Worth it," she replies over her shoulder.

The syrup pump is looking extremely low, with only a small smear of blue across the bottom. Shoot. We're about to piss off a lot of people. "Madison," I call her over with a whisper. "We only have enough syrup for one more slipper."

Her head hangs back in relief. "Finally! Let's get out of here." Pulling off her brown visor, she waves her arms wildly to get our customers' attention. "Excuse me? Hi, hello! So, unfortunately it's twelve o'clock and the Fairy Godmother's spell has been broken; there are no more Glass Slippers today."

The crowd moans with several expletives peppered in as well. One guy throws down all his books and just storms out as people shout their frustrations:

"I've been waiting forever!"

"I never get the special drinks!"

"Isn't the spell supposed to go until midnight?"

I grit my teeth as Madison shrugs with a not-my-problem expression. "Yeah, well, you shouldn't drink caffeine that late anyway!" she replies. "Go, have a great summer! And follow Java Jam! on social for next semester's secret menu!" Amid lots of grumbling the line dissipates, leaving us to clean up the shop for the last time for a while.

"At least no one started crying like the time we ran out of that Eeyore, I Lost My Tail espresso," I observe as I wipe down the counters.

"Oh god, I forgot about that." Madison shakes her head while putting away the leftover muffins. "I have a feeling it was a test, though, you know? Like extra customer service experience for the road ahead." She smiles to herself, biting her lower lip in excitement. I thought she talked about Disney a lot before, but now it's on a whole different level. Every time she even thinks about her future it's like the sun rising within, little beams of anticipation bursting through. She probably doesn't even notice this difference but I do.

Shop clean and closed up, we head out into the warm Chicago summer day, students sprawled out on the quad to soak up the sun. We're both done with our finals, so it looks like we have the rest of the afternoon to hang.

"Do you want to hear your horoscope?" Madison asks, pulling out her phone.

"Do I have a choice?"

"No." She scrolls down her screen before adding, "Aquarius: You have a fun, sexy summer on the horizon. Even though the most amazing person in your life will be out of town, make sure you get out there and explore, kissing that cute boy while making time for yourself."

"It does not say that!" I lunge for her phone but she easily keeps it out of reach.

"The stars never lie. . . . Haven't I taught you anything?" She laughs. "Here's mine. Gemini: Damn, girl, you are really something, killing it on all fronts. Hot girlfriend, hot career, hot everything. Just don't forget to call or text your best friend every day while you're away because, wow, you're really going to miss each other."

I link my arm with hers, resting my head against her shoulder. "Fine, that one I agree with."

"I know you do." She kisses the top of my head. "I do, too."

We walk off campus, talking and laughing about everything and nothing, holding on to each other tight before we head off into the unknown.

It's a magical place to be.

The End

ACKNOWLEDGMENTS

I grew up with Disneyland in my backyard. Not literally, of course (although how cool would that have been?!), but growing up in Southern California, I spent a significant chunk of my formative years exploring the Happiest Place on Earth. Those adventures definitely helped shape the person I am today, and I'll never stop dreaming about my next trip to the parks. Thank you, Disneyland, for inspiring me to never (fully) grow up.

Thank you to the entire Disney Books team for entrusting this story to me. Having the opportunity to shape a new Disney resort has been an absolute dream come true, and I am so, so honored I was chosen to bring this idea to life. This book is my love letter to the parks, and I will always cherish this magical experience.

To Brittany Rubiano and Cassidy Leyendecker: Thank you for your amazing insight and talent. I loved geeking out about all things Disney with you two, and this story truly thrived with your guidance and feedback. Maybe someday we can meet up at the parks! I appreciate you both so much.

To Jess Regel: Thank you for continuing to believe in me and for always supporting my goals. You helped me realize my dream of writing for Disney, and for that I am forever grateful!

To Wendy Anderson: Thank you for chatting with me about Imagineering and your experience designing Disney parks. Your insight was invaluable in shaping the rules for Happily Ever Island, and I absolutely loved learning about behind-the-scenes Disney magic! I hope I didn't fangirl too hard on our call.

To all my early readers, including my sprinkle sister Stephanie Kate Strohm: Thank you for your honesty and wise feedback. I could not have reached the end without you!

To all my family and friends, who never stop supporting me and cheering me on when things get rough: Thank you for being there. Todd, thanks for making me tacos and scrambles to power me through deadlines. Cam, thanks for giving me bursts of encouragement when I need them most. Molly, thanks for making me laugh with your bouncing spirit.

And to my sister, Tiffany: Thank you for being my Disney soul mate. Whether we're running down Main Street in tutus or screaming down Splash Mountain at 1:00 a.m., my favorite place to be is at Disney with you. Believe!